Cindy,
Enjoy!
Carleen

It's Me, Hannah

Carleen Bunde

Cawing
Crow
Press

For permission requests, email the publisher, at:
inquiry@cawingcrowpress.com

Published by:
Cawing Crow Press LLC Dunlo, PA

ISBN: 978-1-68264-029-6

Library of Congress Control Number: 2017933383

Visit us on the web at: www.cawingcrowpress.com

To Strudel and Pretzel, my sidekicks through many a long night of writing.

And for Douglas, Steven, Lynne, and my husband, Jerome

The author wishes to thank Cawing Crow Press for making this book possible

CHAPTER 1

Mama was murdered that windy, cold North Dakota morning, but I didn't know it yet. I remember it all too clearly. Papa hung up the phone and shouted, "Hannah, hurry up, get in da truck, jou're coming vit me." I snatched my purple jacket off the hook in the foyer, dashed out the door and bounded into the front seat beside Papa.

"Isn't Mama coming with us?" I asked.

"She had an appointment at Edna's Beauty Parlor and left about a half hour ago." Papa rammed the truck in gear and sped down the prairie road, leaving a trail of dust behind. The smell of fresh-plowed fields filled the air.

The next thing I knew, we were out of the truck, and Papa had hold of my hand, pulling me alongside him. We ran so fast against the powerful North Dakota winds, my black button shoes barely touched the ground, and my long red hair blew, every which way, in my face .

Dr. Knightley was already at the site when we got there. His small frame was bent over a broken figure, but when he looked up and saw Papa and me, he brushed a tuft of gray hair off his forehead with the back of his hand and scrambled our way. He reached out, shook Papa's hand and spoke in a hushed tone, "I'm sorry, Johan, I'm so sorry."

I reached up, pushed the hair out of my eyes and looked at Papa; a wave of panic crossed his face. Trembling, I held my hands over my ears to stifle the earsplitting screech of the siren. The acrid smell like that of pig blood filled my nose.

Dr. Knightley stood by Papa with a powerless look on his face. "Oh, Johan, if only I knew of ways to keep tragedies like this from happening."

Papa nodded his head in disbelief.

I overheard an onlooker, "Who would think something so ghastly could happen on Country Road Nine?"

Another squeaky voice, "It's hard to make sense of such a tragedy. Such a shame, such a shame."

A statuesque woman wearing a red box coat that hung open stood amongst the crowd, ringing her hands and shaking her head. "Such good people too. What is to become of Cajsa's little girl is more than I know."

Cajsa's little girl, that's me. They're talking about my mama.

A stranger in the crowd shouted, "Jesus Christ, did you see what I just saw? The blood spurted out of that man like a stream, and I swear to God, his whole damn head was cut off."

Another voice, "he's not from around here. His truck had Montana license plates."

Delilah's Bakery door burst open, and out Delilah bolted waving her big doughy hands in the air and screeching, "Good God, what in the hell is all the ruckus about?" In a flash, the muddy thruway was packed with horrified lookers-on and storeowners.

A dizzy feeling overpowered me when the annoying harsh sound of the big red fire truck sped in. It almost rammed into a group of spectators before it came to a screeching halt beside Mama's smashed blood splattered car.

A bystander whooped, "By jingle, the Badger Towing Service sure as hell didn't waste any time getting here."

I watched the truck pull up. Two powerful men in grey coveralls jumped out, the driver hollered, "Move back folks—make room." Quickly, they loaded the demolished pickup onto the flatbed, inched their way around the mob, and sped off rattling through town.

That's when I spotted the gold-ruby bracelet lying in the rubble. Shaking, I hollered out and jabbed Papa, "Look, that's the bracelet you gave Mama for her birthday." But, I didn't want to believe it was her lying there. Benumbed, I stood, helpless, staring at the shattered body, its bloody skull sliced open like a ripe tomato on the gravel road, surrounded in a pool of blood.

I looked up at Dr. Knightley. "Will Mama be OK?"

He patted the top of my head. "Honey, an ambulance is coming."

The doctor looked the other way, his eyes fixed on Papa. "Johan, she didn't stand a chance. The only good thing, it was instant."

Papa's face showed pain, the likes of which I had never seen before. He mumbled under his breath, "This cannot be happening. Yust yesterday, my Cajsa came running to greet me, smiling when I drove into the jard on my tractor. And now . . . now she is gone."

I looked around in total confusion. Folks scrambled, crying hysterically and bumping into one another to get out of the way when the ambulance came barreling down the street with its lights flashing and siren screeching. I shrieked an eerie high-pitched cry and collapsed on the ground. I could feel Papa's body tremble when he bent over to help me up with one hand, all the while smoothing back my rumpled hair with the other.

The last thing I remembered was the long white ambulance driving up to the body, and the medics lifting Mama onto the stretcher.

***

The next morning Papa sat on a wooden chair in the kitchen, hunched over the heavy oak table. He opened the *Grand Forks Herald* wide and read Mama's accident report out loud.

> Arnold Logan, a Montana native, was driving a 1944 Ford pickup with a camper attached when he swerved and collided head-on into Cajsa Jonesen's 1946 Buick. Cajsa Jonesen was killed instantly.
>
> This accident happened around nine o'clock a.m. on County Road Nine, two and one-half miles out of Munich.
>
> Arnold Logan was driving under the influence of alcohol. The smashup threw him through his truck windshield—He was pronounced dead at the scene of the accident.

Papa threw down the paper with a snort.

"What does driving under the influence of alcohol mean?" I asked.

"Och, I don't vant to talk about dat right now, Hannah."

The night before Mama's funeral service I rode with Papa to Baston's Funeral Home for the viewing. Walking into the parlor I froze in my footsteps. Papa's hand pulled at mine. I couldn't bear the thought of seeing Mama dead like this. Papa pulled a bit harder. I felt beads of sweat forming on my forehead. I wanted to fall on the floor crying, but I pulled up my strength from deep inside and allowed Papa to lead me to the coffin.

Mama looked nothing like I had imagined. Her cheeks were rosy, and she looked sweet, placed in a beautiful, hand-carved, wooden casket. Her head rested on a white satin pillow trimmed in little pink rose buds, and her pretty slim hands were folded over her chest—peaceful.

Papa bent over and gave Mama a little kiss on her forehead.

***

On June 6, 1945, folks jammed the Zion Lutheran Church in Munich to attend Mama's memorial service. Grandma Bamford, a devout Catholic, sat in the front pew.

Besides lots of perfume, Grandma had on the same black dress she wore to Grandpa's funeral. Her sparse gray hair, pulled back in a bun and tucked in tightly under her black hat, shook along with her roly-poly body. All she could do was fling her rosary beads around and howl.

Grandma's best friend, Tova, dressed in black as well, sat beside her, on the edge of the seat with her lanky arm flung over Grandma's shoulder. I overheard her say, "I'm so sorry, Lieula, I know your heart is breaking, but please try to get hold of yourself. You know it hurts me too, and to think I will never see Cajsa's cheerful face in my mercantile again is very sad."

Sobbing, Grandma nodded. "I know, Tova, I know."

I sat on the other side of Grandma, wedged between her and Papa with Papa's arm, large and warm, around me. Dr. Knightley came rushing in at the last minute and squeezed himself in at the end of the pew, his arm poking out into the aisle.

I leaned my head on Grandma's shoulder, looked up into her sad face and whispered, "Don't cry, Grandma." I pulled my white linen handkerchief out of my pocket and handed it to her. "Thank you dear." Grandma whispered under her breath. An awful mournfulness welled up inside me and I started to sob. Grandma poked me and gave me back my hanky. I crouched in the pew blubbering and wiping my face, but I managed a crooked grin when out of the corner of my eye I saw Annabelle and her mother ushered in.

Annabelle and I spent our first-born days lying side by side in the baby nursery at the Devils Lake Memorial Hospital after our mothers gave birth one day apart. My mom and Annabelle's mom were best friends so naturally we became the best of friends as well. I couldn't imagine life without Annabelle.

After the service and during the luncheon held in the church basement, Grandma and Tova were huddled together when Mrs. Bengtsson and another lady, both dressed in pitch-black, gathered around them. Grandma talked in a hushed tone, "And can you believe Johan took little Hannah with him to the scene of the accident? Why, the idea. Seeing her mother lying on the street, covered in blood, will affect her for the rest of her life. Yah, and how in the world is Johan ever going to care for Hannah by himself?"

Every time I passed by Mrs. Elsie Hall she reached out and hugged me. She declared, "Hannah, we are all going to miss Cajsa. It's so sad. Your mother was a first-class lady if ever there was one."

Mrs. Bengtsson cried out, "Poor little Hannah. She and her mother were inseparable."

I stood by the large table full of flavorsome looking homemade buns, ham, chicken and casseroles of all kinds that folks had brought, but I was too upset to eat anything. Wiping my eyes with the backs of my hands, I wandered next to Papa, poked his arm and murmured, "Papa, will I become an orphan?"

Papa grasped my hand and cleared his throat. He bent over and talked in a low voice, "No, Hannah, as long as I'm alive jou vill never be an orphan. Ve vill make it togetter, Hannah, jou and me. Ve have to."

Mrs. Murger nudged Papa's arm. "Sorry to be taking off so soon, Johan, but Wenzel needs me at home, he's not feeling well at all." She hugged me good-bye and on her way out, she turned and said, "We'll be by to see you and Hannah soon, Johan."

"Jou bet, Dakota."

After the memorial luncheon, we headed for the South Salem Cemetery. Papa, a lean, strong, jovial person who always stood straight, now sat stoic and disheveled behind the steering wheel. I looked back and watched Tova and Grandma following us in Tova's new, black Chevrolet and held back the tears.

The undertaker was already at the gravesite, standing alongside Mama's coffin when we walked up. I was delighted to see a gorgeous cross of white roses placed on top of her wooden casket. But, I let out a loud shriek and I thought I was going to tumble over when I saw the hole the *menfolks* had dug, and knew Mama would be buried deep under the ground, all smothered with black dirt when she really wanted to be with us.

5

Grandma stood beside Papa and me with her black pocketbook hanging over one arm as she wiped away her tears with a pretty lace handkerchief.

Tova ambled over in her new black patent leather pumps, moved in between us and put her arm around Grandma.

The scent of roses was everywhere.

Tova exclaimed, "You know, Lieula, seeing those roses on Cajsa's casket makes me think of the time, and I hope this gives you some comfort, it was a beautiful, sunny day, and I stood beside Cajsa in her backyard watching her watering her rose garden, when she looked up at me, and started to laugh and said, 'You know, Tova, I wouldn't mind dying, if I could be buried in a bed of roses.'"

"My word, did Cajsa really say that?"

"Yes, she did."

When all was said and done, with Mama's grave covered in North Dakota prairie roses, it did look beautiful.

Papa and I were getting in the car to leave the cemetery when Grandma came wobbling across the way, her black hat set cockeyed on her head. She gasped for breath and whined, "Johan, don't go running off, let me take Hannah. Tova will drive us home."

"Vell, no Lieula, Hannah is coming vit me."

***

Papa changed out of his black three-piece suit into bib overalls as soon as we got home.

"Hannah, dake off dat pretty dress, jah and hang it up, svitch into play clothes, Sissy Pie, den come vit me to the barn vhile ve do da chores, jah."

"OK, Papa, but don't go until I come back downstairs."

I ran up the steps to my bedroom and slipped out of my good dress—when I reached for the clothes hanger, the memory of Mama standing in my little closet, hanging my freshly ironed dresses overwhelmed me. I tossed the dress I was holding on the back of the rocking chair and flopped on my bed. Big tears streamed down my face.

Papa shouted up the stairwell, "Hannah, are jou coming or aren't jou?"

I wiped my face on the pillowcase and uttered, "Papa, wait up for me."

The scent of fresh-cut hay loomed when Papa pulled the barn door open. He had fourteen Holstein dairy cows that he milked promptly at six a.m. and six p.m. He had different names for all of them. There were sheep, horses and a pigpen full of pigs to tend to as well.

Bessy the cow turned her head and looked at me from her stanchion with what could only be described as a sweet smile on her face. I walked over, reached through the boards and scratched her under her chin. Bessy stretched her nose way out and closed her friendly brown eyes in appreciation.

I picked up Mittens, my calico cat with one front paw missing, and hugged her before she squirmed, jumped out of my arms, and hurried back to her litter of kittens. The kitties' eyes were just beginning to open, and their fur felt like velvet when I gathered them in my hands and held them against my cheek. I looked at Papa sitting hunched over on his three-legged milk stool with his forehead pressed into the cow's flank. Papa had tied Daisy's tail onto her leg with a piece of twine to keep it from swinging and smacking him in the face. As sad as things were, when Daisy's tail flopped around in a loop, it struck me as funny.

Suddenly, Papa's body started to jerk. His chest wrenched, but he made no sound. I didn't know what to think. It scared me. Papa gasped. He looked up and tears were running down his cheeks. I had never seen a grown man cry like that. I knew Papa wouldn't have liked being seen.

I walked away, climbed up the ladder to the hayloft, grabbed hold of the pitchfork, and began heaving loose hay down to the cows and horses. Out of the blue, I heard a cackle from behind me. I tossed the pitchfork aside, flopped down, lay smack on my belly and stuck my head through the haymow hole as far as it could go. To my surprise, Rosy the hen sat perched in the horse's grain-feed box—of all places.

She stood up, spread her feet wide apart and raised her tail feathers. Out popped a large white egg. Just imagine eating that egg, yuck! I went tearing down the ladder, hollering, "Papa, I just now saw Rosy lay an egg!"

Papa stopped milking and looked up at me, all teary-eyed. He spoke in a quiet voice, "Dah heck jou say, it isn't too often you see something like dat." He wiped his eyes with the back of his hand. "I tink it's gotta be some kind of omen."

Papa finished up his chores and hollered, "Vell, dat's all done, let's head on up to da house den, Sissy Pie."

"I got an idea, Papa. Why don't you help me carry Mittens and her kittens up to the house? We can keep them in a basket by the cook stove. I'll take good care of them, please Papa?"

"Och, Hannah, dat's a silly notion, cats belong in da barn. Come along now."

"Grandma lets Rhubarb come inside her house."

"I don't care vhat jour grandma does vit her cat."

Papa trudged along. "Looks like ve're in for a rainstorm, yust look up dere at the dark sky, Sissy Pie."

I stomped along behind Papa.

I didn't feel like looking up—who cares if the sky looks dark?

Maggie, our brown-and-white collie mix, nosed my palm joyfully, and lumbered after me on the way to our big white farmhouse.

It wasn't too long before Maggie curled up in front of the potbelly stove and fell asleep. I sat in Mama's oak rocking chair, slowly moving to and fro. Across from me was Papa who slouched on the davenport, his long legs stretched out in front of him, staring at the tips of his shoes, blubbering, "Cajsa, the laughing center of our life, of our home and family, gone, leaving Hannah and me behind. Oh, Cajsa, how could you leave us? Ve've alvays banked on Cajsa for every ting, dat I don't see how ve can go ahead. I almost feel like dere is noting to go ahead for."

Then, flat out, Papa sprang up off the davenport, grabbed his red handkerchief, blew his nose hard, and hurried out the back door. Looking over his shoulder, he hollered, "Hannah, I'm going down to da blacksmith shop. I'll be right back."

I couldn't push the sight of Mama lying in the wooden coffin with a satin pillow under her pretty head out of my mind. Oh, how I wished with all my heart that I could slide in bed next to her and listen to her soothing voice while she read me a story. Gone was my mother who would sweep me into her arms and whisper love words, silly nicknames.

Papa came back carrying a jug of red wine, plunked it on the table, and reached for a glass from the big wooden cupboard shelf. The legs made a grating sound when he pulled the chair away from the table and sat down. He lifted the jug, poured the glass full, and took a long, slow swig.

"Ja, a little red vine is goot for the old ticker."

The sweet scent of cherry tobacco swirled from his pipe.

"Och, your grandma and dat goddamn awful loud bawling she did today. She should have kept dem damn rosary beads in her purse at the Ludheran church for Christ sake.

"And vhere do jou suppose Mrs. Olofsson ever found such a big hat vit black feathers like dat?"

"What did you say?"

"Och, I vas yust talking to myself, Sissy Pie."

Papa had never quite got over his silly habit of talking to himself.

His voice grew louder.

"Lieula means vell I guess, but she better not tink she is going to come around here and tell me how to run tings like she did Cajsa, or I vill tell her a ting or two. If she ain't bitching about how Elis vouldn't let her drive it's someting else. No vonder Old Elis guzzled dat moonshine. Hannah, jou are staying vit me, dat's for damn sure—dat's vat your modder vould vant too."

Grandma lived down the road a quarter mile from Papa's place, in the little cottage she and Grandpa shared until he died a few years back at a relatively young age from cirrhosis of the liver.

Papa kept on mumbling, "Ja, tings vill never be da same vithout Cajsa."

I kept an eye on Papa, and watched him reach into his shirt pocket and pull out the gold chain fastened to his pocket watch. He wound the watch back and forth a few times in slow motion. I dozed off, and the next thing I knew Papa was playfully pinching my nose.

I sat up with a jerk.

"Jou better go on up to bed, Sissy Pie."

I leapt out of the rocker, put my arms around Papa's neck, and clung to him.

He hugged me and whispered, "Oh, Sissy Pie, I can feel jour heart breaking. Jou run along now and get to bed. Tomorrow vill be a better day. Tings can't get any vorse den dey already are."

"Good night, Papa."

"Good night, Sissy Pie, sleep tight and don't forget to say your prayers like Mama taught you."

Maggie rose from the rug, yawned and followed me up the stairs to my bedroom. I lifted the covers, slipped into bed and folded my hands together.

> Now I lay me down to sleep,
>
> I pray the Lord my soul to keep.
>
> If I shall die before I wake,
>
> I pray the Lord my soul to take.
>
> God bless Mama, Papa, Grandma, and all the animals.
>
> Amen

Sleep wouldn't come. I thought about when I would lay in bed in the mornings, snuggled under the covers, listening to Mama's pretty voice singing along to songs coming from her little kitchen radio. Eddy Arnold strumming "Make the World Go Away" was her favorite.

I'd wait for her call, "Wake up, my little angel, I have rabbit-ear pancakes fresh off the skillet for you." Then, I'd hop out of the covers and scamper downstairs. I loved the clean clothes smell of Mama's skin when she wrapped her arms around me.

Poor, sweet Maggie rested on the floor beside my bed, making little whimpering sounds. I reached down and rubbed her head.

I heard Papa stomp in the back door when the first gray light of dawn began to appear in my bedroom window.

I hollered downstairs, "Where were you, Papa?"

"I ended up spending da night down in da blacksmith shop, sitting on da old wooden bench trying to make sense of it all."

"So, I was in the house all by myself all night."

"You had Maggie."

When I came downstairs, Papa was sitting on a kitchen chair with his elbows on the table and his face buried in his hands. For a dreadful moment I thought he was bawling again. Slowly he drew his hands from his face. I saw he wasn't crying, but his eyes were filled with anguish that looked like it was worse than tears.

What's going to happen next? What if Papa thinks he can't take care of me by

10

himself, and sends me to Grandma's house? Dear God, I hope that never happens. I don't want to leave Papa all by himself. And I don't want to live away from Maggie and the farm animals, either. There are times Grandma can be cranky too.

Grandma was a real entrepreneur when it came to running her Rhode Island Red chicken business. In early spring she would order baby chicks out of the seed catalog, diligently tend to the brood, then sell some for fryers; others she held onto for egg-layers.

I heard Mama say one time; "There was no woman in the whole neighborhood as shrewd as Grandma when it came to running a chicken business. Why, her hens laid eggs year-round, bringing in lots of money. Grandma was a very self-sufficient, independent, and wise woman. I hoped to do things on my own like her, when I grew up."

Just a few days after Mama's funeral Papa left me off at the Halls' big rambling farmhouse to spend the day. As soon as we drove into their yard, Elsie came running out with a big smile on her face and pulled me into her arms. "Oh, Hannah, my sweet little one, it's so good to see you. Tom just left for town with a load of grain. I expect him home soon. I know he'd be awful disappointed if he don't get to see you."

"I don't think Papa will be back to get me until late. He wanted to finish combining the wheat before he quit working in the field today, that's why he brought me to stay with you, Elsie." She liked for me to call her Elsie, not Mrs. Hall.

"It's so sad without Mama."

"I know it is, Sweety, I miss your mama so much."

Elsie was canning fresh green beans from her garden, and she let me help her sort the good beans from the rotten ones.

"Put the bad ones in the bucket here, Hannah. I'll feed them to the pigs."

Elsie packed the beans in Bell glass quart jars and placed them inside the pressure cooker, before she set it on the burner of her gas range.

"Those beans are going to take lots of time before they're done cooking."

"I like beans. Do you, Elsie?"

"I sure do, next to corn, they are my favorite vegetable."

Elsie was one of those women who are built little on the top and who have a big rump, and she giggled over everything. She wore black, square-heeled oxfords like Grandma. I never saw her without a big apron tied over her pretty flowered, cotton-starched housedresses that she ironed perfectly.

Her husband, Tom, was bald-headed, and a little bent over from when a horse kicked him and broke his back. He always had on tan work pants and a red plaid flannel shirt come winter or summer.

I overheard Elsie telling Mama one time that she regretted never having children of her own, yet Tom and Elsie seemed to be so happy together.

Elsie didn't drive, so Mama would stop and pick her up and take her everywhere with us.

That day was the first time I saw Lassie, Elsie's collie that she had recently ordered out of a farm catalog. Elsie and Tom already had the name Lassie picked out before the dog arrived at the Munich depot in a big wooden crate. Lassie was the friendliest dog, and acted like she knew me as soon as she saw me. When I heard her whimpering outside while we were sorting the beans, I asked, "Can I let Lassie in?"

"No, Tom doesn't think it's a good idea to fuss over her too much or let her inside, because then she won't make a good cattle dog."

Papa thought it was the silliest thing he'd ever heard of—buying a dog and spending all that money, shipping costs and everything when most likely that collie wouldn't be any better a cattle dog than if they had picked up some old stray that needed a home, and Lord knows there were plenty of them around.

The day wore on; it was way past milking time, and Tom hadn't come home. Elsie began to fret. She felt helpless because she had never learned how to milk cows. She scampered around the house, looking out the windows for Tom. She started wringing her hands and running her fingers through her short brown, tightly curled hair. Mama had given her a Toni permanent just a few weeks ago.

I sat on the kitchen stool and looked into Elsie's anxious face as she stood leaning on her kitchen counter, and I didn't know what to do. I wished Papa would get there soon. When all at once the kitchen door flew open and in stumbled Tom, disheveled and happy as a lark, carrying a Hershey candy bar and a three-pound roll of fresh butter.

Elsie took one look at him, glanced up at the kitchen clock hanging on the wall, and shouted, "Tom, do you have any idea what time it is?"

"What time is it, Honey?"

Like a shot, she turned and picked up her Elsie-the-cow ceramic cookie jar, a birthday gift from her husband, and threw it full force onto the kitchen floor, whooping the whole time. "Don't honey me, you goddamn drunken sonofabitch, get out in the barn and milk your cows before their bags burst."

Tom smirked. "Sweetheart, I thought you'd be happy to see your old man."

He put the candy and butter on the kitchen table, spun around, and out the door he went.

In my nervousness it struck me funny, and I busted out laughing, then Elsie started to giggle with repeated short catches of breath, and together we picked up the broken pieces.

"Elsie, I wish your cow cookie jar didn't break."

"Be careful so you don't cut your fingers, honey."

The old pressure cooker whistled on the stove, giving off the aroma of green beans cooking and sounding like it would explode any minute.

Elsie walked out the back door, carrying the broom in one hand, the dustpan full of broken glass in the other, and hollered over her shoulder, "Hannah, I'm warning you, don't ever marry a drunkard. I'm telling you, there is nothing I hate more than my husband walking in that door drunk, and not getting those poor cows milked on time."

I grinned nervous like.

I had no idea Tom got drunk like that.

Elsie dropped everything, threw her arms around me and squeezed me hard before she got busy, taking the jars out of the pressure cooker.

It wasn't long until I heard Papa's truck drive up, and I hollered, "Good-bye, Elsie, Papa's here to get me."

Elsie followed me to the door. "Good-bye, Hannah, come back and see me soon."

I never was so happy to see Papa in my whole life, and I couldn't quit thinking about Elsie. It shocked me to hear her cuss at Tom like she did.

***

Papa took to walking ; he said it calmed his nerves and made him forget. He'd swing his arms and move at a fast pace all around the farmyard and down in the pasture sometimes until two or three in the morning. When Papa got back from walking he always came into my room. I would wake a little when he tugged on my covers and whispered, "Good night, Sissy Pie," but when I opened my eyes he was gone. Papa lost fourteen pounds in three weeks. Now and then I found him sleeping on the davenport in his clothes and work shoes. If anyone happened to ask him about Mama, Papa would nod his head and start talking about something else. Coburn, the old red rooster, crowed so loud early one morning he woke me. I heard the putt, putt of the John Deere and knew Papa was out in the field already. I still hated the thought of being alone all day, so I called for Maggie, and we took off running through the field to be with him. From way off Papa saw us coming, and his dust-covered face broke into a big grin under his straw hat, pulled low to hide the sun. He slowed the tractor way down when I caught up to him and motioned for me to hop on.

I jumped up, grabbed onto the back of the tractor seat and bounced along. Papa spun the big steering wheel around and shouted over the noise of the tractor, "Hang on tight vit bot hands, Hannah."

I gripped the seat and yelled against the wind, "OK, Papa."

I loved watching the seagulls fly behind the plow, swooping down to dig in the freshly- plowed soil and soar away with long wiggly worms dangling from their beaks. Maggie scampered along behind the tractor, stopping every now and again to rub her face in the dirt, and she rolled over and over in the cool furrow.

I stayed in the field with Papa all day, and when we got home and went inside, the first thing Maggie did was run into Mama's bedroom.

"Papa, have you noticed when Maggie comes in the house the first thing she does is run into your bedroom, by Mama's side of the bed?"

"Jah, Maggie is looking for Cajsa, poor ting. Maggie was Cajsa's dog, dats for sure. Jah, your mama was a real animal lover, alright."

"Just like me, huh, Papa?"

"Jah, Sissy Pie, yust like jou."

Not only did I talk to sweet Maggie, I thought she talked back.

***

14

Most of the time it all felt like a bad dream. Papa visited Mama's grave often, but I didn't want to go.

One lazy afternoon as I lay on the davenport, listening to the familiar sounds of the windmill singing in the brisk breeze, I heard Papa whistling and pounding on something out in the backyard, so I threw myself off the couch and ran outside.

"Hi, Papa. What are you doing?" I hollered.

"Vorking on da tractor, Sissy Pie."

There was a grunt of exertion, a flash of metal as the wrench flew and clattered off the chassis. "Sonofabitch, I need a bigger vrench to finish dis yob."

Papa's knuckles bled. He picked up an old grease rag off the tractor and wiped his hands, mumbling something about, "Goddamn haying season."

Maggie was in the backyard digging deep into an old gopher hole and kicking up dirt. I ran past her toward the rope swing that hung from the old oak tree. I jumped onto it and began to swing.

"Look Papa, see how high I can go."

Papa looked up at me sitting on the weatherworn swing seat. "Jah, you better slow down, Sissy Pie, or jou'll fly out of dat swing and get hung vay up dere in dem dere branches, and I'll never see jou again."

Wouldn't it be something if I could swing up into the sky, above the clouds and see Mama in heaven?

Swinging high and looking down, I was thrilled when I saw Mrs. Murger drive into our yard. I slowed the swing, leapt off and ran to greet her. Annabelle's little face bobbed up in the passenger-side window. Her perfect white teeth showed when she grinned at me, and her thick, long, curly brown hair hung from under her straw hat. Her mother's big sunglasses dangled on her nose, covering her eyes. Everyone noticed Annabelle's sparkling brown eyes and long eyelashes.

Annabelle shouted, "Hi, Hannah, I've been missing you."

"I miss you too, Annabelle."

Dakota Murger, an attractive, tall, slim woman, stepped out of her green 1941 Buick Super Sedan, shading her gray-blue eyes from the sun. She beckoned for me to come, and I dashed into her arms. Mrs. Murger had that same clean clothes smell of her skin like Mama.

Papa stopped what he was doing and shouted, "Goot morin, Dakota, goot to see you!"

"Johan, how are you doing? I would like to take Hannah home with me if it's all right with you? She and Annabelle can play, and it will give you a bit of respite."

"Jah, I am doing as goot as a fella can, Dakota. It's okay vit me if Hannah goes vit you. Jou run along, Hannah, and be a goot girl. I appreciate your offer, Dakota."

Papa turned and went back to working on his John Deere tractor.

I grinned when Dakota gestured for me to hop in the backseat. Annabelle smiled and glanced over her shoulder. "Hannah, how come your dad always says goot instead of good?"

"I guess because he's from the old country."

"What's the old country?"

Mrs. Murger spoke up, "Johan and his parents emigrated from Stockholm, Sweden, known as the old country, Annabelle."

The smell of summer heat and dust blew off the prairie road as Dakota steered her car down the bumpy road.

As soon as Mrs. Murger stopped the car in her yard, Annabelle and I hopped out and took off running through the soft thick grass and plopped down on the lawn in the backyard. I put my hands behind my head and felt the blades dig into my fingers. We lay side by side, studying the clear blue sky and the pretty white clouds floating above.

Annabelle rolled over on her tummy and looked at me. "Hannah, you seem sad. I know it's because you miss your mom."

"Oh, Annabelle," I whined.

I sat up, rested my forehead on my knees, and started to cry and couldn't stop.

"Hannah, what can I do?"

I kept sobbing into my folded arms.

Annabelle shifted over and put her arm around me.

"I'm sorry."

"You don't have to be sorry."

The heat bore down on us. Annabelle swatted a mosquito biting on her arm.

"You could always come and live with us, Hannah."

"I know, but I could never leave Papa."

"My mom misses her best friend, Cajsa, a lot too, you know."

"I think of Mama the minute I wake up in the morning, and she's the last thing I think of before I go to sleep at night."

Just then, I saw a little green bug leap out of the thick grass and land on Annabelle's arm. Annabelle giggled, snapped up the creepy-crawly little guy and nestled it in her hands. The bug began to sing a low cracked chirp. Annabelle held it close to her ear and listened, then opened her hands wide.

We watched the pretty little bug fly away.

***

Later on we took turns riding Thunder, Annabelle's brown, shaggy, bad-tempered Shetland pony, through the woods and all around. Too soon, Mrs. Murger called, "It's time for you to go home, Hannah. Wenzel will give you a ride."

Mr. Wenzel Murger worked as the depot agent at the Munich Great Northern train station. He drove up in his work truck, reached across with his big muscular arm and held the passenger-side door open. Smiling, he said, "Hurry, Hannah, get in. I'm heading to the depot, and they tell me it's time you get home to your pa." I hopped up into the cab and plunked down on the hard cushion.

Mr. Murger turned and looked at me, "Hannah, I want you to know you're welcome to come and play with Annabelle at our place anytime."

I gave a happy grin. "Thank you, Mr. Murger. We sure had fun riding Thunder today."

"You did, huh? You got to be careful when you're around Thunder. He's a feisty little pony who'll bite you if he gets a chance."

"That's what Annabelle said too, but so far he's never bit me."

Mr. Murger shifted gears. "I hope he never does."

I could hear the cream cans rattle in the back as Mr. Murger drove slowly down the familiar country road.

If I were to live anywhere other than with Papa and could choose, it would be with the Murgers. They were a wonderful, fun family. Annabelle was the only girl and the baby of the family with five older brothers. I often wondered what it would be like to have a sister or a brother.

CHAPTER 2

Fall made me feel like everything was starting again. Mrs. Swenson was the only teacher I'd ever had. I was delighted to know she would be our teacher again, because every year when the school year ended rumors started that Mrs. Swenson was retiring and moving back to Minnesota.

Mrs. Swenson had a reputation as a first-rate teacher who took a genuine interest in each and every one of her pupils.

I thought about the Friday afternoons when she sat at the old Baldwin piano. A fall of white hair framed her heart-shaped face as she pounded on the keys—her foot tapping, with us kids gathered around her, singing, "Detour (There's a Muddy Road Ahead)." I hoped we'd get to sing like that again.

Mornings before school I'd brush the snarls out of my long hair real good, and Papa would braid it into two thick French braids. One Tuesday, shortly after school started, all the kids went out to play during recess while I stayed at my desk, looking over my new, thick arithmetic workbook and wondered how I would ever get through all that, when out of the blue, Mrs. Swenson asked, "Hannah, can you read what I just wrote on the blackboard?"

I strained my eyes and attempted to read the words.

"No, Mrs. Swenson, I'd have to move up closer to see to read it."

"I've noticed you've been doing a lot of squinting, Hannah. I think you better tell your father that it would be a good idea for you to have a comprehensive optometric examination."

Puzzled, I looked at Mrs. Swenson.

"Tell your father you need to have your eyes examined by an eye doctor."

"OK, Mrs. Swenson."

***

Papa sat on the Davenport reading the *Grand Forks Herald* when I walked in after school.

"Hi Papa!"

"Hi Hannah."

"Guess what? Mrs. Swenson told me today that I should have my eyes examined by a doctor."

"Is dat right? Vhat's da problem, Sissy Pie?"

"I can't see the blackboard that good."

Papa threw the paper down, rushed to the telephone and called Dr. Murphy's office. Mrs. Wengle, the receptionist, informed Papa that it was impossible to fit me in for an appointment until October twenty-first, on a Friday—two weeks away.

My face broke into a pout. "Papa, do you mean I have to wait two whole weeks to see Dr. Murphy? It's embarrassing to have to sit way up in the front of the classroom."

"Dere ain't much I can do about it, Sissy Pie, Dr. Murphy is da only eye doctor we have around here, and ve're damn lucky to have him."

The kids laughed when I screwed up my eyes, but I thought if I squished them hard enough maybe this whole eye problem would fade away. I yearned for Mama to be with me at the dreadful doctor's visit.

***

When the day finally arrived, Papa picked me up at school. I felt on edge all the way to town, and when I walked into Dr. Murphy's office my heart really started to race.

Just as Dr. Murphy pointed for me to have a seat in the big leather chair in the small examination room, I looked back at Papa who was sitting on an over stuffed chair in the waiting room, thumbing through an old *Time* magazine. My body trembled.

"Hannah, have you visited an eye doctor before?" Dr. Murphy asked.

I shook my head, no.

In a kind voice, he said, "Well, you have nothing to be afraid of."

Dr. Murphy was a man who looked like everyone's favorite uncle. He had a head of thick graying hair and a gentle face that could reassure even the most nervous patient.

The examining room smelled like alcohol. Dr. Murphy gestured for me to have a sit. I anxiously climbed up onto the high black leather chair. He placed a gruesome machine before my eyes that reminded me of the anvil Papa kept in his blacksmith shop.

"What in the world is that?" I exclaimed.

"It's an optometry machine that allows me to examine the patient's eyes and tells me if they need glasses."

"It's too big for my face." I blurted out as I scooted forward on the cold chair.

Dr. Murphy cracked a smile, and went on about his business, testing one eye at a time. "Hannah, tell me what letters on the chart you can see best."

The machine clicked when he flipped the glass lens. I shouted, "E." At the same time, Papa pounded on the door and shouted, "Hey, Doc, are Hannah's eyes going to be OK? She ain't going blind or any ting like dat, is she?"

"Hannah will be out in a few minutes, Mr. Jonesen."

Dr. Murphy explained to Papa that I had a severe case of myopia—nearsightedness. A condition in which close objects are seen clearly, but objects further away appear blurred. Dr. Murphy turned to me. "A pair of glasses with the correct prescription will take care of that problem just fine."

There were so many frames to choose from—after some time, I settled on a pale blue pair.

Papa grinned. "Dey look goot vit jour blue eyes, Hannah."

I had to wait another long week before we could pick my glasses up.

As soon as we walked into Dr. Murphy's one week later, Mrs. Wengle got up from behind her desk and dug my new glasses out of a drawer behind the counter. She indicated for me to take a seat and assisted in adjusting the frames just so. She chuckled, "I don't know if your little pug nose can hold them up, Hannah." Then she picked up a big mirror and held it for me to look into. When I saw myself I burst out, "I love my new glasses." My goodness, I couldn't believe how bright and crystal clear everything looked.

When Papa and I got outside, I shouted, "Papa, let me hang onto your arm. It feels like the sidewalk is going to come up and hit me in my face." To see each slender blade of lush green grass was magical.

***

I couldn't wait to show Mrs. Swenson my new blue glasses on Monday. But if I'd known what was about to happen, I would have put on different bloomers.

It all began when Mrs. Swenson stood by the side of the room, gathering grades one through three together, and instructed us to hold hands and form a circle.

We were going to play ring-around-the-rosy.

Mrs. Swenson's oxfords squeaked when she walked heavily toward the Motorola phonograph and selected the 10-inch, 78-rpm setting. Then she grabbed hold of the crank on the side of the phonograph with her short stubby fingers and wound her up. Away we went, running and skipping round and round to the tune of:

> Ring around the rosy
>
> A pocketful of posies
>
> Ashes! Ashes!
>
> We all fall down!

How fun! The faster we'd go, the better I liked it. Until the elastic in my bloomers snapped, and I felt them sliding down my skinny thighs. When I tried to jerk my hands loose, Olaf and Isabel squeezed them tighter.

I tugged and hollered, "Please, let go." Oh, God! My bloomers fell down and landed in a heap around my ankles. Only then did the kids let go of my sweaty hands. I quickly bent over, grabbed hold of my daisy-print bloomers that Grandma had sewn for me, and took off running to the restroom in tears.

Annabelle scurried behind me, touched my arm and whispered, "Don't cry, Hannah." Then she darted back beside Mrs. Swenson, who stood with her hand outstretched, a pile of gold safety pins in her palm.

Annabelle grabbed the pins, bounded into the bathroom where I stood mortified in the stall, and gave them to me. I snatched them up, quickly fastened my underpants together the best way I could and pulled them back on.

I held my head high when I marched back to my desk, but I felt my face turning red.

Akecheta, who happened to be fifteen years old, and still in eighth grade, sat stuffed in his desk with his long legs poking out, gawking right at me with a big smirk on his face.

"Are you sure your bloomers are going to stay up, Hannah?"

I ignored him.

His mop of black hair fell over his dark brown eyes when he swung his head back, slapped the top of his desk and roared with laughter.

The look on Mrs. Swenson's face was enough to make one's hair stand on end. Her broomstick skirt blew up in the air, showing her white slip when she scrambled across the room, huffing and puffing, heading straight for Akecheta.

"I'll teach you not to laugh and make fun of people," she bellowed. She swung her fleshy arm and slapped Akecheta's face so hard he reeled backwards. Mrs. Swenson's pretty cameo broach fell to the floor.

"If I'd seen it coming I would have ducked," he whooped.

Shy little first grader Beulah Johnson sat in her desk—scared silly, yet she jumped up, snatched the broach and handed it to Mrs. Swenson.

"I didn't want anyone to step on it," she whispered.

"Thank you, Beulah."

Mrs. Swenson pinned it back on the front of her white blouse and sat down behind her desk.

It grew silent. You could hear the scraping sound of the hands on the big school clock that hung above Mrs. Swenson's desk. I counted the minutes until four o'clock, and wished Mama would be looking out the kitchen window, watching for me when I got home. If she were there she would have seen to it that I never put on those underpants with the worn-out elastic in the first place.

Mercy, I was so humiliated I didn't know how I could ever face the kids at school again. I felt such hatred towards Akecheta. There were times I felt angry with all the kids in school because they could go home to their mothers. I'd hear them talking about how: "My mom patched this. My mom cooked that. My mom bought me this." Big deal! Most of the time I went home to an empty house except for sweet Maggie, who came to meet me with her tail wagging a hundred miles an hour and running round and round in circles.

***

Snow blew across the road in front of the truck that Tuesday afternoon in November when I rode along with Papa to the little country school where the Cavelier County election took place.

Papa hurried up the broken-down steps while I waited for him, and in no time he was back outside—done voting.

He stood by the side of the truck and took his pipe out of his shirt pocket, stomped the tobacco with his pocketknife, and lit it up before he hopped in and slid behind the steering wheel.

"Boy, that was fast. Papa, who did you vote for?"

He looked at me real stern, reached up and took the pipe out of his mouth.

"Don't ever ask me vho I woted for."

"Why not?"

"Because, dat's my business, and nobody else's."

Why was that such a big secret? I wondered.

Hooray for Harry S. Truman. He won the presidential election that year.

***

Christmas time became more meaningful than ever for me that year, mainly because Mrs. Swenson chose me to act as Mary in the Christmas pageant.

I told Annabelle, "I think she chose me because she felt sorry for me because my bloomers fell down."

"No, Hannah, she chose you because she knows you'll be a good actress."

I got excited just thinking about it, and the best part was, I could bring my magic skin doll to play Baby Jesus. I started marking the days off on the calendar until December seventh got there.

The play took place on a Friday evening. I was sitting on a bale of hay in the center of the stage in front of the Nativity scene, with Baby Jesus lying in the manger, when Mrs. Swenson walked over and reminded me to "sit still, no laughing, and keep your eyes focused on Baby Jesus."

I nodded my head.

It was really hard not to crack a smile when I peeked out at Grandma and Papa sitting in the front row, looking happy and smiling up at me. I imagined Mama sitting with them.

My neck felt itchy against the prickly wool shawl that wrapped around my head, over my shoulders, and hung to the floor. When I glanced at Mrs. Swenson she looked amused.

The minute Annabelle walked in with her mother and saw me in my Mary garb with Baby Jesus in the little wooden manger, she busted out laughing. Mrs. Swenson reached out and put her hand on Annabelle's forearm, signaling her to be quiet. Then Annabelle and her mother walked over and seated themselves in the second row. Playing Mary was easy. I was coached by Mrs. Swenson to sit still on a bale of hay, behind the manger with my eyes fixed on baby Jesus and act serious—no laughing, and I didn't even have to learn any lines.

When the play was over, I ran behind the curtain, took off my costume and hurried back out onto the stage. Everyone began to clap, and I couldn't stop grinning.

"Thank you," I cried.

Papa chuckled, "Vell, here comes Mary." Grandma smiled. "You looked as cute as could be up there on the stage, and you did an excellent job, Hannah."

"Grandma, maybe I'll be an actress someday."

"Remember, Hannah, you can be anything you want to be."

***

It was a beautiful spring day when I took off running to Grandma's house. Maggie bounded ahead. Grandma stood stooped over weeding her vegetable garden when Maggie and I ran up behind her.

Grandma turned our way. "Why, the idea. I didn't expect to see you today."

"We wanted to surprise you, Grandma."

"Surprise me, you did."

She removed her yellow garden gloves, pulled a pretty hankie from her apron pocket and wiped the perspiration from her brow.

"Does your pa know you're here?"

"No." I smiled up at Grandma. "He left for town before I got up."

Grandma shrugged. "Does he leave you alone often?"

"No, but I can take care of myself just fine."

"You think so, huh? Have you had breakfast?"

"No."

"Come along, Hannah. I will make you something. Would you like some scrambled eggs?"

"No."

"What would you like?"

"Grasshoppers," I said and laughed, as if I'd said the funniest thing in the world. Grandma chuckled.

"I would really like oatmeal with raisins."

"Are you sure you want to eat oatmeal on a hot day like today?"

I grabbed onto Grandma's soft plump hand. "Yup, that's what I would like."

Maggie collapsed on the porch in a cool shady spot.

"Go in the house, Hannah, and get a bowl of fresh water for Maggie."

"What bowl should I use?"

"The small blue dish setting on the counter, dear."

Grandma wiped her hands on her apron on the way to the butler's pantry. I scooted my fanny up on the high-back chair, leaned against the large oak kitchen table and watched as Grandma picked the Quaker oats off the pantry shelf, poured some water in the pot, sprinkled in some oatmeal, a little cinnamon, and a pinch of salt, then stood in front of her cook stove, humming and stirring the pot.

"Grandma, after watching you, I think I know how to cook oatmeal."

"You do, huh? You know, it's not a good idea for you to cook oatmeal if you are home alone. I'd worry about you handling the boiling water."

"I know."

The aroma of cinnamon spice filled the air. I sat, stroking the linen tablecloth with the palm of my hand. *Someday I want to be a good cook like Grandma.* The next thing I knew, Grandma plunked a big bowl of oatmeal sprinkled with brown sugar in front of me, and sat down on a chair on the other side of the table.

"Hmmmm, Grandma, it tastes just like Mama used to make. I miss Mama's good cooking so much."

"I bet you do, dear."

"Papa makes us good suppers, but his cooking is nothing like Mama's."

"From what I've heard, your pa took over the cooking when his mother was ill. He was her only child. His father had already died the year before. Bless his heart; he saw to it that his mother was well taken care of until the very end.

"Why, I can just see Cajsa standing on the kitchen stool, covered in flour from head to toe and rolling out pie dough with her little rolling pin while I sliced the apples. She loved to be in the kitchen, and by the time she married your father she was a splendid cook."

"How did Papa get to know Mama?"

"Well, when it got too much for Johan with the farm work and all, he ran a help wanted ad in the paper, and Cajsa answered it. The plan was that she would work for the Jonesens that summer and go back to teaching in the fall. She had just finished her first year of teaching in the little schoolhouse you go to, Hannah. The next thing we knew, Johan and your mama were in love and planning a wedding. Your pa didn't want his wife to work out of the home, so that ended her teaching career. I remember all your mama could talk about that fall before they got married was your papa."

I looked at Grandma and smiled.

"With Cajsa being my only child, it was hard to let go. I know your pa resented me because of that and still does. The day she died, part of me died too."

"Mama was an only child just like me?"

"Yes, she was an only child just like you, Sweetie, and you are the spitting image of your mama when she was your age."

"Grandma, is Tova our relation?"

"No, it seems like she is, and she's young enough to be my daughter, but she's just a real good friend. We both came from Wisconsin—not from the same town. I understand she purchased the Munich Mercantile with inheritance money. She graduated from business school before she moved to North Dakota—a real entrepreneur, that gal. It worked out really well for her too, with the nice little apartment above her store as living quarters."

"Every time I go into the store she gives me a peppermint candy. I don't like peppermint, but I take it anyway."

Grandma chuckled, "Is that right? Now, as soon as you finish eating, you better head on home, so you're there when your pa gets back from town, and don't go lollygagging and get into any kind of mischief on your way home. Do you hear me?"

"Don't worry, Grandma."

Grandma lightheartedly pinched my cheek and walked out to the porch with me.

"Good-bye, Hannah. Come back and surprise me again real soon."

I ran down the prairie road with my long braids flying in the breeze. Maggie ran ahead through the tall weeds and grass alongside the road, chasing a gopher back into its hole. Every few minutes she looked to see if I was coming.

I glanced over my shoulder when I reached the first curve in the road and saw Grandma sitting on the old stone bench beside the lilac bush in the middle of the garden, with her head resting wearily in her hand. I must go see her often.

When I got to the cattail marsh, I stopped and sat down by the side of the road. Maggie plopped beside me while I rested my elbows on my knees, my chin in my hands, listening to the frogs croak. It felt so nice and peaceful. Looking off in the distance I saw beautiful cattails, and I thought about how Mama and I would go on long walks by the water and pick them. Maggie poked at my arm with her nose.

"Yeah, Maggie, I know you're here." I rubbed her head. *Wouldn't it be fun to pick some cattails today?*

Without another thought, I took off my red sandals, tossed them by the side of the road and slid down the slope. Wild ducks rose with a whirr of wings. Maggie looked up at them and barked. I plodded over sharp rocks and clumps of mud and jumped over the small gurgling creek that feeds the pond to get to the cattails that grew along its rim. Maggie's long pink tongue dangled out of the side of her mouth as she dallied along, sniffing all the strange scents.

I loved the feel of the soft water lilies brushing against my legs as I waded through the water. I had to climb on top of a huge boulder and stand on my tiptoes in order to reach the furry spikes. In no time at all my arms were full of beautiful, soft, fuzzy cattails.

I spun around and hollered, "Come on, Maggie, let's go home."

Boom! My scrawny legs slid out from under me, and I skidded off the slippery boulder. The cattails flew out of my hands and their brown fur flew in my face and everywhere else before they landed in the murky water. My blue glasses slid off my nose, and I ended up flat on my back in the swamp, barely able to hold my head above water.

I screamed and struggled underwater for what seemed like forever before I managed to get hold of a big elm branch in both hands, and pull myself up into a sitting position. I squinted to get a look at my left foot that was hurting something awful—that was when I discovered my foot was stuck underneath the boulder and I couldn't jerk it free no matter how hard I tried.

Could it be cut off?

"Oh mercy, God, somebody please help me," I cried.

My straw hat had blown off my head, my face felt blistered from the heat. I could barely see what was going on.

Maggie stood on a rock beside me with her long pink tongue hanging out of her mouth, panting.

"Oh, sweet Maggie, what are we going to do?"

She stretched over and licked my face and my neck.

Suddenly, Maggie raised her head, pricked up her ears and dashed up the embankment, barking loudly. A car screeched its brakes. I squinted and could tell it was Mr. Murger in his shiny black Ford; most likely with a cigarette drooped from between his lips.

Mr. Murger got out of his car, and Maggie darted up the slope to meet him.

He reached out—Maggie licked his hand, and he shouted, "Well, I'll be darned! Hannah, what in the world are you and Maggie doing way out here, for God's sake?"

Maggie woofed and ran back by me, then back up the hill to Mr. Murger, back and forth, back and forth she went.

I waved my hands and cried out, "Please help me, Mr. Murger."

He turned to look, and saw my thin, bare flailing arms and my small, sunburned, panicked face gawking at him from the swampy waters.

"Oh, now I know what Maggie's trying to tell me. Hannah, what's going on? You silly girl. What are you doing down there anyway?"

"I was trying to pick cattails, and I slipped off the rock. My foot is stuck under a big boulder, and I can't get up."

Mr. Murger talked in a loud voice, "Well, just give me a minute. I'm on my way down to help you out of this mess you got yourself into."

"Oh, thank you, thank you." *He sounds mad.*

Mr. Murger rolled up his tan pant legs and followed Maggie.

I saw him snatch the cigarette out of his mouth and throw it in the water. When he got down beside me, he clamped his palms in his armpits and stood for a minute or two to collect himself. Next, he drew a deep breath, bent over and struggled to lift the rock off my foot, but that didn't work. Finally, he was able to squeeze his strong hands in between the slick boulder and my skinny leg, and gently tugged, little by little until my foot was free.

I held back the tears when he picked me up and sat me down on top of the boulder.

An old Chevy truck loaded down with russet potatoes went rattling past.

"Mr. Murger, can you see my glasses anywhere?" I whimpered.

"Just a minute, I want to look at your foot first."

I held my hands over my eyes; afraid I'd see blood. Ever since Mama's horrible accident I couldn't stand the slightest sight of blood.

"Is it bleeding?" I cried out.

"I don't see any blood, but your ankle is a little swollen and black-and-blue. Dr. Knightley better have a look at it. Oh, I see your glasses stuck in the muck. They look a little twisted, but the lenses aren't broken."

He reached to pick them up, and stood for a bit, straightening the frames and wiping the lenses, then poked his handkerchief back into his pocket and handed them to me.

"Oh, thank you so much, Mr. Murger, now I can see again. " I felt weak and shaky. "I don't know if I can stand up."

"Here, let me help you, Hannah." He grabbed hold of me and tossed me over his broad shoulders, then carried me up the slope and carefully laid me on the backseat of his car.

Maggie started howling like a wolf, and scampered round and round the car—scared we were leaving her, I guess.

Mr. Murger snapped his fingers, signaling for Maggie to come. She leaped into the car, plopped onto the front seat, and shook. Water sprayed all over Mr. Murger and everywhere else. He just laughed and wiped his face with the sleeve of his shirt before he put the key in the ignition. Maggie quickly spun around and fixed her eyes on me.

Mr. Murger jammed his car in gear with such a jolt I was almost flung onto the floorboards. I grabbed onto the seat and rolled over on the soft tweed car cushion that stank like cigarette smoke.

"I'm taking you straight to our house, Hannah. Dakota will help you."

"OK, Mr. Murger."

Papa is going to be very upset with me, I know. What if he gets so mad at me that he won't let me go to the County Fair with him and Grandma? Or what if he thinks I should go and live with Grandma after all?

Maggie walked alongside me, nudging my leg with her nose as we made our way into the house. Mr. Murger turned to Maggie, "You're welcome to come in too, Maggie," and he held the door open for her.

Dakota immediately called Dr. Knightley and ordered me to lie down on the davenport before she placed a big pillow under my bruised foot.

Maggie plopped on the floor beside me.

Annabelle carried a dish of food and some water over for Maggie, then sat down on the edge of the davenport and brushed my forehead with her hand. "Hannah, what were you doing?"

"I was trying to pick some cattails."

"You're going to be OK."

"I know."

I smiled when Dakota tucked a soft, warm blanket around me. "Thank you, Mrs. Murger. I'm so happy that Mr. Murger came along when he did, and that my foot is OK."

Mrs. Murger chuckled. "I bet you are."

In no time Dr. Knightley drove up and walked in carrying his big black doctor's satchel. I started to get up, but he gestured for me not to bother. He took off his jacket and threw it on the arm of a chair.

"Well, my goodness, Hannah, what have we got here?"

Maggie jumped up and walked over beside Dr. Knightley's black satchel and sat down, watching, unblinking.

Dr. Knightley gave my foot a good going-over, felt the bones and everything.

"No broken bones. In no time you'll be good as new, Hannah."

Feeling scared and a little shaky, I mumbled, "Thank you, Dr. Knightley."

"You're welcome, Hannah. It's best you stay out of the swamp waters."

"I know."

It was getting late when Dr. Knightley left. Dakota had tried calling Papa several times, but the party line was busy. When she finally got through. I heard every word he said from where I lay on the davenport. Papa had this habit of talking loud on the telephone. "Tanks for calling, Dakota. I vas starting to get really vorried about my Hannah. How is she anyvay?"

"Oh, she's doing just fine. She was more scared than anything."

Papa and Dakota agreed it would be okay for Maggie and me to spend the night.

Dakota heated up a bowl of chicken-noodle soup for me, and I ate every spoonful.

Dakota even allowed Maggie to come up to Annabelle's bedroom with us. She plunked down by the side of the bed. Annabelle must have been really tired because we hardly had a chance to talk before she was sound asleep. I lay awake, tossing and turning. If only I'd listened to Grandma.

When it seemed to me it must be morning, the clock struck one a.m. Sleep just wouldn't come. I listened to Maggie's heavy breathing by the side of the bed and thought about Mama. I wanted her by me so bad right then.

***

Amazing, when I got up in the early morning my foot hardly hurt at all, and I could walk as good as ever. Mrs. Murger gave Maggie and me a ride home before Annabelle woke up. As soon as we entered our driveway, Maggie spotted a badger running through the yard. She couldn't get out of the car fast enough to chase it. Luckily the badger got away and burrowed into his hole. I was glad because badgers had always frightened me—just seeing their long claws scared me to death.

I hollered, "Good-bye, Mrs. Murger, thanks for everything."

She smiled. "You're welcome, Hannah."

I felt lucky to have my foot feeling better and so happy to get home, yet I was a bundle of nerves at the thought of facing Papa. I ran inside and peeked in at him. I could tell he'd already finished the morning chores. He who looked so peaceful sitting in the living room in his big oak rocking chair. The smoke from his pipe circled in the air as he listened to the news on his fancy Philco radio. The *Grand Forks Herald* lay on the little end table beside him.

Maybe he's not going to say anything after all.

I headed up the stairs to my room when the sound of Gabriel Heater's voice, "Hello out there in radio land," startled me. But when Papa hollered, "Vhere do jou tink jour going, young lady? I vant to talk to jou," I spun around, ran back down the steps and plopped on the davenport across from him. I couldn't bring myself to look Papa in the eye.

Papa turned the radio off and the whole house went silent. I could hear flies buzzing outside the screen.

Papa took the pipe out of his mouth and placed it in a glass ashtray on the end table. He locked his hands together and stretched them over his head. "Vell, Hannah Marie, after I got done talking to Dakota last night, I vent ahead and rang up Dr. Knightley."

"You talked to Dr. Knightley?"

"Yah, I did. I vanted to hear it from the horse's mout. I'm glad jou didn't get hurt any vorse den jou did. Jou know I've told you over and over not to go in da vater, but no, jou vent ahead and vent anyvay. Vhot do jou have to say about dat?"

A big lump formed in my throat. Words wouldn't come out.

He shifted in his chair. "Vell, den, let me ask jou dis: Did you learn someting?"

My lips trembled like I was going to cry—in a faint voice, I answered, "Yes, Papa, I learned a lot. My foot hurt something awful, and I thought for sure it was cut off. I was scared I would drown and no one would ever find me. Papa, from now on, I promise I'll do whatever you say."

Papa chuckled, "Dat's an awful big promise."

"I'm sorry I made you worry."

"Vell, I certainly hope so. If you learned someting from jour foolhardiness, dat's punishment enough, den. I can understand jou wanting to pick cattails. I remember vhen jou and jour Mama vould go on walks and bring dose long fury tings home. Cajsa vould put dem in dat big green vase. I tink da vase is still up dere in the cupboard somevhere, but Sissy Pie, it's too risky to go in da swamp vaters by jourself."

"You're the best, Papa," I cried.

Papa smiled. "Jou think so, huh?"

Overwhelmed with grief, I walked outside and plopped down on the back steps. I glanced over at the sunflowers growing alongside the fence; some of them were as big as little trees. They reminded me of Mama.

Without any warning the tears started streaming down my cheeks. I covered my face with my hands and wailed, "Oh, Mama, why did you have to die?"

Maggie plodded over and jabbed my hand with her wet nose. I pulled her into my arms and sobbed into her soft, doggy-smelling fur. I hugged her with all my might and whispered, "I love you so much, Maggie Boo."

Her tail smacked the porch rail, she swished it so hard, and her whole body shook when she raised her head, looked at me with those sad eyes, and licked my face until the weeping stopped

***

Papa was looked up to and respected in the community as a good man who took pride in his family homestead and worked hard on the land. His farm animals were of utmost importance.

The barn became my haven, and I spent more time than ever in the warm, high-ceilinged, spacious building. I loved feeding the baby calves from a big glass bottle, covered with a long black nipple. The little "boonzies" sucked up the milk and made little moo sounds. The baby lambs felt soft and warm when I sat down on a pile of hay and nuzzled them in my arms. Cute, furry kittens of all colors had the run of the barn.

Sally, my palomino, was most special. When she heard me tramping through the straw bedding in her stall, her ears perked up and she neighed, showing enormous teeth. I loved to snuggle against her big warm neck and lay my cheek on her soft nose.

I taught Sally ground manners and how to accept the bit. Things I'd learned from being around Papa and his horses. Papa said Sally had the most perfect temperament he'd ever known in a horse.

Sally was one of a team of workhorses who hadn't been broke to ride. Yet right from the start she trusted me, and allowed me to jump on her back and ride her all around. If I did happen to fall off, she stopped and waited for me. Then I'd grab onto her mane, toe-walk up her long legs and slide back on. I remembered Mama saying, "Hannah's a natural when it comes to training Sally."

Little did we know how useful Sally would become when the school bus stopped running, and again when the pastureland was destroyed after a long spell of dry weather.

Sally was an unusual horse. Such as the time we trotted down the narrow prairie road on a beautiful, sunshiny day. A warm breeze blew in my face as we rode against the wind. I loved looking at the dandeloins growing down the center of the road, even if Papa hated those yellow weeds—to me they looked pretty.

I clicked my tongue and shouted, "giddy-up." Just like that, Sally took off at a full gallop, and I was thrown off. I landed in the ditch by the side of the road, but lucky me, I settled on a pile of thick, soft grass.

Sally stopped immediately and looked down at me sprawled on the ground—right off she hoofed it down the slope and stayed right by my side.

I leaped up and hollered against the wind, "Stand still, Sally," before I scrambled to the top of the dusty road, took one big leap and landed smack-dab on Sally's back.

Sally neighed, and clambered up, out of the ditch with me grasping onto her long, coarse mane and at a slow gait she headed for home.

I felt safe when I was with Sally. She was one of my best animal friends—for sure.

CHAPTER 3

On a brilliant, clear day in mid-April Maggie and I ran out the squeaky barn door after throwing down hay for the cattle. We were headed for the house when Maggie stopped dead in her tracks. Her ears pricked up and she yipped.

"Maggie, what is it?"

Another little yip.

Clear to me came the single, thin squeal of a little pig. I made a beeline in the direction where I thought the squeal had come from and caught up to the old hog shed, with its red paint beaten by the sun. My heart sank when I saw a helpless baby pig stuck in the slop, way over in the corner of the pen with his little-bitty pink eyes peeking out.

Maggie nosed my leg when I grabbed onto the wooden fence and jumped over. I held my nose as I tromped through the pigpen and scooped up the grubby fella in one hand.

Bewildered, I stood in the middle of the pigsty, holding the weak, pink little pig in my arms, and counted one, two, three, four, five, six, seven piglets snuggled up to their mama—nursing. The selfish old sow glared at me and grunted.

I carried the piglet up to the house and into the bathroom. I could feel the little guy's heart beat when I wiped him clean with a damp washcloth. It was hard for me to believe that a pig could be so tiny.

I wrapped him in one of my baby doll blankets and laid him in an old wooden orange crate, then placed the crate in a safe, warm corner of the barn and ran to the tool shed where Papa stood, bent over his workbench, fixing the handle on an old hay fork.

"Papa, come quick, I have something I want to show you."

Papa wrinkled his brow and nose. "Vell, vhat could dat be?"

He took one look at the runt pig and shook his head. "It doesn't look like he's going to make it, Sissy Pie. Let me tell jou someting, dose big sows are known to lie down on their sickly runt pigs and squash them to death."

"How could any mother do such an awful thing? Can I keep him, Papa?" I cried out.

"Ja, Sissy Pie, it's OK vit me."

I fed the runt pig warm cow's milk out of a pop bottle attached to a rubber nipple, and carried him around like a little baby. I named him Baxter. In no time Baxter looked like a normal pig, and he loved to nibble corn off the cob. I had more fun giving Baxter Joy dishwashing detergent bubble baths in the old washtub. He'd make happy squeals when I scrubbed his little belly with the scrub brush. And his coat sparkled after I dried him off with a big, soft bath towel.

I know if Mama were here she would help me take care of Baxter. I wish she could see him.

Papa was getting ready to go to town when Annabelle came riding in on her bike. "You be goot girls, jou hear? Don't suppose I'll get home till around chore time."

Papa leaped into the cab of his one-and-a-half-ton International truck, loaded down with wheat to sell at the Munich Grain Elevator. I watched him pull out of the driveway, and noticed a big tumbleweed blow across the dusty road in front of his truck.

Annabelle always asked me the minute we were home alone, "What can we do that's different, Hannah?"

I looked with excitement around the cozy kitchen—my eyes landed on the big sack of Dakota Maid flour setting on the cupboard shelf.

"Well, we've never made bread dough."

"Mixing up bread dough sounds like fun."

I reached up, pulled the big white mixing bowl out of the cupboard and plunked it on the kitchen counter. Annabelle read loudly from Mama's old Betty Crocker recipe book, "We need flour, sugar, salt and yeast."

I dashed to the butler's pantry next to the cookstove and began gathering yeast, salt and flour. When I picked up the sugar sack and shook it, it felt like it was almost empty. A little bottle of blue coloring setting on the shelf caught my eye, so I snatched it up and poured in a few drops while Annabelle laboriously stirred the dough with a big wooden spoon.

The blue dough stretched warm and elastic-like in our hands when we rolled it between our fingers. Wow! It even smelled like the bread dough Mama made.

Annabelle dashed to the kitchen sink to wash her sticky, doughy fingers, and happened to look out the window. "Hannah, guess what? Your pa is driving into the yard."

"It can't be, Papa told us he wouldn't be home until chore time."

I peeked over Annabelle's shoulder. Sure enough, it was Papa, big as life.

"Oh, mercy, what are we to do now? Papa's not going to like it one bit if he sees the sugar sack plumb empty. Just the other day he told me to take it easy on the sugar, 've vont get more ration stamps for anodder couple of veeks.' We can't possibly let Papa see the dough."

"I'll bury it in here, Hannah."

Annabelle snatched the comic section out of the *Grand Forks Herald* and wrapped the dough up. "Now, where should we hide it?"

"Oh my God!" I heard Papa's work boots, STOMP, STOMP up the back steps.

I snatched the dough, dashed out the back door, and ran like the wind. Annabelle scrambled behind me, and we didn't stop until we got to the old farmhand's dilapidated pickup, parked out beside the barn. I shouted, "Open the pickup door, Annabelle." She grabbed the door handle and swung it wide open, and I heaved the dough onto the dusty seat. WHAM, I slammed the pickup door shut and leaned against it—out of breath, I announced, "OK—we'll leave the dough here until Papa goes back to town."

I thought Papa would go back to town right away, but instead he raked old stalks and leaves in the garden. He patched a big tire on his truck and made a few trips down to the old blacksmith shop.

Later on, Annabelle was helping me tidy up the kitchen when Papa ambled in. He sat down at the table, leaned back on the chair legs, crossed his fingers behind his head and started to laugh. "Girls, do jou have any idea vat dat big, blue, bubbly-lookin stuff is doing in Ted's old pickup? Or am I seeing tings? By God, I tink I'll go down dere and dake a damn goot look."

"WHAT STUFF? WHAT ARE YOU TALKING ABOUT?" I hollered over my shoulder as

I bolted out the door.

"Oh my God!" The dough had risen so high it reached the top of the cab inside the pickup, floated out the broken window and down the side of the door.

I pushed the soft dough back inside the cab, seized the chrome door handle and flung it open. Next, I gathered the dough in my arms and shot across the yard as fast as my legs could go, and I didn't stop until I came upon the foul-smelling pigpen. WHOOSH, I heaved the blue dough, newspaper and all, into the trough.

The pigs squealed with joy and clambered over one another to get at the dough. Annabelle and I hung on the high fence, peeking through the wires, doubling over in laughter as we watched the fat baby pig, squished in between two big sows chomping away. And it only got funnier when the baby pig looked right at us with blue dough stuck on his snout, in his eyes and running down the side of his mouth.

Annabelle nudged my arm. "You know what? Those lucky pigs just ate the best supper they'll ever get, and your pa will never know the difference."

I jumped down and slapped my knee. "Yeah, and what he don't know won't hurt him."

I spun around when I felt a little jab on the back of my leg. There stood curious Baxter.

"Baxter you just missed out on a good supper."

He oinked and took off running towards the barn. I looked up, and saw that Papa was walking towards the barn too, with Maggie running alongside him. Annabelle and I darted through the tall grass and caught up with them.

I shouted over the loud wind, "We came to help you with the chores, Papa."

"Jou can start by gathering the eggs den."

Annabelle and I gathered the eggs, threw down hay and tossed grain to the chickens.

Papa finished up the barn chores, walked up to the house and went right to work in the kitchen.

Soon, Papa called, "Jour supper is ready, girls."

We gathered around the kitchen table. Annabelle grinned and picked up her hot dog, then set it down. "I love eating at your house, Mr. Jonesen."

Papa chuckled, "There is Fig Newtons dat I just picked up at the store for dessert, girls, help jourself."

And he never mentioned the blue stuff in Ted's pickup again.

It was dark and dreary the next morning when I rode along to take Annabelle home. Papa drove into the Murgers' yard, slammed on the brakes, shut off the engine, and just sat there for a bit before he rolled the car window down, looked out and shouted, "Vat in the vorld is going on?"

The Devils Lake ambulance came barreling around the corner and stopped in front of the Murgers' house. Right away, two medics jumped out, ran around and opened the back doors of the ambulance.

I looked over my shoulder at Annabelle, who was staring out the back window with wide-open eyes. She screamed, "Oh my God, they're taking my brother, Radovan."

I jumped up and spun around. Kneeling on the seat, I reached over and threw my arms around her.

Papa got out of the car and leaned into the half-open window. "Come on, Girls, you might as vell get out too."

The three of us stood side-by-side on the front lawn in total shock. My heart began to race.

All we could see was the tip of Radovan's dark brown hair from under the white flannel blanket when the medics carried him out of the house on the stretcher, and slid him inside the ambulance. Quickly, they slammed the double doors shut.

I grabbed Papa's coat sleeve.

"Did you see blood coming out of Radovan?" I cried.

"No, Hannah, I didn't see blood."

Dakota Murger, dressed in a rose-print terry cloth robe and wearing sheepskin slippers, stood on her front porch, leaning against the pillar. Her hands trembled when she reached to push her auburn hair from her eyes. In a low, hoarse voice she spoke.

"I didn't worry about Radovan that much when he first said he had headaches and a sore throat, but during the night he developed a high fever. I tried every home remedy I could think of, yet he only grew weaker and sicker."

Tears ran down Annabelle's face as she darted across the yard, and into her

41

mother's arms.

Mr. Murger stood stoic beside Dakota and murmured, "Dakota, hurry, get dressed, dear. We've got to get to the hospital as soon as we can."

Papa made an impatient gesture, "Hannah, let's get going, ve aren't doing anybody any good standing around here."

We watched the ambulance roll out of the driveway with the siren screeching.

"OK, Hannah, get in da car."

Papa started the car and drove down the well-known road toward home. My body shook. I crouched against the pickup door. Sobbing, I asked Papa. "Why do you think the ambulance took Radovan? I hope he doesn't die. Why do people have to die? Why did Mama have to die?"

Papa drove in silence, slowly turned into our driveway and slammed on the brakes. Looking at me, he rumpled his hair with a quick, nervous motion. "Sissy Pie, ve'll never know why jour Motter died. He pulled his red hankie out of his pocket. "Here, let's vipe dose tears avay. I tink dere's a Hershey's candy bar vaiting for jou in da house."

Trembling, I rubbed my eyes with the back of my hands, and walked alongside Papa. He put his hand on the top of my head. "Sissy Pie, don't go vorrying about Radovan dying. My insides tell me, he vill be OK."

Later, I saw Papa standing outside by the windmill, and I snuck into his bedroom. I opened Mama's top dresser drawer and the scent of rosemary leaves filled my nose. I dug around looking at all her pretty lingerie. I found a pair of brand new nylon stockings in a box, stuck underneath all her hankies. One big pearl earring lay in the corner. I picked it up and examined it.

I remember Mama wearing those earrings. She loved pearls.

I put the earring in my jeans pocket.

Papa wouldn't care, but he wouldn't like it if he caught me snooping around in his bedroom either.

When I opened the second drawer, it was empty.

Papa must have cleaned it out. I wonder what he did with Mama's stuff.

On the way out of Mama's bedroom, I reached way down in my pocket and ran my fingers over the smooth pearl.

Maybe if I carry Mama's pearl with me I won't ever be sad.

After days of anxiously waiting by Radovan's bedside, Dr. Roxwell informed Mr. and Mrs. Murger that the test results confirmed Radovan had infantile paralysis, also known as polio. Twelve-year-old Radovan would need to wear rigid braces on his legs and walk with the aid of crutches for the rest of his life.

The world was in the midst of the biggest polio epidemic in history. Some schools closed. Parents panicked, and the public grew desperate for a vaccine. Various hospitals declined to admit polio victims.

A few days later, I rode along with Papa to pay the Murgers a visit, hoping to see Annabelle. Mr. Murger came out of the house and met us as soon as we drove into their yard. Right off, Papa started in, "I vant to do vhatever I can to help, Venzel. If anyvon needs a ride or anyting, I'll be glad to take dem. If jou need to use my car, dat's OK too."

"Don't worry, Johan. We are managing OK. Dakota and Annabelle are at the Fargo Hospital with Radovan right now. Northern Pacific has transferred a young man from the Bisbee Depot to fill in, so that Dakota and I can take turns staying with my son."

I felt sad for Radovan and the Murger family; still, I couldn't help but miss playing with Annabelle.

***

"Vell, Sissy Pie, I'm pretty vell caught up vit the harvesting. Vhat do jou say ve go to Devils Lake tomorrow morning? I'm tinking about trading my old John Deere tractor in for a new one, and ve'll get jou some school clothes vhile ve're dere."

"I'd love to go shopping in Devils Lake. I want to look at the jewelry in Woolworth's Five and Dime too. I still have birthday money to spend, Papa."

"I tink dat can be done."

Papa believed in shopping local, but there were some things you couldn't purchase in Munich. It was a special occasion to shop in Devils Lake, fifty miles from our farm.

"Papa, I can hardly wait."

"Vell, jou'll have to. How's jour foot anyvay?"

"It's fine." I stuck my bare foot up for Papa to see. "Maybe I can get some new shoes too."

After the chores were done the next morning, Papa and I took off for Devils Lake.

Our first stop was at the John Deere implement store outside of town. Right off, a salesman wearing a nametag that said Clarence on it came running out. He shook Papa's hand and followed us all over the big sales lot, talking a mile a minute, trying to convince Papa to buy the large John Deere Model D tractor. Papa moseyed around, taking his time to look at all the different models.

"Vell, Clarence, vit a big purchase like dis, a man has to dake time to tink it over before he makes da deal."

"Oh, I understand, Johan, but that Model D is the best tractor out there, and let me tell you, they are moving fast. You could walk in here tomorrow and they could be all gone."

"Da hell jou say?"

Papa left with the promise he'd be back.

Next stop was J. C. Penney. I ran straight to the shoe department and stood in the aisle with boxes of pretty shoes all around me, shilly-shallying.

"Papa, do you like 'em?"

Papa grinned and glanced down at my feet in the red Mary Janes.

"Do jou like 'em is da ting?"

"Yes, I love them, and I know Mama would like them too. I can't wait to wear them."

"Dey are for school, Hannah."

"I know, but can I wear them home?"

"Okay, Sissy Pie, but try not to get dem dirty."

Papa sat in the car, smoking his pipe, and waited for me while I went into Woolworth's and spent all my money on a beautiful birthstone ring, something I'd wanted for a long time.

On my way out to the car, I held up my hand for Papa to see, and I couldn't quit smiling.

Papa grinned. "Did jou get everyting you wanted, den, Sissy Pie?"

"I sure did, Papa, and I'm ready to go home."

While Papa and I traveled down Highway 2, headed home, I looked out the car window and read the Burma Shave advertisements along the highway.

The hobo

Lets his

Whiskers sprout

It's trains—not girls

That he takes out

—Burma Shave

When we came upon Greske's Gas Station and Saloon, Papa slowed way down, pulled up in front of the gas pumps and came to a creaking stop. He jumped out of the pickup and shouted, "Fill her up."

I heard frogs croaking from off in the swamp when I got out of the pickup and traipsed alongside Papa into the high-ceilinged, dimly lit, smoke-filled saloon that smelled like stale beer.

A sign on the door read, "No minors." But Papa paid no mind. The place was hopping. All the booths and most of the tables were full. I climbed up on the high wooden stool next to Mrs. Runa Hagebak and sniffed her lilac perfume.

Runa Hagebak smiled at me. "Well, Hannah, don't you look pretty in your pink pedal pushers and matching polka-dot top, and my goodness, just look at those Mary Jane shoes."

Blushing, I leaned my elbows on the long smooth mahogany bar and looked into Mrs. Hagebak's lovely oval-shaped face, heavily rouged and powdered. I held out my hand for her to see my new ring.

"Well, that has to be the nicest blue topaz stone I've ever seen."

"I know, it's my birthstone."

"Mrs. Hagebak, did you know that Mama's birthday was the same day as mine?"

With a sweep of her hand Mrs. Hagebak brushed the hair out of my eyes. "No, I didn't know that, Sweety, but I do know it's hard with your Mama gone, and I'm sorry. I wish there was something I could do."

I nodded. "I wish Mama could see my new ring, and my red shoes."

"Honey, she sees them. She's looking down on you from heaven and watching everything you do."

I smiled. "Really?"

Papa spoke up, "A bag of pretzels for Hannah, please, and a bottle of orange pop."

Mr. Greske plunked a bottle of my favorite, Orange Crush, and a bag of pretzels in front of me. I took a big, long drink, hmmmmmm.

Someone shouted, "You got any good jokes, Johan?"

Papa chuckled and plopped down on the stool next to me. He motioned for the bartender to bring him a Hamm's beer. "Jah, send a drink, vhatever she's drinking over dere to da lady while jou're at it."

Mrs. Hagebak reached around me and nudged Papa's shoulder. "Thank you, Johan."

"Jah, how jou doing, Runa?"

"It's awful to lose your husband after thirty-eight years. I sure do miss the old bugger, but all in all I'm doing OK."

"I understand yust how jou feel, Runa, for damn sure."

Papa started tapping his foot when a Hank Williams tune flowed from the jukebox and shouted, "Turn her up."

I loved to people-watch and believe me, there was no better place than Greske's bar to look at people. I gawked at the short plump fella, dressed in bib overalls. He looked funny with his egg-shaped head sunk way down into the collar of his red-checked shirt as if he had no neck. He dropped a few nickels into the jukebox, hung onto a nearby doorjamb and swayed to the tune, "Hey Good Lookin'."

Papa perked up when a blonde lady came prancing through the swinging barroom doors, wearing red wedge heels. When she looked at Papa her chubby face broke into a smile. Papa smirked, looked down and kicked at the peanuts on the floor, then slid off the bar stool and motioned for me to come.

"You taking off, Johan?" Mr. Greske asked.

"Ja, I gotta get home, dose cows don't milk themselves."

Papa and I hurried out of the saloon, hopped into his yellow pickup and sped off. As we traveled down the long, straight road, I slithered close to Papa on the seat and twisted around to look him in the face. I blurted out, "Papa, I hope you never get married again."

"I don't tink you have to vorry about dat, Sissy Pie. Jour motter was the first and only voman I ever loved. I adored dat woman. I know dere's no one like her out dere anyvhere. Now don't jou go telling your grandma I had you vit me in Greske's bar, do ja hear?"

"I won't tell anybody."

Now and again Papa wiped the fog off the windshield with the back of his hand and leaned forward to peer through the hole he had rubbed clear.

I couldn't quit looking at my new ring.

"Papa, how come you keep your wine jug down in the blacksmith shop?"

"Vell, dat started vhen I married jour motter. She didn't vant her motter to know dat ve had vine in da house. Cajsa vould have a little vine vit me every now and den. She liked to drink from a pretty vine glass, but she didn't vant jour grandma to know. Your Grandma Bamford was dead set against drinking alcohol of any kind, it was a fright."

"How did you meet Mama?"

"Oh, Sissy Pie, I don't feel like going into all dat right now. Ask your nosy grandma, she'll tell jou everyting."

"Grandma told me already."

"Vell, vhy did jou ask me den?"

I giggled. "Papa, who was that little fella with the pelican neck, playing the jukebox?"

"Oh, ja, now, dat's Mr. Crabgrass. His chin tilts vay up in the air from a big goiter. He likes to drink whiskey and chase it down with beer and throw his quarters in the jukebox. Jah, he's quite a character, alright."

"He looked drunk to me. You know, Papa, they won't let anyone visit Radovan at the hospital, except his family, and I sure miss being with Annabelle."

"Yah, it's yust Annabelle and her parents who can wisit him, vit dis polio outbreak going on. I'm sure jou do miss her, but she vants to be vit her brotter and help take care of him, and dats a goot ting."

"I know, but I have lots of stuff I want to tell her. I hope her mother lets her come to the fair with us."

I walked beside Papa to the barn, but when it came time to water old Chester the bull,

Papa told me, "Hannah, it's best to get in da house and stay dere vhen I dake Chester out of his pen."

Papa took hold of the heavy yellow rope and hooked it around Chester's big neck. I scampered into the house, climbed up onto the backless kitchen stool and peeked out the window. Even though Chester scared the daylights out of me, I still liked to look at his huge, rugged body when Papa pulled him along. Chester bellowed and pawed the soft earth with his horns on the way to the big, round wooden water tank. The water ran off his nose ring when he tossed his head and rolled his eyes after guzzling gallons of water.

I heard farmers from all around say to Papa, "Let me know if you're ever ready to sell your bull, Johan, I'd pay top dollar for a bull like Chester." Chester was a handsome bull and a purebred too.

***

It was a very special day when Annabelle and I got together after what seemed like a very long time.

"Your hair sure has grown, Annabelle—it looks prettier than ever."

"Thank you, Hannah." She pulled me close with tears in her eyes and confided, "You know, my own legs ache when I look at Radovan's shriveled legs. I pray that someday he'll be able to walk without crutches."

I didn't believe that could ever happen, not from what I'd heard about the horrible, crippling disease. It broke my heart to see Radovan struggling along on his crutches, but he didn't want sympathy. Radovan persevered—made the best of it, and was glad to get back to school after four long months.

On a gloomy Saturday afternoon, Annabelle, Radovan, and I were on our way to the depot when a convertible jalopy, painted gold, pulled up beside us. A smart-aleck kid, dressed in a black leather jacket with long, greasy black hair, jumped out of the driver's side. Three of his buddies followed behind.

The smart aleck stomped toward us and got right in Radovan's face, swinging his fists and yelling, "Hey, cripple, can't you move any faster?" Then he grabbed for Radovan's crutches. The rest of the gang gathered around and hooted with laughter.

Without any warning, Annabelle picked up a rock, held it above her head and charged after him shouting, "You leave my brother alone or I'm throwing this rock at you."

"Hey, guys, did you hear what she said? She's going to throw rocks at us? Well, I don't believe in fighting with girls. Let's get the hell out of here."

They took off running like a band of orangutans. Annabelle threw the rock as hard as she could and hit the smart aleck between the shoulders.

The thugs piled in the convertible and sped off, laughing and hollering.

"Hey, Sis, that's some throw you got there," Radovan yelled.

"Well, what else could I do? I wasn't going to stand there like a dummy and let those punks steal your crutches or hurt you."

My face reflected the anguish in Radovan's eyes. Annabelle put a hand on her brother's shoulder. "Let's go home."

***

Come rain or shine, we never missed going to the County Fair—the biggest event of the year. It took place in June. Farm folks entered their prize sheep, cows, pigs, chickens, ponies, foodstuffs and crafts.

Sometimes, Grandma sewed off and on all year on a project to exhibit at the fair. I loved to watch Grandma's fingers, short and sturdy, working on a hand-sewn quilt. She made tiny stitches, ripping out entire squares and starting all over if she made the slightest mistake.

Baxter had grown into an adorable, curious, smart, strong pig by then. I don't think he thought of himself as a pig; he acted more like an old farm dog. Oftentimes, he snuggled up to Maggie in the barn while we were doing the chores and slept. I was delighted when Papa suggested that we enter Baxter in the pig competition. And I was happier than ever when I heard Annabelle was coming along with us to the fair!

Midmorning, on a Friday, Papa loaded Baxter into the trunk. He tied a small twine rope onto the trunk lid to hold it open so Baxter could breathe fresh air, and we all piled into the car. Grandma sat in the backseat between Tova and Annabelle, holding her double-ax pattern duvet on her lap. I sat up front with Papa and hung my head out the window, listening, and hoping Baxter was doing OK back there.

When we got to the fair, Papa lifted Baxter out of the crate and carried the squealing pig under his arm across the fresh mowed grass to the big Animal Exhibition Barn.

"Och, dat dirty pig," Papa grumbled as he bent over, pulled his big hankie out of his pants pocket and wiped the muddy streaks off his gray trousers.

"Jou girls stay together. Don't go talking to any strangers, ja hear?" Papa hollered over his shoulder as he turned around and hustled toward the racetrack.

Tova, her hair pulled up in an elaborate twist on the back of her head, carried Grandma's duvet draped over one arm and hung onto Grandma's arm with the other. Grandma's solid black chunky-heeled oxfords squeaked as they hurried towards the craft exhibit booth.

Annabelle and I treated ourselves to cotton candy and wandered through the dusty fairgrounds, pulling on the gooey pink stuff and shoving it into our mouths. The smell of peanuts roasting and candy apples filled the air.

Bells clanged and lights blinked. People of all ages crammed into the fairgrounds. Farm boys strolled the grounds, puffing on cigarettes, ogling the girls.

The Ferris wheel seats were filled with kids screaming and waving at their friends below when we hopped on and went for a ride. We looked at each other in surprise when the Ferris wheel came to a full stop and the greasy-looking operator grinned through missing teeth and gestured for us to stay put. We plunked back down on the hard seat, giggling and swaying our legs back and forth in the crisp air, and the next thing we knew, we were going round and round again.

When the Ferris wheel stopped once more, we leaped off, hollered, "Thank you," and began running through the midway. The jolly operator waved his arm and nodded.

"Let's ride the carousel," I shouted above all the hubbub.

"Oh, no Hannah, the carousel is for the little kids."

I loved the carousel music and the joy of sitting on top of the polished brown-and-white painted horse. Annabelle shouted from the crowd, "Hannah, hurry up and get off of that kiddies' ride. There is so much more for us to see." She took my arm when I leaped to the ground, and pointed at all the people carrying big stuffed panda bears and tigers. "Hannah, let's try our luck at winning something."

A Gypsy fortune-teller, dressed in a long orange skirt with a multicolored scarf tied on her head, peered out of a tent, beckoning with her long, slim fingers to come inside.

The likes of her looked scary. We bolted around the corner, not watching where we were going, and I crashed into a creepy-looking character with skinny arms hanging out of a grimy sleeveless shirt. I looked up and saw his face was covered with tattoos. Oh, my God, he grabbed hold of my arm and shouted, "Stay right here, girlies. Take your chance on ring tossing. You win every time. Step right up, pretty girlies."

I jerked away and we hit the ground running. I hated the feel of his dirty hand on my arm.

Why would anyone want tattoos all over their face?

Clowns stood on every corner, handing out balloons and candy. I noticed a yellow balloon flutter through the air, followed by a child's long wail.

Annabelle said, "Someday, I'd like to be a clown and entertain kids, maybe at a children's hospital or something."

"That sounds like fun."

Further on down the fairgrounds, we saw a huge sign hanging on the outside of this humongous tent that read: "BIGGEST FREAK SHOW IN THE WORLD." At the bottom of the big sign in small letters—"adults only."

"Come on, Hannah, let's go see the biggest freak show in the world."

"No, we can't go in there. See the small letters at the bottom?"

"Oh, come on. It will be something different. Look how the wind blows big gaps below the tent. We could sneak under there real easy."

"I hate going into closed-in places, but, hey, why not?"

We plopped down on our bellies and crawled over dirt and weeds that stunk like pee, and wormed ourselves into the big freak tent.

When I got inside and stood up, I happened to glance down and saw that my white blouse was smeared with dirt. I whispered, "What will I tell Grandma when she sees my muddy blouse?"

"Tell her it's from holding onto Baxter."

People stood shoulder to shoulder inside the noisy hot tent, staring up at the stage, and didn't even notice us slip in. I held my hands over my mouth to keep out the stink of perspiration.

The "Fat Lady" waddled off the stage, in an aqua-sequined dress. She looked back, waved her fleshy arms and gave a fake smile. The crowd clapped. An old man hollered, "Fat lady, pretty fat lady, come on back. I love fat women."

What's next? I wondered, when out from behind the big canvas curtain popped a giant of a man, wearing a big, red-striped short-sleeved shirt and baggy blue pants. His huge brown shoes looked like bedroom slippers.

I whispered in Annabelle's ear, "He is the ugliest freak I've ever laid eyes on."

She nodded and laughed like crazy.

In a thunderous voice the monster shouted, "So what you are about to see, ladies and gentlemen, is a rare sight indeed, one of the last traveling sideshows in America today. You don't want to miss it. It might amaze you. Yes, it might even disturb you. But, come, witness it with your own eyes for tomorrow it too may vanish."

I stood alongside Annabelle with my arms crossed, goggle-eyed.

The monster loosened his trousers—they dropped to the floor. He didn't have underpants on. BOOM—his huge pecker flopped out and dangled on the stage.

The sight of it gave me a shock.

Oh, my God. I held onto Annabelle's arm and whispered, "Can you believe this?"

Annabelle stood dumbfounded, howling with laughter. "Well, that beats anything."

The monster's shoe flew off when he spread his legs apart and lifted one foot in the air. He didn't miss a beat, but quickly took his pecker in both hands and pulled it way out for everyone to see, shouting, "Look close, ladies and gentlemen. The best is yet to come."

He sprawled his legs even wider, and gestured with one big hand. "Look, look right down here. You don't want to miss this, ladies and gentlemen."

Good God, he had big, soft-looking flabby girly parts down there too. Flabbergasted, I stood with my hands over my mouth, and stared at the weird whatchamacallit.

The freak rubbed his stubby, ugly face and looked amused, as he stood smack-dab on the middle of the wooden stage. Then he shouted, "Now, let me tell you something, ladies and gentlemen, my big pecker has never got hard, but if it does I am going to have me one hell of a good time."

The crowd roared. An old farmer in bib overalls cupped his hands to his mouth and yelled, "Hey, buddy, make it work."

I whispered in Annabelle's ear, "If Grandma knew I crawled in here and saw this rotten dirty stuff, she'd have a cow. Let's get out of here."

"Well, what if my mom knew we were in here? I don't want to even think about that."

"Mrs. Hagebak told me that Mama is watching me from heaven. I don't want to think about that either."

Lickety-split, we ducked under the tent and crept out into beautiful fresh air and sunshine.

Annabelle laid her fingers on the inside of my elbow and spoke in a little voice, "Hannah, I think the freak's big long wiener and all that other ugly-looking stuff was really made out of rubber."

"You don't think his *cock* was real?"

"Oh, my God, Hannah, I can't believe you said that."

Annabelle had a lively laugh. Looking at me, she let it rip. And, then, I started laughing so hard I thought I'd pee my pants. We promised each other then and there we would never, ever tell a soul that we had snuck into the adult freak tent.

Just then, I saw Papa coming our way, stooped over and reaching for his tobacco pouch.

"Hi Papa!" I shouted.

"Oh, hi dere girls. I been looking for jou. Ve got to get along now. Did you girls have a goot time, den?"

Annabelle grinned from ear to ear and rolled her eyes. "I had the time of my life and I'll never forget it. Thank you for taking me, Mr. Jonesen."

"Jour velcome. I'm glad jou could come vit us, Annabelle."

I smelled beer on Papa's breath.

We spotted Grandma sitting on a wooden armchair in the craft building. Her face broke into a big smile when she saw us, and she held up a pretty blue ribbon.

On the way to the car, Papa stumbled over a tent stake sticking up out of the dirty, paper-strewn fairgrounds. "Goddamnit," he muttered.

Grandma shrieked, "Tova, get the car keys from Johan. You are going to have to drive us home. Let him behind the wheel and we'll all be killed."

"By God, dat might be a good idea. I don't feel like driving anyvay." Papa muttered as he leaned against the side of the car, pulled the keys out of his pants pocket and handed them to Tova, then wormed his way into the passenger seat.

Annabelle and Grandma got into the backseat, and I climbed in between them. I plopped down on the cushion, leaned my head back and busted out laughing. I couldn't help it. Just thinking about us crawling under the tent, and seeing that outrageous stuff, and how Annabelle laughed when I said "cock." *Oh, my God, please help me.*

Grandma poked me with her elbow.

CHAPTER 4

Tova scooted behind the steering wheel and fit the key into the ignition. She sat there with her hands on the wheel for a moment before she turned the engine, then drove at a slow speed over the potholed street.

Papa was feeling good and couldn't quit jabbering, "Ja, I saw Yacob and his missus at da racetrack, jou know Lena hardly goes anyvhere vit him, but it looked like she was having a good time watching dem horses run. I saw lots of people I knew, but I really didn't drink dat much, maybe two beers at da most."

Grandma shouted from the back seat, "Oh, you didn't really drink that much? Huh?"

Papa's pipe hung precariously from the side of his mouth when he turned and talked over his shoulder.

"Jou know vhat jour problem is, Lieula? Jou vorry too damn much about notting. Alvays making a mountain out of a mole hill."

Tova gripped the steering wheel and yelled, "Would you please quit your silly arguing, right now."

I looked at Annabelle who sat jammed in beside me, snickering with her hand covering her mouth. And I busted out laughing all over again and couldn't stop. Grandma reached over, yanked my ear and scolded, "Stop that silly laughing. Do you hear me?" Then she pushed herself up off the thick seat cushion, tapped Johan on the shoulder and shouted, "Hannah is going home with me tonight, Johan."

"Lieula, don't even start vit dat."

I held my hands over my ears.

There goes Grandma again, overreacting and making a big deal out of nothing. Didn't she see that Papa stumbled over an old tent state, sticking up, out of the ground?

Papa liked to drink a few beers and have fun, but I'd never seen him drunk. And, I know he let Tova drive just to please Grandma.

Tova hollered, "It's hard enough driving a strange car without you guys yelling at each other, so shut the hell up, both of you."

Oh, my God. We forgot Baxter?

I shouted from the backseat, "Papa, guess what?"

"Vhat is it, Sissy Pie?"

I grabbed onto the front seat behind Tova and pulled myself up. "Tova, you have got to turn around RIGHT NOW and go back to the fairgrounds, PLEASE."

"What's the matter with you anyway, Hannah? You know better than to shout in my ear when I am driving."

"WE FORGOT BAXTER."

"Oh, for Christ sake, how da hell could ve do dat?"

The pink wart by Grandma's nose quivered when she bellowed, "Why, the idea."

I imagined Baxter sitting inside that strange, little pen amongst all the strange animal sounds, wondering why we never came to get him by now.

"It's no use going back now. Da stock barns are closed up for da day, sure as hell."

"Can't we go and see for sure?"

Grandma chimed in, "Let it be, Hannah, your pig will be OK."

"Pipe down back dere, Hannah Marie. Ve'll get up early in da morning, and me and you vill drive back to Cando and pick up jour pig. Don't go vorrying your pretty little head about Baxter. He vill be yust fine."

After a restless night, I leaped out of my bed before it was even daylight and ran down the stairs, calling, "Papa, wake up."

Papa pushed his body upright, swung his feet onto the braided rug by the side of his bed, shrugged into his overalls, and headed straight for the barn. He hurried through the milking and farm chores before we took off in his pickup.

We got to the Cando fairgrounds so early that the stock barns hadn't opened yet. Papa parked in the shade under a big oak tree, leaned back on the seat, and puffed on his pipe.

I rolled down my window and hung my head out, watching and waiting for the big, crooked stock-barn doors to open. A narrow-chested guy wearing nothing but a pair of black shorts and black rubber boots caught my eye.

He sat spread-eagled on a long wooden bench next to the barn, picking his nose, rolling it in his dirty fingers, and throwing it. Ping: a booger landed on a tin can. Oh, my God! I'd never seen the likes, and I cracked up.

Now I knew for sure what Papa meant when he'd say, "People vill do anyting."

Papa took the pipe out of his mouth. "Vat's so damn funny, anyvay?"

SCREECH! The barn doors opened—I leaped out of the truck and took off running, stumbling over the dirty paper cups and stinky cigarette butts, and laughing so hard I almost fell.

As soon as I entered the barn, I spotted Baxter laying in the little pigpen on a pile of yellow straw, sound asleep. A blue ribbon hung on his cage. When he heard my footsteps his eyes opened.

I got down on my knees to get at the strange latch, and I wrestled with it for a bit before I got it to open. I gently pulled Baxter into my arms, snuggled him against my chest, and whispered, "Baxter, you are the prettiest pig in the whole wide world. I'm so proud of you."

Papa caught up to me and stood beside the pigpen with a big grin on his face. "Jah, Baxter, jou are a real vinner, alright."

Baxter made two little oinks that sounded like, "Thank you."

Papa loaded Baxter into the back of the pickup, and then hopped into the cab. I bounded in beside him, and we took off. It was good to hear Baxter's happy squeals coming from the back of the pickup as we rumbled down the road.

Papa reached up and turned the wipers on when little misty raindrops landed on the windshield. Grandma was standing out in the drizzle by the chicken coop, watering her chickens and throwing out cracked corn, when we caught up to her house. Papa slowed down and turned in. She had on a thin blue sweater, buttoned crooked, and wore an upset smile. Cloris, the hen, waddled in the grass, pecking near her feet.

Grandma crossed her arms over her chest and walked up to Papa's side of the pickup. I scooted over and stretched around Papa to get a better look at her grouchy face. She looked right at Papa with her dark brown eyes and started complaining to him again about him drinking too much beer. Was he ever going to quit?

Papa paid no mind. He hopped out of the truck and chased the laying hens that had wandered onto the side of the road back into the chicken coop. Then he jumped back in his truck, and we took off down the narrow, dusty prairie road towards home. Papa drove along mumbling something about how goddamn crabby Grandma was all da time.

"I know, Papa, if things don't go her way, she gets grumpy."
I rolled the window down, looked back and gave Grandma a happy wave. She smiled and waved back. I felt a little angry with Grandma too. She could have at least pretended she was happy for Baxter. After all, he'd survived the night in that big barn with all the weird animals around him, and he'd won a blue ribbon!

***

Later on, I felt guilty for thinking bad thoughts about Grandma, so I called for Maggie, and we headed back to Grandma's place. I took my time and walked slow by the side of the road. I reached in my pocket for Mama's pearl earring and twirled it around in my fingers. I kicked at a stone here and there, and I thought real hard about Papa, Grandma and me. I think Grandma is jealous because Papa and I get along so good. I love Grandma a lot, but it's not like Papa and me. And, I thought about the time Papa told me he thought, "Grandma vas trying to live Cajsa's life through me." Maggie snapped me out of my trance when she jumped straight up and barked loudly at a crow flapping and cawing in the air.

Grandma saw us coming and walked out onto her sagging porch, waving her apron before her as if she were shooing chickens.

"Hurry, get inside before it starts to rain again," she shouted.
Maggie looked up at Grandma with her intelligent eyes. "Yes, Maggie, you're welcome too." Grandma patted Maggie on the head.

I plopped down on a chair by the kitchen table. The smell of tomato soup simmering made my stomach rumble.

"Where did you get the pretty flowers?" I asked when I spotted the beautiful bouquet of sunflowers on the table.

"Tova brought them over the other day. She picked them out of her garden. Did you and Annabelle have a good time at the fair?"

I giggled. "Annabelle and I had a blast. Aren't you glad you chose the quilt you did to enter, Grandma? I love how you and Baxter both got blue ribbons."

"All my hard work paid off."

"Well, no one can make quilts like you can, Grandma. That's for sure."

Grandma filled a big ceramic bowl full of tomato soup. She spread butter on fresh-baked bread, poured a glass of ice-cold lemonade and placed the plate and glass in front of me.

I looked up at Grandma. "You can always tell when I'm hungry, can't you?"

Grandma smiled.

"Remember the good corn pudding Mama used to make?"

"I sure do. It's an old family recipe, passed down."

"I wish I had some right now."

"You do? Well, let me know when you're coming next time, and I'll have it baked for you. It probably won't taste like your mama's, but we'll wait and see."

"Grandma, I found this pearl earring of Mama's." I took it out of my pocket and showed her.

"Where did you find it? That belonged to my mother, your great-grandma."

"It did? Well, there was only one earring in Mama's top dresser drawer, and I took it. I carry it with me and it makes me feel good—like Mama is close by."

"Well, I'm glad it helps you, dear. Your mama felt so bad when she lost the one earring. It's a real keepsake. You hang onto it."

"I will." I put it back in my pocket. "I wonder how old it is, Grandma?"

"Oh, I have no idea."

When I finished my second helping of soup, I wiped my face with the big white linen napkin and told Grandma, "I have to get on my way. Mr. Murger is dropping Annabelle off to spend the night with me." The chair creaked when I slid myself away from the table.

***

I just got home when Annabelle came dashing up our driveway on a brand new bike; with her hair bobbing in the breeze and a big smile on her face. She hung onto the handlebars with one hand, and in her left hand she clutched a twine handle wrapped around the cardboard box that served as her suitcase. Stepping hard on the pedals, the bike wobbled slightly. I ran out to meet her.

"Hi Hannah! I thought your dad was giving you a ride."

"Well, he planned to, but since I got my new bike I wanted to ride it."

"Wasn't it hard riding and hanging onto your box too?"

"No, not at all. I can ride my bike with both hands off the handle bars."

Annabelle's new bike was a white 1947 Schwinn with pink trim and the seat was brown and white leather.

"How come you got a new bike? It's not your birthday or Christmas." Laughing, Annabelle responded, "Well, since you got a new bike, I wanted one too. No, Dad surprised me when he came home with it yesterday. I heard him say to mom, 'it's time Annabelle has her own girl's bike, and it counts as part of an early birthday present too."

"Your bike is beautiful, Annabelle."

"It's quite a change after riding a boy's bike all my life. It pedals so easy too, and I love it. Hannah, I was thinking on my way over, why don't we make a tent and sleep in it tonight?"

"That sounds like fun, but first, let's bake a cake to take with us. I made a spice cake for Papa the other day and it turned out quite nice."

Annabelle sat on a kitchen chair and watched while I mixed up the cake in Mama's big blue mixing bowl and popped it in the oven. While the cake baked, Annabelle and I ran up to the attic and snatched some old Indian blankets out of the age-old wooden trunk. The smell of spice cake filled the air.

We draped the blankets over the barnyard fence, and Annabelle ordered me to hold them in place while she hammered big nails into each corner. She left a wide opening for us to crawl in and out of, and we tossed quilts, pillows and some old Indian blankets inside.

The sun was going down when I packed my pajamas and a big flashlight into a grocery bag and picked up the delicious looking frosted cake.

Annabelle looked at the cake. "Hmmmm, I love cream-cheese icing." She grabbed her cardboard box and out the door we went.

Papa hollered, "If it starts to rain or gets cold out dere, jou girls get back in da house right avay before jou catch a deat of cold. Do jou hear me?"

"Don't worry, Papa."

I clambered inside the tent, and Annabelle handed me the cake, my bag, and her stuff before she crawled in and plopped down on the blankets.

"This is so much fun, Hannah."

"Yeah, just think, we can eat cake for breakfast and stay awake all night if we feel like it."

"Eating cake for breakfast is really different"

We snuggled under the quilts, put our arms under our heads and looked at the shiny stars through the big hole in the top of the tent, and we spotted the Big Dipper. We had a high old time, giggling and singing silly songs. And we talked and talked, and talked some more.

"Hannah, Dad told me that we are going to have a man teacher this fall. Did you know that?"

"No, I didn't, but I'll be glad to go back to school, won't you?"

"Hmm-mmm. I miss seeing the other kids."

The howl of a far-off dog rose in the night air. Maggie lay outside by our tent and answered with a fainter howl.

Crickets chirped.

Annabelle whispered, "Did you know I have a rupture?"

"Of course not. What are you talking about, a rupture?"

"Mom took me to the doctor the other day after I showed her my lump."

"What lump?"

"I noticed a bulge on my—well, let me show you." She leaped out of the blankets, grabbed hold of the flashlight, and pulled her panties down.

"What are you doing?"

"I'm showing you, it's down here, Hannah," and she shone the light on her lump.

"Oh, my God, Annabelle. You call it a rupture?"

"Yeah, a rupture is the same thing as a hernia."

"I thought just old men got hernias."

A lump the size of a walnut popped out.

"Does it hurt?"

"No, but it feels weird. Do you want to touch it?"

"No. What did Dr. Knightley say?"

"He told my mom to keep an eye on it, and if it grew any bigger to bring me back in, but he didn't think it was anything to worry about. Then again, it could disappear on its own."

"I hope so. What do you think caused it?"

"Dr. Knightley really doesn't know why these things happen. Mom said she thinks it's from sitting on top of Lightning and riding him with my legs stretched so far apart, but I don't think that's the reason. I mean, you ride Sally more than I ride Lightning and you don't have a rupture. It doesn't hurt or anything. Most of the time, I don't even think about it."

"Well, I hope you don't have to have an operation."

Annabelle giggled. "Hannah, did you notice I have hair growing down there?"

"Yeah, I did."

"Have you?"

"Have I what?"

"Got hair down there?"

"No. I wonder why you do and I don't when we're both eleven."

"Mom told me I'm growing into puberty, and girls grow into their adolescence at different ages. I'm getting hair under my arms too. Mom said it's a sign I may be getting my period soon. Did you know you could get your period when you are as young as nine years old?"

"Oh, my God! I don't have any of that stuff happening to me yet."

Once more, the jealous, mean feeling came over me, and I couldn't help it. Sometimes I felt so envious of Annabelle and her mother. It seemed Annabelle could talk to her mother about anything. They were like best friends. And I didn't have anyone. I couldn't go to Papa and ask him about girl stuff, and I felt awkward talking to Grandma.

Just then, a strange noise coming from outside the tent snapped me out of my mean, jealous streak.

I poked Annabelle.

"What is it, Hannah?"

"Shhhh. Listen, it sounds like a man's big footsteps coming toward our tent."

The heavy footsteps grew closer.

"Who could it be?" Annabelle whispered.

I sat up and pushed my hair back away from my ears. "What if it's some lunatic who escaped from the crazy house in Jamestown with a butcher knife, and he's going to stab us both? Be quiet and lay still."

I heard insects humming, and more footsteps—CLOP, CLOP.

"Hannah, whoever it is, he must have humongous feet. Should we holler for your pa to come?"

"No, that would only make him crazier."

Annabelle and her big ideas, always wanting to do something different.

All of a sudden, Annabelle brought herself up on her elbows and started laughing hysterically.

I screeched, "What's wrong with you? I told you to be quiet."

"Look," she shouted and shone the flashlight on the opening in our tent.

Oh, my God! Sally's big head poked through. She had somehow managed to stretch her long neck over the barnyard fence and look in at us.

I started laughing and crying at the same time. "You silly horse, you scared us half to death."

Sally curled her lips and made a whinnying sound before she galloped away.

"Hannah, let's eat some spice cake right now."

"OK. Hand me the flashlight, will you?"

I let out a bloodcurdling scream when the light landed on the cake—"Annabelle, look! Our nice spice cake is covered with ants. We can't eat it."

Little, creepy ants were crawling everywhere.

Annabelle shrieked, "Good God, ants are crawling up my legs too. Let's get out of here, right now."

We busted out of the tent and ran through the back door, into the kitchen, and headed upstairs to my warm, comfortable bedroom.

Papa woke up and hollered, "Is dat jou, Hannah?"

"Papa, we got attacked by ants."

"Ants, jou say? Vell, quiet down now, and go on up to bed. It's a long time till morning."

***

The days grew shorter and colder, orange and yellow leaves covered the grass, and once again it was time for school to start.

I didn't sleep a wink the night before the first day of school. I just lay in my bed, listening to a fly buzzing on my ceiling and turning over in my mind: *What would the new man teacher be like? What should I wear and what to take to school the next day?*

I was up and ready long before it was time to go, dressed in my new yellow-flowered shirt and short denim skirt. Finally, it was time to catch the school bus. When Baxter saw me walking down the driveway, he came scampering after me.

I spun around, pushed on his bristly backside, and struggled to get him to go back where he belonged. I coaxed, "Go home, you silly pig, go home, baby," but he only grew more agitated and squealed bloody murder, until Papa hurried along and chased him back into the farmyard.

I hopped on the school bus, walked down the aisle and turned to wave at Papa and Baxter before I plopped down on the seat next to Annabelle. As soon as the bus stopped in front of the schoolhouse, I scrambled off and ran up the steps, two at a time.

All of the students, grades one through eight, seated themselves at the desks where they had sat the year before. There were sixteen kids in the country school.

The teacher, a grave elderly man, queerly shaped with a round body set on short legs, turned from the blackboard and looked cross-eyed over his bifocals.

"Now, children, I want you all to sit up just as straight and pretty as you can and give me all your attention for a minute or two. My name is Mr. Knute Iverson. You are to call me Mr. Iverson."

I hadn't watched where Annabelle went after she hopped off the bus, but she came strutting in just on time, and quickly removed her hat. Mr. Iverson put down the eraser and gazed stupidly at her shiny mass of hair. "My God, girl, what a head of hair!" he exclaimed, sounding innocent and foolish.

Annabelle looked at him, blushed, and drew in her upper lip, then quietly sat down.

Mr. Iverson had a gold watch chain like Papa's hanging from his light-green plaid shirt pocket, and he went on to say, "Children, it's OK to sit where you are for now, but I will assign you different seats soon."

Olaf, an eighth grader, spoke up, "Oh, really? Where are you going to seat us, Mr. Iverson? Out on the back forty?"

"Now, now, young fella, I will have none of that sarcasm in my schoolroom."

I realized after the first day with Mr. Iverson, I never should have worried so much. *Things are going to be OK.* When I got home and climbed off the bus with my arms full of new books, Maggie was waiting right by the mailbox to greet me. And Baxter came scurrying down the rutted driveway, squealing happy squeals.

The minute I walked into the kitchen, I smelled food cooking. Wow! A hot supper of roast pork, carrots and potatoes sat on the back of the stove.

Amazing, Papa must have come in from the field earlier and cooked our supper.

I kept my ears open for the *putt, putt* of the John Deere tractor while I set the oilcloth-covered table with Mama's plain white dinnerware. Later, Papa sat across from me, slowly cutting his pork roast into little pieces, listening to me.

"Papa, the new teacher seemed a little strange, maybe it's because I've never had a man teacher before, but I think I'll get to like him. He has a pocket watch like yours and his name is Knute Anderson, and he is sort of funny-looking."

Papa reached for the butter dish and muttered, "Ja, I don't recall Newville ever hiring a man teacher. Jou say his name is Knute Iverson, dats a goot Swede name. He should fit in real goot around here, den."

Exactly four weeks after school started on a chilly Saturday morning, I sat by the kitchen table, dressed in my favorite pink-flannel pajamas decorated with hearts and devouring a bowl of hot oatmeal with raisins and cinnamon, when I heard a strange truck rattle into our driveway. I laid my spoon down, pushed the white lace curtain aside, and peeked out.

The little guy driving the clunker of a truck was the man I saw in Greske's bar with the pelican neck.

He jumped out of his truck and stood looking towards the barnyard, massaging his chin, before he hustled around to the back of the truck and threw open the tailgate. Then he took off running into the barnyard and grabbed hold of Baxter. Baxter squealed like never before when the man shoved him into the back of his truck.

I didn't want to believe it, but I knew the man was taking Baxter away to market. I felt like storming out there and slapping his face. I could see Baxter's pink snout peeking through the wooden truck-bed slats, and when I heard him squeal as the truck barreled out of the driveway, I started to cry.

Why didn't Papa tell me Baxter was going to market?

I ran outside where Papa stood by the well, throwing all his weight on the pump handle as it went up and down. With my hands planted on my hips, I yelled as loud as I could.

"Papa, how come you didn't tell me you were selling Baxter? Baxter was my pig."

"Hannah, I knew if I vould tell jou, jou vould get upset, maybe talk me out of it too. Maybe I vent about it in da vrong vay, but, jour a big girl now, Hannah, jou know on da farm ven pigs fatten up, dey go to market. Jou vouldn't vant to have him butchered and eat his pork chops, vould jou?"

"Oh, Papa, don't say that. I don't want to ever think about anyone eating Baxter. You know, he seemed like another Maggie to me."

I stomped my feet and yelled some more, "You know that if I hadn't picked up helpless little Baxter out of that dirty pigpen when his mother tossed him way over in the corner and didn't want him, he never would have grown up to be a big, fat pig."

Oh, Lord, God, what am I going to do?

"Jou stop dat damn screaming right now, Hannah Marie. Jou know better den to holler at jour pa like dat. Jou should be ashamed. Now, get back in da house and behave jourself."

I trudged back to the house, walked up to my bedroom and picked up the first thing I could get my hands on, which happened to be my long-handled hairbrush, and I threw it against the wall and I swore something awful, "God damn it, sonofabitch, bastard." I didn't care if Papa heard me or not. Then I flopped down on my bed and bawled my eyes out.

***

As sad as I was about Baxter, I was excited to go back to school on Monday. Mr. Iverson had chosen me to help the younger kids with reading and spelling. And, it would take my mind off of losing my pig. I loved teaching the little kids and even dreamed of becoming a schoolteacher like Grandma. Grandma taught school for sixteen years before she married Grandpa. I'd always loved books. I don't remember learning to read, it was just something I always did. I was hungry for knowledge, I guess.

Three or four students would gather around me in a little alcove behind the piano. I stood with great importance, pronouncing the spelling words slow and clear. My heart went out to Roger Blackbird, a shy, diminutive third grader with eyes so brown they looked black behind thick glasses. Every time we gathered together, Roger ran over and plopped himself down in the chair facing mine.

One snowy, cold afternoon, we took turns reading from Roger's favorite book, *Black Beauty*. When Roger's time came, he smiled self-conscious like and shuffled his feet before he began to read loud. He pronounced the words perfectly.

I was sitting on a little wooden chair, looking at him and feeling proud, when all at once, his little face shrank up like he was about to cry. His words became slurred, and oh, my God, yellow pee ran down his pant legs and all over the hardwood floor.

Roger's *Black Beauty* book dropped to the floor with a thud. Mr. Iverson stomped across the room, snatched Roger by the ear and marched him into the restroom.

My heart hurt for timid Roger, and my dream of becoming a schoolteacher quickly vanished.

Annabelle poked my arm and made a weird face when Mr. Iverson announced he would dismiss class early on Friday to show us kids his Fire-Eating Act.

"Fire-Eating Act? I bet it's going to be something," she mumbled.

Before show time began, Mr. Iverson left the room for a few minutes. Then he quickly strutted back in, proud as a peacock, dressed in a black suit and top hat. He carried a lit torch and started his act by taking a wide stance to keep his balance. He tilted his head back while holding the torch above and placed it in his mouth.

Next, he stuck his tongue on the wick and closed his lips around the torch in an O shape and swallowed. I noticed his overly large ears shone bright red when he pulled the torch out of his mouth.

Laughing, he shouted, "That's fire-eating in a nutshell, boys and girls."

The kids clapped and roared with laughter.

Roger nudged me. "Hannah, I seen a fire-eater at the fair once."

"Was he as good as Mr. Iverson?"

Roger squirmed and gave a shy little smile.

Later, when Papa and I were sitting at the kitchen table eating our supper, I told him, "Mr. Iverson dismissed class early and showed us kids how to eat fire."

"He showed jou how to eat fire? I've never heard of such a crazy ting, sure don't sound like teaching school to me."

***

A couple of months later, I walked into the schoolroom and found Mr. Iverson sitting slouched at his desk, sound asleep while the rain gushed down from the roof and splashed onto the wide windows.

Olaf walked in, took one look at Mr. Iverson, and busted out laughing.

"Hey, guys, watch this."

Olaf snuck up behind Mr. Iverson with a spitball in his hand, aimed it right at him and flung it full force. The spitball skimmed Mr. Iverson's head, yet he didn't budge. Soon all the boys were flinging little clumps. The air grew thick with paper wads. To top it all off, when Mr. Iverson woke up, he just sat there grinning like an idiot.

But nothing could have prepared me for what happened next. It took place on the Friday before Christmas vacation began, when Mr. Iverson stood in the front of the classroom, quizzing the sixth-grade kids.

His thick black eyebrows wiggled, and his eyes riveted on Annabelle. "What city is the capitol of California? I'm asking you, Annabelle."

Annabelle shifted in her seat, tossed her head to flick her hair off her face and glanced down at the floor. I leaned over and whispered, "Sacramento."

That's when all hell broke loose.

Mr. Iverson bounded across the room, headed straight for me. His creepy eyes, both the crossed and the good, settled on me, unblinking. His face flushed and his upper lip quivered. He shouted, "You sneaky scoundrel, don't you ever whisper the answers to anyone." He grabbed my arms in his clammy hands and pulled me forward.

Ouch! My chest hit the front of the desk and I was stuck, but that didn't stop him. He came at me from an angle, yanked me out sideways and started swinging me round and round. My body fluttered in midair.

George Olson stood up, openmouthed. Elvira Hanson, who tended to act hysterical, began to cry. I shut my eyes, said a little prayer, and that's when I heard Mr. Iverson's pocket watch hit the floor.

"Oh, my God," I wailed, when at long last Mr. Iverson let go of my spindly arms and I toppled to the floor. He bent over, picked up his watch and strode out of the classroom. I lay there for a moment or two before I got up, stumbled to my desk, sank down and buried my face in my arms.

Annabelle smelled like school soap when she wrapped her arms around me. "Speak to me, and tell me you're OK, Hannah."

No use to tell Papa when I get home. He would say, "You had to have done someting bad to cause Mr. Iverson to get so upset." It was accepted in the community that the teacher had power over the children.

So I never told Papa. After that day, oftentimes, I'd sit at my desk, staring at Mr. Iverson over the top of my book and think, *You wacky asshole. I can't wait for the school year to end.*

***

I missed Mama more than ever when I walked into an empty house after school on those cold, wintry days. Sometimes, I'd be so overwhelmed with grief I didn't feel like doing anything but cry. I'd shove the tall wooden stool up to the kitchen window and sit by the warmth of the radiator, watching the flying snow, and sob my eyes out, wishing Papa would get home soon. Maggie lay on the floor beside me, whimpering.

I spent more time than ever at Grandma's house that winter. I loved it when we'd sit in her warm, cozy living room watching the fire; now and again, the lignite coal burned so hot, both sides of the potbellied stove turned red.

I'd snuggle next to her on her brocade davenport while she patiently taught me how to darn socks. First I threaded the darning needle with thick, black thread, and then placed a light bulb inside the sock where the hole was and made little vertical running stitches while Grandma sat and watched me, with her glasses propped up on her head.

Rhubarb lay on the back of Grandma's chair. "OK, now turn the sock upside down, Hannah, and make another row of stitches going the other way."

"OK, Grandma."

Grandma reached over and smoothed the hair from my face. "Promise me you'll stay the good little girl you are, Hannah."

I scooted close to Grandma and whispered, "I hope so."

Grandma hugged me. "Oh, Hannah, my heart, what would I do without you?"

"Be sad."

Grandma confided, "I took quite a tumble last fall and ever since, my hip aches more than ever. I guess some things just take time to heal. Come warm weather, I'll be fit as a fiddle again."

I rubbed her arthritic hand and said in a little voice, "I hope you never die, Grandma."

Grandma chuckled and looked at me. "Your old grandma is too ornery to die."

***

I loved when springtime rolled around. Seeing the snow melt and the tulips and all the other spring flowers popping up out of the ground made it my favorite time of year.

As soon as I got home from school, I'd pull on my jeans, climb up on Sally's bareback, grab a handful of mane, give a nudge with my heels, and off we'd go, riding through the lush green pasture, listening to the sound of the meadowlarks whistling and rounding up the cattle for milking time.

In mid-April, Mr. Wenzel Merger, president of the school board, announced that due to budget cuts, the county would no longer provide school-bus service. Most of the parents took turns driving their kids back and forth, mornings and afternoons. Lucky me, I got to ride Sally.

Papa hauled plenty of hay and oats to the school barn for Sally to eat, but there was no water tank, so during recess, I hurried out back to the barn, grabbed a bucket and led Sally across the dirt road to an old, rusty abandoned well, where I pumped bucket after bucket of water and held it up for her to drink.

Most of the time, I took the shortcut across the field, alongside the railroad tracks. Sally's ears stood straight up when she heard the long, low moan of the train whistle. The conductor would grin and wave at us from the caboose.

When some of the kids passed me by in a car with their mother driving them, they wouldn't even wave back at me. One day, Olaf put his face up to the window and stuck his tongue out. *I guess they're jealous because I get to ride my horse to school, and they can't.*

***

On a windy spring Saturday afternoon, I started across the bright flowered pasture. When I caught up to the cow's salt block, I stopped and chopped off a good-size piece, then stood barefoot on the soft green grass, licking the salt chunk and watching the baby colts jumping around. Suddenly, I heard a little moo far-off in the distance, or was it the wind?

I held my hand over my eyes to shade the sun and strained to see. To my surprise, Buttercup the cow stood in a state of anxiety as another Holstein looked on. Buttercup slowly lay down on the grass, but right away got back on her feet. In disbelief, I caught a glimpse of what looked like feet and nose appear inside a wet-looking, crystal clear sack before she lay down on the ground again, and began to toss about and moan something awful.

CHAPTER 5

It was horrible to look at, but my curiosity grew. The Holstein nibbled the grass, then took off running through the muddy slough and headed to the other side of the pasture, where she joined the herd. I kept my eyes on Buttercup, and watched as she got up on her feet and whiffed her newborn. Stimulated by his mother's soft mooing and the stroke of her tongue, the baby calf lifted his head, emerged from the pouch and strained to stand up, but his spindly legs wouldn't hold him. He rested a bit and tried once more. Oops, he tumbled backwards. The poor baby had a dreadful time getting his scrawny legs coordinated.

Finally, with instinct and his mama's coaxing, success! Buttercup waited patiently while the famished calf attempted to find a nipple. He stumbled around, sniffing. He knew it was somewhere. Even so, he grew tired and sank on the ground once more.

The proud mother leaned over her newborn as he lay helpless on the soft grass and continued to lick his ears, his chest, his belly and wherever she could reach. It wasn't too long before his soft black-and-white coat was dry and fluffy and he was up on all fours, nursing vigorously.

Oh, my God! I didn't know a baby calf was born inside of a big sack.

The minute I started up the school steps on Tuesday morning, I was taken aback when I saw Mr. Shoemaker, the school superintendent, a thin gentleman with short sandy hair, standing at the top of the steps. He motioned with his lanky fingers for me to stay where I was. "No need to go inside," he said.

I stopped in my tracks.

Mr. Shoemaker appeared shaken as he leaned against the wooden railing. The skin on his neck wobbled when he cleared his throat and, in a powerful voice, announced, "Students, due to a crisis within our Newville school system, there will be no book learning today. You are welcome to go home and you will not be counted absent. However, school will take up tomorrow as usual. I hope to see you then."

Holy cow! What was that all about?

I looked around for Annabelle and spotted her standing off by herself with a puzzled look on her face. She grinned when she saw me and waved.

I motioned for her to come and shouted, "Hurry, Annabelle, I'll give you a ride." Together, we ran out back to the school barn.

"Hannah, what do you think is going on? We don't have school today, and we won't be counted absent, yahoo!"

"Yeah, who would've thought? Wait here, Annabelle, I'll bring Sally around."

I quickly bridled Sally and led her outside. "Whoa, baby, whoa."

I boosted Annabelle up on Sally's back, then led Sally over by a big tree stump near the swing set and swung my right leg forward over the horse, careful not to bump Annabelle.

"Grab hold of me and hang on tight when we get going, OK?" I shouted over my shoulder.

Annabelle gripped my shirt with both hands.

I clicked my tongue, and Sally took off on a fast run, her hooves smacking the hard dirt road. I gave the reins a jerk, and steered Sally away from the edge of the roadway. It frightened me when Sally galloped close by the powerful waters that flowed down the gaping ditch.

Just as we turned into the yard, Mr. Murger came roaring past us in his truck and headed straight down to the blacksmith shop, where Papa was pounding metal on an anvil. Mittens lay on the ground, stretched out long and lazy by Papa's feet.

Mr. Murger slammed on his brakes and came to a screeching stop right in front of Papa's shop. He rolled his window down, stuck his head out and shouted, "Hi, Annabelle, hello, Hannah. I'm surprised you girls got here ahead of me, but I guess Sally doesn't waste any time once she gets going."

Mr. Murger jumped out of his truck and began to tell Papa what had happened to Mr. Iverson. Annabelle jumped down and ran over, and stood alongside her father. I stayed put and held tight onto Sally's reins.

Mr. Murger's voice grew louder and louder. Papa knocked his pipe against the heel of his shoe to dislodge the tobacco and lent an ear.

"Yeah, Johan, I was out in the front yard raking leaves when the kids came walking up the driveway after school yesterday. I noticed the sheriff's car speeding past my house, kicking up dust. I watched it pull up and stop in front of the schoolhouse, so I took off in my truck and hightailed it over there. The county sheriff, Orvin Pearl, you know him. He just built that big, brick three-story house outside of town. Well, he'd already slapped the cuffs on Iverson and was shoving him into the sheriff's car by the time I got there."

"The heck jou say."

"Johan, I leaned over and peeked in at Iverson stuffed into the backseat and I tapped on the window, but he wouldn't look my way."

"Jah, I saw jou going by last night like a bat out of hell, Venzel, but goddamn it, I never dreamt something like vhat jou're yust telling me vas going on. Yesus Christ, vat's dis vorld coming to anyvay?"

"It's hard to believe, Johan, but Sheriff Pearl showed me the report where Mr. Iverson stabbed a little Chippewa Indian kid with a scissors — almost killed him at the Belcourt Indian Reservation when he taught there. The Turtle Mountain Band of Chippewa Indians held a jury trial in Belcourt. The verdict: to put him in the loony bin in Jamestown and keep him in a straitjacket rather than send him to the prison."

Chills ran up my arms, and I felt Sally's reins slide through my fingers.

Good God, Mr. Iverson could have killed me that dreadful day.

Mr. Murger went on to say, "How the lunatic escaped and got hired to teach in Newville is more than I know. Come to find out he's not a real Scandahoovian, and Knute Iverson isn't his real name either. The sheriff took him to the county jail last night. Yeah, he's a sly character alright."

There was a chill in the air, and you could see Papa's breath when he talked. "He doesn't got dat fox's face for notting. Like I alvays say, people vill do anything. Tank God dey got rid of him before he killed one of our kids. Och, it scares the hell out of me to tink about dat. I hope the law puts him behind bars where he belongs and dat he's locked up for goot."

"Yah, that's for sure. I told Dakota when I got home, but I didn't say anything to the kids. Then, early this morning the school board got together for a special meeting. Johan, Mrs. Norlander will teach until school is dismissed in the spring. I'm glad she has agreed to help. It's never easy to find someone willing to teach way out here in the boondocks, especially during the cold winter months. She's with child, you know, so she won't be coming back in the fall. Hopefully we'll find an excellent teacher by then."

"Vell, jou sure got dat situation taken care of in fast order. Jah, Venzel, if it ain't one damn ting, it's ten more, but vit a man like jou on da school board, I'm not vorried one damn bit."

Boy, was I happy to hear Mr. Iverson was gone, but I wasn't too excited about the idea of another new teacher. Once again I got ready for school, picked out my clothes, gathered my books, and hoped the new teacher wouldn't be mean. I couldn't wait to get through the eighth grade and go to high school in town.

The following morning, Wednesday, Mrs. Norlander, a petite, vivacious lady dressed in a pale green two-piece suit with a pretty floral scarf swung over her shoulders, stood in the doorway and greeted each scholar enthusiastically. She asked our names and how to pronounce them correctly before we all settled in at our own familiar ink-stained wooden desks.

I grew to like Mrs. Norlander more every day. She was bubbly and full of life, and she made learning fun, such as singing the multiplication tables to "Mairzy Doats." Even so, she didn't put up with any foolishness, like the time Annabelle sat at her desk, smacking her gum. Mrs. Norlander abruptly stopped what she was doing, marched over in front of Annabelle, and stood with her arms crossed.

"Annabelle, are you chewing gum?"

"No, Mrs. Norlander."

"What do you have in your mouth?"

"Nothing."

"Whatever you are smacking on, take it out of your mouth."

Annabelle tossed her curly hair, bunched up her mouth, and blew a huge Bazooka gum bubble that covered her whole face.

A blast of giggles filled the schoolroom, but I wasn't laughing, and my heart started to pound. *Will Mrs. Norlander get upset and act like Mr. Iverson did with me?*

Mrs. Norlander gestured for everyone to be quiet, and the room grew silent.

"Annabelle, take that gum out of your mouth, stick it on your nose and leave it there until I tell you different."

Turning ten shades of red, Annabelle did what she was told. Mrs. Norlander went back to writing on the blackboard in perfect cursive letters.

I never understood why Annabelle acted like she did. At times, it seemed she would do anything to get attention.

I really liked geography class. I loved learning about different places and all the states. California sounded so pretty with all its sunshine, flowers blooming year around, palm trees, and the beautiful ocean. I couldn't help but wonder what it would be like to live where there was no snow.

When I told Papa one time that I'd like to live in California some day. He told me, "Jou live any vhere jou vant to, Hannah. Dere's no future for a joung person on da farm any more."

Just when I was getting to know Mrs. Norlander really good, the school year came to an end. I felt sad the day I told her good-bye. *Will I ever see her again?*

But, oh how I loved the freedom of summer! I rode my bike to Annabelle's house on the first day of summer vacation to spend the night. I could feel my thick braids bouncing on my back as I pedaled like a maniac and looked at my watch every now and again to see how quick I could get there.

Annabelle, her brother, Triston, and his friend Herbert were standing outside in the yard when I rolled up. "Fifteen minutes," I shouted.

"Fifteen minutes, what?"

"It took me fifteen minutes to get here."

"Oh, big deal. I've got to your house faster than that, riding my bike," Annabelle yelled back.

Right off, Triston hollered, "Hey, would you girls like to come and see my brand-new tent?"

We both hollered, "Yeah," at the same time.

I ran over and peeked through the flap of the door, then turned around and yelled, "Annabelle, this tent is really something."

Annabelle gave me a little shove. "Well, don't just stand there, go inside."

Gracie, Herbert's girlfriend, a free spirit with big boobs, was sitting on an old wooden orange crate, dressed in short shorts and smoking a cigarette. She threw the cigarette butt on the floor of the tent, stomped on it with her shiny red cowboy boot and cracked a big smile.

Triston ran ahead and signaled for us to have a seat. I sat down on the cinder block that leaned against the wall and Annabelle plunked down beside me. She started to giggle and jabbed my arm.

"What?"

"Look." She pointed at Triston, who was bent over, digging through an old army trunk with the crack of his butt showing.

I whispered, "That's nothing after what we seen at the fair, remember?"

Annabelle laughed, "I guess you're right about that, Hannah."

Triston quickly jerked up his pants and looked at us with a smirk on his face. He pulled out two Camel cigarettes and waved them in our faces.

"Interested, my darlings?"

Annabelle fidgeted. "What do you think?"

I shrugged my shoulders and made a silly face. "Why not?"

Gracie, her hair so blond it looked white, picked up a box of farmer's matches and slid it open. I heard a scratching sound against the brown sandpaper strip when she struck the match. She held the flaming matchstick in her long, slender fingers and danced all around. At the same time, Herbert pulled a Zippo lighter stamped with a picture of a naked lady bent over out of his jeans pocket and offered to give me a light as well, but Gracie beat him to it.

Honest to God, I shocked myself. *Here I am, eleven years old and smoking a real cigarette.*

Herbert dropped down on the floor, crossed his legs and began to blow perfect smoke rings that floated through the air like little clouds.

Triston pushed up the brim of his battered hat and yanked the cigarette out of his mouth.

"Hey, would you girls like to hear a dirty joke?"

Annabelle giggled and wrapped one arm around my shoulder. "Yah, go ahead, tell us a dirty joke."

"Do you know what the Mason jar said to the lid?"

I looked up at Triston—dumbfounded.

"You can't screw me without a rubber." And he exploded with laughter. Gracie sat beside him, laughing her head off.

With a disgusted look, Annabelle nudged me with her elbow, jumped up, and stalked out of the tent. I followed right behind her.

Triston shouted, "Hey, someday you'll know what I'm talking about. I'm warning you, don't you girls ever come into my tent when I'm not here."

"Yah, as if we'd want to, you dumb shit," Annabelle hollered back.

On our way to the house, Annabelle jabbed my arm again and whispered, "I have something to show you, Hannah."

I loved going to the Murgers' house. It was a happy place to be. In the kitchen windows hung sheer white curtains, pots of red geraniums sat on the deep sills, and it always smelled like something good cooking. That day Mrs. Murger had one of my favorites, a big pot of ham and beans simmering on the front burner of her kitchen stove.

We gathered around Dakota's large kitchen table at suppertime and ate delicious bean soup with fresh baked bread and butter, and apple pie a la mode for dessert.

"Thank you, Mrs. Murger, for the nice meal. Everything tasted so good," I exclaimed when I finished eating.

Dakota gave me a little hug. "You are welcome, my dear. We like having you at our house, Hannah."

"And I love coming here."

After supper, Annabelle and I helped with the dishes before we scampered upstairs to her room. Annabelle sank on her flowered, padded bed coverlet and patted the space next to her, and I plopped down. She stretched her arms above her head and pushed herself up enough to sit against the pillows that she'd punched behind her back.

We flipped through movie-star magazines, stopping to get a second look at Rock Hudson, and we talked about guys. I always got crushes on dark-haired guys and Annabelle liked boys with blondish hair.

Suddenly, Annabelle sat up. "Hey, Hannah, remember, I told you I had something to show you." She jumped off the bed and escaped into her closet.

I lay with my hands behind my head; looking at all the family pictures on Annabelle's dresser, and wondered what it would be like to have all those brothers.

What is she up to, anyway?

At last she pranced out of her closet, giggling and wearing a tight white T-shirt over huge breasts.

Wow! I wasn't expecting that. I held my hands over my face and rolled on the bed with laughter. Annabelle had on her aunt Stella's big brassiere, stuffed full of old nylon stockings.

She pulled the T-shirt tighter around her big boobs and did a little jig. She looked hilarious with her small narrow hips and great big top.

I giggled, "Be careful, you could tip over."

"I hope my breasts grow this big, then the boys will really fall for me."

"Oh, jeez, Annabelle." I slapped the bed with my hand.

"Haven't you noticed how the boys get all goggle-eyed when they see a girl with big boobs?"

"Yah, I guess so. Boys are so stupid."

"Hannah, have you got your period yet?"

"No, but I don't feel like talking about that now."

Annabelle went on to say, "I can't wait to go to high school in town and meet new guys." The thought of going to Munich High thrilled me, but I dreaded freshman initiation.

Dakota tapped on the bedroom door. "Quiet down, girls, it's way past your bedtime." We crawled under the blankets, covered our heads and talked barely above a whisper until we fell fast asleep.

The next day, in the early afternoon, I hopped on my bike and started for home. Just as I got to the end of the Murgers' driveway and turned left, Triston and Herbert leaped out of the ditch, running with a dead gopher attached to a rope and swinging it. They scared the daylights out of me.

Too scared to look back, I kept on pedaling as fast as I could. I felt the dead, cold

80

gopher hit my neck. My heart shot into my throat and I yelled at the top of my lungs, begging them to "please stop." Next thing I knew, I hit loose gravel and landed in a heap by the side of the road. I cried and screamed bloody murder.

Dakota heard my shrieks, and she and Annabelle immediately ran out of the house to see what was going on. The boys took off.

Between sobs, I told them what happened.

"Where are Triston and Herbert?" Annabelle asked.

I pointed. "They went that way."

Dakota looked at my bloody knee.

"We've got to get that skinned knee taken care of."

I saw blood running down my leg when Dakota helped me up off the ground. Annabelle picked up my bike and rode it to her house.

Lucky she can still ride it, after it fell so hard on the ground.

My muscles felt weak as I hung onto Dakota's arm and stumbled along. As soon as we got inside the house, I plopped down on a kitchen chair. Dakota scuttled around the kitchen, gathering a washbasin of water, a washrag and some hydrogen peroxide.

I leaned back, shut my eyes and broke out in an awful sweat.

Dakota gently washed the wound and whispered, "I can see bone."

"You can see bone?" I shouted. And, I slithered off the chair. *I'm dying. I just know I am dying.*

Later, when I woke up on the davenport with a wet washcloth on my head. I sat up and yelled in agony, "What happened?"

Dakota exclaimed, "You fainted, my dear. You're going to be just fine."

I started crying all over again, not because my knee hurt, but, I wanted Mama. I told Dakota, "Any time something bad happens, I want my mother."

"That's understandable, Hannah. You know, we all miss your mama. She was my best friend, and I will never have another friend like her."

It was so hard, oh so hard.

***

I found out if I kept really busy, I didn't get sad. Oftentimes, I'd sit beside Papa in the big

International truck and watched him shift the gears, so one morning after Papa left; I decided to take the truck for a spin.

Papa always left the keys in his vehicles. I hopped up, slipped in behind the huge steering wheel, and before I could even get the door shut, Maggie jumped in, right over the top of me with her long tail flopping in my face. I shoved her away with my elbow and turned the key in the ignition. I had to scoot up a little on the ripped leather seat in order for my foot to reach the clutch before I shifted into low gear. A warm breeze blew through the half-open windows as I held onto the big steering wheel with both hands and drove carefully out of the yard. Away we went, rattling down the prairie road.

I better not go by Grandma's house. Oh God, if she saw me driving the big truck, she'd have a cow for sure.

I turned at the end of the driveway and headed straight east. Maggie shifted over by the passenger's side window, sat with her head hanging out. She didn't miss a thing. Oh, boy! When she spotted a wild turkey running up out of the ditch, through the weeds, and headed directly at us, she let out a loud cry.

Oh, my God! The frightened gobbler zigzagged across the road right in front of me. I thought for sure I felt the big wheels going over him, but when I peered through my side window, I caught a glimpse of his brown wings flapping in the breeze as he flew down the side of the road. Thank the good Lord. I didn't kill him.

Amazing! I could handle the truck just as well as Papa did, but after that turkey scare I wanted to go home. I forged ahead for about three miles, and when I found a good place to turn around, I did. Then I pulled the big International into the yard and parked it in the exact tracks where Papa had it. In no time I was tootling around the farm in the truck, operating the pedals with my feet and the levers with my hands.

I was at Grandma's that summer day when she walked out to her mailbox by the side of the road and came back grasping a letter from her sister Hortense. We went inside, where she opened it carefully. There was a light in Grandma's eyes that I had never seen before when she stood in the middle of her kitchen, holding onto the letter and reading it.

Grandma exclaimed, "My word, my sisters Hortense and Cassandra, we call her

Cassie plan to pay a visit soon. They are traveling from Fox Lake, Wisconsin, my childhood home. The last time I saw them, Cajsa was five years old. Now, that's a long time ago."

Grandma hadn't gone back to Fox Lake since she came to North Dakota, and she never talked about her family. Would Grandma's sisters look like her? I couldn't wait to see them.

Grandma named off all the things she wanted done before they arrived. "Hopefully, you can help me, Hannah."

"Just tell me what you'd like me to do and I'll do it."

When I got home, I asked Papa if he knew Grandma's family.

"Vell, if I remember right, jour mama mentioned something about her aunts Hortense and Cassie wisiting von time vhen she vas a little girl, but no, I don't know dem, except for Dudley, who shows up every now and den vhen he's not locked up in yail. He's a character, all right."

"Who's Dudley?"

"He's jour grandmotter's brotter. She calls him 'da black sheep of da family.'"

Grandma called Papa the morning Hortense and Cassie were to show up, and asked him if he would pick up the oranges and bananas she had called in and ordered at the Mercantile while he was in town. Right away, I took off on my bike for Grandma's place when I heard they were arriving.

In the early afternoon, Great-Aunt Hortense came barreling into Grandma's yard, driving a gray Ford. The tires screeched when she slammed on the brakes.

Grandma sprang up off the davenport, wrestling her apron over her head and tossing it on a chair, then rushed outdoors to greet them. I trailed behind her.

Hortense, a tall, stout, big-bosomed woman with a long narrow face, dressed in a white cotton shirt and tan gabardine slacks, bounded from the driver's seat.

Great-Aunt Cassie, a much shorter and plumper woman, scrambled out of the passenger's door and lagged behind Hortense. Her purple dress blew in the wind against her bowlegs. A big red handbag hung on her arm.

Neither one of them looks as pretty as Grandma.

Grandma was delighted to see her sisters, and proudly announced as she swung her arm around my shoulder, "Standing beside me is my granddaughter, Hannah."

Aunt Cassie smiled and stroked my hair. "You look just like your mama."

"Everyone tells me that."

"I can't believe how grown-up you are. Your grandma has told us so much about you in her letters and I'm thrilled to finally meet you."

I grinned. "I'm glad to meet you too."

After greeting one another, we walked up onto Grandma's sunken porch and plopped down side by side on the old wooden bench.

Cassie twisted her chubby self around and looked right into Grandma's face. "Tell me, Lieula, how are you anyway? I know it's been hard with the loss of your daughter."

"Thanks for asking. Of course, I was heartbroken after losing Cajsa, but you know, it's unbelievable how everyone came forth, gave support and truly cared. I'm very grateful for all the good things in my life, and there are many. Especially my Hannah, I have to stay strong for her."

"It makes me happy to see you doing so well, Lieula."

Hortense interrupted, "There's a heavy sweet smell in the air. Do you have lilac bushes growing nearby, Lieula?"

"Oh, yes, there's a cluster of bushes on the west side of the house. I've always loved the smell of lilacs blooming. I guess I got that from Mama. Remember the big lilac bushes she grew in her front yard? Are they still there?"

"Yes, Lieula, they bloom every spring, beautiful as ever."

"It seems the older I get, the more I miss Fox Lake. It's been ages since I've been home."

"Sh!" Great-Aunt Hortense put her fingers to her lips.

A pair of mallards landed before us on the front lawn. The drake's lovely, shiny green head wobbled when he mounted the female; then right after, he flew to the sky.

Aunt Hortense swiveled about like a worm and muttered, "Oo-ooh, my goodness."

I sat beside Grandma, swinging my legs back and forth, and listened to them talk. Suddenly a banged-up Watkins truck rumbled into the yard and came to an abrupt stop. Grandma leaned her head back against the porch wall. "Well, I never!" her words exploded. "Is that you, Dudley?"

A small-headed, bearded man with a large belly got out of the truck. He wore a red vest over a black-and-white checkered shirt. His white hair blew around like cotton as he rushed towards the porch with his arms full of little packages. He gave each of his sisters a little bottle of Watkins vanilla and handed me a package of sweet-smelling Wrigley's gum. I noticed his fingernails were stained with nicotine and on his wrist was an ugly purple scar.

Grandma smiled and thanked him. "Where have you been keeping yourself all this time?"

He looked down. "Lieula, I thought you'd have heard by now. Believe me, I'm not one bit proud to tell you the system released me from the state penitentiary just two months ago. I spent close to a year in jail for bootlegging Moonshine. And would you believe? I was lucky enough to land a job right off with the Watkins Company. Did you know that the Watkins Company has grown so big, it now has offices in the United States, Canada, Australia, New Zealand, South Africa, and England?"

"I don't really care how many offices the Watkins Company has. You never even had the decency to respond to the telegram I sent you, informing you of Kajsa's horrible death."

"Lieula, I know, I have lots of apologizing to do, but we're all together now, so let's have a good time."

"Hmm," Grandma sighed.

Hortense spoke up, "I found his address and sent him a note to let him know we planned to visit North Dakota and what time we would be here. Lieula, let's try to enjoy the short time we have together, OK?"

Cassie chimed in, "Yeah, I can't remember the last time we were all together."

Shortly, Papa pulled up on his John Deere tractor. He looked as surprised as Grandma was to see Dudley. Papa leaped down, reached around and grabbed the brown grocery bag filled with oranges and bananas, and walked onto the porch.

Dudley leaned on the porch pillar. His bushy white eyebrows wiggled and his yellow teeth showed as he laughed nervous-like and reached out his hand. Papa gave him a hearty handshake, and handed Grandma the grocery bag, then turned and cheerfully greeted Hortense and Cassie.

Grandma's big orange marmalade cat, Rhubarb, sat perched on the wide porch rail, carefully licking each paw and wiping it over her ears and head. She jumped down, meowed at my feet, then leaped up on my lap and arched her back against my chest before circling three times to find her cozy spot. As I cuddled Rhubarb, she made a rumbling purr.

Cassie looked up at Papa and smiled. "Johan, it's so good to see you again. My word, I can't believe how grown up Hannah is. You've done a wonderful job of raising her on your own."

Papa chuckled, "Jou tink so, huh? Vell, jou have to give Lieula a lot of credit too. Ve're mighty proud of my Hannah, dat's for sure.

Hannah vas telling me yust da otter day how she'd like to live in California some day. And, believe me, I support her in vhatever she vants to do. Sad to say, dere's not much of a future in farming anymore. Vit the cost of da machinery and low grain prices, it's hard to get ahead dese days. Not like it vas vhen ve first came to America.

I was tickled to hear Great-Aunt Cassie and Papa saying those nice things about me, yet I got all bashful feeling, and nuzzled my face against Rhubarb's fury cheeks.

Dudley nodded, and muttered. "My, you have a pretty cat there, Lieula,"

Grandma smiled and looked at Rhubarb. "Yes, Rhubarb is lots of company, but I have to keep an eye on her because she likes to get in the chicken coop and eat the eggs.

"Come on, kids, let's go inside before the mosquitoes eat us up alive. I have the table set, a roaster full of fried chicken, potatoes cooking, and a whole supper including bread pudding with caramel sauce."

I smiled at Grandma. "I thought I smelled cinnamon."

It felt so good to sit at the table with family gathered round me. Grandma looked happy as well. I watched Great-Uncle Dudley fill his plate and eat like he hadn't had a meal in days.

We had barely finished eating when Papa wiped his face with a napkin and scooted his chair away from the table. With a big smile on his face, he patted Grandma on the arm. "Lieula, I hate to eat and run, but I got chores dat have to get done. Tank you for the mighty fine supper. It's been great to see everyone."

Grandma gave me a little hug. "Try to get back early in the morning, Hannah. I need your help."

I looked at Papa.

"Dat's okay vit me, Hannah."

"I'll see you in the morning, Grandma."

I followed Papa out the kitchen door, jumped up on the tractor behind him and grabbed onto the backseat. Hortense, Cassie, Dudley and Grandma stood out on the front porch, waving at us as we drove away.

Maggie heard the John Deere putting up the driveway and came running to meet us with her tail wagging, making happy barks.

Papa took off for the barn, and I scurried to the milk house, grabbed the buckets and ran down to help him.

I loved it when it was just the two of us in the big, cozy warm barn. I looked over at Papa sitting on his stool, milking Elsie, and I asked him, "Papa, what does bootlegging Moonshine mean?"

"It's when someone makes white lightning or other high-proof distilled spirits and sells it. It's illegal in da first place."

"Oh, before I forget, Hannah, vhen I was in town today, Tova told me dat the Southern Baptist church is planning a Bible school session dis summer at the little red country schoolhouse over in Towner County. I tink jou should go, give jou someting to do and keep jou out of trouble."

I often wondered what the red school with the big steeple and bell on top was like on the inside. Well, now was my chance to find out.

As soon as I got to Grandma's early the next morning, Dudley announced, "I better get going. I got lots of delivering to do."

Grandma mumbled to herself, "Good riddance."

The following Saturday, Great-Aunt Hortense, Great-Aunt Cassie and Grandma stopped at my house and picked me up. Great-Aunt Cassie hollered from the backseat, "Hurry, Hannah, get in, we're going to Langdon for a fun day!" Cassie had a sparkly way of talking, and she laughed a lot.

When we got into town, Aunt Hortense looked at her watch and announced, "Why, it's already lunchtime. Hannah, would you like to eat at Nick's Drive-In? I just drove past it."

I smiled and answered, "Yes, I sure would." Hortense quickly spun the car around and parked in front of Nick's Drive-In. The smell of French fries filled the air.

I stretched my neck to get a better look at the menu posted on the drive-in window. An Everly Brothers song, "Bye Bye Love," blared from outside speakers.

A slender teenage girl in a spotless flowing dress bustled out to our car. Cracking a smile, she asked, "May I take your order, please?"

"I'd like a cheeseburger, some French fries and a vanilla milk shake, please," I said.

Grandma and her sisters ordered the same, except Grandma asked for coffee.

In no time the carhop was back, carrying a metal tray filled with sizzling-hot cheeseburgers, mouthwatering thick vanilla milk shakes and golden French fries.

The cheerful carhop looked at Great-Aunt Hortense. "Would you please roll your window down halfway?" She attached the tray to it. Aunt Cassie leaned over in front of Aunt Hortense, straining to see. "Is there catsup on that tray, Hortense? I can't eat fries without catsup, you know."

Hortense passed the plastic catsup container to Cassie, and from the front seat she handed Grandma and me a handful of napkins, along with the good-smelling cheeseburgers. I watched Grandma slowly unfold her napkin and spread it on her lap, and I did the same.

When I had finished eating, I crunched up my napkin and wrappers and handed it all up to Aunt Hortense to discard on the tray, calling to her, "Thank you, it's fun to eat in the car and Grandma likes it too, don't you, Grandma?"

Smiling, Grandma replied, "It's certainly different."

Hortense chuckled. "I'm glad you enjoyed it."

I would like to be a carhop someday.

One afternoon while Great-Aunt Cassie and I sat on the porch swing, I handed her my little red autograph book and asked, "Would you please write in this before you go?"

She poked her stubby fingers into her handbag, took out a purple pen and began to write a delightful little message that went like this:

Roses are red

Violets are blue

Sugar is sweet

And so are you

She handed the autograph book back to me. I giggled when I read what she wrote and thanked her.

We had many good times together before Hortense and Cassie's vacation came to an end. Grandma grew melancholy after her sisters were gone, and all she wanted to talk about was Fox Lake and the good old days.

When I told Papa that Grandma talked a lot about the "good old days," he guffawed. "I vonder how goot da goot old days really vere? I told jou, Hannah, jou're grandma's getting a little senile."

I didn't want to think about Grandma growing old and senile.

"Hannah, Bible school starts on Monday."

"Papa, Radovan has appointments at the clinic in Fargo next week to get fitted with new leg braces. Annabelle is going along, and I don't really feel like going to Bible school if Annabelle can't go with me."

"Vell, it vould do jou goot to go vitout Annabelle. Jou two are togetter enough da vay it is."

It surprised me that Papa suggested I go to Bible school in the first place. Even though Papa was baptized and confirmed a Lutheran, he never got up on Sunday mornings and went to church.

Papa always said, "Jou don't have to go to church to prove anyting to nobody." He'd tap his chest. "I got God right here. Dat's enough. Most of dem churchgoers are notting but a bunch of hypocrites anyvay."

I'd imagined the little red schoolhouse all wrong; turned out it was much smaller and darker inside than my regular schoolhouse. Bible school classes were held outside in the beautiful sunshine, and we were allowed to sit on the swings or wherever we felt like. I loved that part most of all.

There was a little corner blocked off, with a makeshift bookcase, full of bible storybooks. My favorite was this big book, called, "A Golden Stamp Book," full of tales from the Old and New Testaments with forty-eight beautifully painted picture stamps and black and white drawings on every page. Miss Hankins would allow me to take that book, and sit in the swing and read to my hearts content.

One of the first lessons Miss Hankins taught us was the Ten Commandments. "'Thou shalt not steal'—stealing is a dreadful sin," she preached. "Now, for instance, if you so much as swipe one cookie from the cookie jar without permission, that's stealing, and you will have to pay tenfold."

Little Clayton Blackfoot sat quietly, listening. His dark brown eyes bugged out. "I'm taking back Grandpa's red-handled hammer as soon as I get home today," he cried.

Miss Julie Hankins told us to be sure to inform our parents that there would be a Bible school program when the session ended, and she expected all the parents to attend. I felt nervous at the thought of singing in front of everyone, yet I was excited because I knew Papa, Grandma and Tova would be there.

CHAPTER 6

Papa told me before he left in the morning, "Sissy Pie, I have to go to the annual Farmer's Union meeting and dake care of some business in town, but I'll stop by on my vay home and be dere to hear jou sing."

"I'll be watching for you, Papa."

Grandma made arrangements for Tova to give us a ride.

Miss Hankins slipped through the flimsy curtain drawn across the make-believe stage and prompted the taller students to stand in the back row, the shorter in the middle and the really short kids in front. Then she gave us each a white candle. "Children, I want you to hold up your candles and sing so everyone can hear you."

Miss Hankin's short blond hair bobbed up and down while she sat, pounding the piano keys with her long slim fingers. Some of the kids got stage fright from standing in front of an audience for the first time. There were giggles—others couldn't sing a word.

I held the burning candle in both hands and sang the words to *This Little Light of Mine* at the top of my lungs. I peeked between the kids in the front row and looked around for Papa, yet I never missed a beat. I saw Tova and Grandma sitting up front. Grandma smiled and made a little motion with her hand. Rows of chairs were filled with parents, grandparents and little children, but I didn't see Papa.

I bet he's not going to make it after all.

I kept singing.

BOOM—the back door banged open and slammed shut, and here came Papa bustling in with Runa Hagebak by his side.

Heads turned.

Why is Runa with Papa?

Papa looked at me and nodded, then grabbed a couple of folding chairs from the back wall. I watched them as they sat down. I couldn't take my eyes off of Runa. Her blond hair was done up in a French twist as usual, and she wore a black skirt with a pretty flower-embroidered white blouse. The four legs on her chair were uneven, and she rocked slightly as she perched on the edge of her seat, sliding a single emerald up and down a chain around her neck.

I felt Miss Hankins looking at me, she smiled. I grinned and sang louder, all the while watching Runa.

"Hi, Hannah!" Runa shrieked.

Papa jabbed her with his elbow. "Shhhh."

Weary, she leaned back and folded her arms across her chest. It wasn't too long before her eyes closed and her head started to bob.

Oh, my God, is she falling asleep?

Whoosh, Runa slithered off the chair onto the floor and landed on her butt. Her slim ankles extended from her skirt.

Folks stared and snickered, but I pretended I didn't notice a thing.

Papa helped Runa to her feet. She sat down with a thump, then gave Papa a big slap on his knee and blurted, "Johan, let me tell you something. Your little Hannah can sing better than any of them Bible school kids up there."

"Shhhh, Runa."

Startled, Grandma looked over her shoulder.

Oblivious to it all, Miss Hankins directed us to sing: *Jesus loves me.* When the program ended, Miss Hankins beamed and rose to her feet. Facing the crowd, she exclaimed, "I think these children deserve a mighty hand of appreciation, don't you?" Papa stood up and clapped long and loud.

On my way out, I ran up beside Miss Hankins, who stood among the crowd, shaking hands. She smiled. "What is it, Hannah?"

I whispered, "Miss Hankins, that lady with my papa is not my mother."

She gave my hand a little squeeze. "I know. You did your part so well, Hannah."

I turned around and saw Papa and Runa leaving out the back door, and I scampered through the crowd to catch up. Papa patted my shoulder. "Good yob, Hannah."

I noticed the black seams in Runa's nylon stockings were twisted all around her skinny legs when she ran towards the outhouse, yelling, "I'll meet you at your car, Johan."

Grandma hobbled out of the schoolhouse as fast as she could go, shouting, "Johan, wait up." Out of breath, she grabbed hold of Papa's arm. "Johan, are you courting Runa?"

Papa stopped dead in his tracks and looked at Grandma like she was out of her mind.

"Vell, since jou are so damn nosy, let me tell jou vhy she vas vit me in da first place. I ran into Runa at the Cando Bar today. She vas drinking Tom Collins and playing shuffleboard vhile she vaited for the brakes on her old Chevy to get fixed. Vell, Ole, da mechanic, couldn't get da yob done in von day, so I did vhat a good neighbor should do and offered her a ride. Seeing dere vasn't time to take her home before Hannah's program, I brought her vit me."

"That's good of you, Johan. How many Tom Collins did Runa drink?"

Papa harrumphed, "Too damn many."

"Why, the idea."

"Jah, it seems ever since she lost her husband, she's taken to drink."

Grandma pursed her lips and strutted towards Tova's car. I ran ahead and hopped in the backseat. As soon as Grandma got in, Tova handed Grandma her battered pocketbook.

Grandma chuckled, "Why, the idea, I hadn't realized I wasn't carrying it. Thank you, Tova. My goodness, who would have thought those children could sing like they did? You'd think Miss Hankins was a concertmaster and they'd been working together for years. Did you see the looks on the children's faces?"

"Yes, Lieula, I never thought we'd see such a performance in the little red school house."

Grandma looked over her shoulder. "Hannah, hearing your sweet voice made chills run up and down my spine."

Tova chimed in, "Hannah, you have a beautiful soprano voice."

I giggled nervous-like. "Thank you."

Grandma straightened up and started rummaging through her purse, mumbling, "I bet Runa is going to be pie-eyed and sicker than a dog tomorrow."

I crouched on the backseat, laughing my head off.

Grandma spun around. "What's so funny back there?"

"I've never heard anyone say 'pie-eyed' before."

I don't know. It all struck me as funny and I couldn't quit laughing.

***

I bridled Sally and took off. Oh, how I loved to get up on sunshiny summer mornings and jump on Sally's back and race over the ground as fast as I could, with the wind blowing in my face and playing in my hair. Before I knew it, we'd galloped all the way into town. So, we rode around Munich, looking at the little houses and their neatly mowed lawns. Mr. Johnson waved and shouted, "Hannah, what are you and Sally doing in town?"

I waved back, "Just going for a ride."

We rode by three churches, the Zion Lutheran, St. Mary's Catholic and the Salem Mennonite. When we passed the elevator, there were six big trucks lined up, full of grain.

Tova rushed out and greeted us with a surprised look on her face when we stopped in front of the Mercantile. She patted Sally's soft nose. "My goodness, Sally, I don't believe I've ever seen you in town before. How are you, Hannah?"

"I'm fine. We didn't start out with the idea of riding into town, but here we are, so I decided to stop by and say hello."

"I'm glad you did."

On our way home, I turned into Grandma's driveway, and we trotted up to her bedraggled porch. I jumped off Sally and tied her to the crab apple tree, then ran over to the well, pumped a bucketful of fresh water and plunked it on the ground for her to drink. Her head barely fit in the bucket, and it seemed like there was no end to her thirst. I filled the bucket four times before she had enough.

I brushed her mane away from her eyes with my hand and kissed her soft nose. "Too bad Grandma doesn't have a big horse tank, huh, Sally? You be a good baby and stay right here. I won't be gone long."

I looked back before I went inside and saw Sally placidly nibbling grass, reins dangling.

I found Grandma sitting in the living room in front of her roll top desk.

"Hi, Grandma! Guess what? I rode Sally all the way into town."

"Well, hi, Hannah! I thought I heard the nicker of a horse, but then I decided it was the sound of the old North Dakota wind blowing. You're telling me that you rode all the way into town? I remember how frightened Sally gets if a car or truck comes near her. I don't think it's a good idea to ride your horse around traffic. What's she doing now?"

"I tied her to the apple tree and gave her lots of water. She'll be OK. What are you up to?"

"I was just getting ready to write a letter to my sister, Hortense."

"Go ahead, Grandma, don't let me stop you. You know something, Grandma, I liked Great-Aunt Cassie much better than I liked Great-Aunt Hortense."

Grandma smiled. "Is that right?"

I giggled. "I like you best of all."

Grandma pulled me close and gave me a little hug.

I was thinking, *now is as good a time as any,* and I leaned into Grandma's chest and whispered,

"Grandma, what does it feel like when you get your period?"

"My word, Hannah, give me a minute." She wiggled nervous-like on her chair, gave me a little push and removed two sheets of writing paper from her top desk drawer, then picked up her best pen and began to write.

I stood with my arms dangling at my sides, waiting and took a deep breath.

Grandma is not going to answer my question.

I felt like a fool. *Oh, God. Why did I ever ask Grandma that question in the first place?*

I covered my face with my hands and wandered into the kitchen, where I snatched a few carrots out of the basket of fresh vegetables sitting on the counter, then ran out to see how Sally was getting along. Her tail swung in the breeze, twitching off flies. She made a whinnying sound and curled her lips when she saw I had carrots, then snapped them up and ground them with her big teeth.

I wiped my slobbery fingers on my shorts, ran back indoors and let the screen door slam behind me. Grandma spun around on her chair with her pen poised over her paper. "Hannah, I want you to hear the last paragraph of my letter."

"OK, I'm listening."

"'Nothing can be lonelier than to be an old widow living on the North Dakota prairie.'"

"My goodness, Grandma, what do you mean by that?"

"Oh, it seems when one gets old, one yearns for their home place. Maybe I should just go to the old folks' home in Fox Lake, Wisconsin, and be done with it."

I bet Grandma wouldn't feel that way if Mama was with us. Sometimes I even forgot what Mama's face looked like when I tried to picture her.

"I hate it when you talk like that, Grandma. Let's think about something good to talk about."

After a long silence, I thought of something and I asked, "Grandma, did you have any boyfriends before Grandpa?"

Grandma shoved her chair back from her desk. "Now, really Hannah, would you stop your badgering? You're getting on my nerves. You know I'm a private person. Why stir up that hornet's nest?"

"Well, excuse me for living."

"You stop with that smart mouth of yours."

She took her old sweet time folding the letter, stuck it inside an envelope and tore a three-cent stamp off a big sheet, licked it and placed in on the envelope.

Grandma handed me the letter. "Now, hurry along and put this letter in the mailbox, Hannah."

I snatched it up, ran outside and down the driveway, then threw the letter in Grandma's huge mailbox and hopped on Sally. Just as I was riding away, Grandma waddled out on her front porch and shouted, "Don't leave without saying good-bye, Hannah, and be careful on that horse."

Sally broke into a trot. I looked back, waved and shouted, "Don't worry, Grandma, I know all about riding horses."

Geez, what in the world did Grandma mean by telling me not to stir up a hornet's nest?

Ever since I'd attended Bible school, I couldn't get the "Thou shalt not steal" commandment off my mind. Even when Papa was plowing in the field and I was home alone, I didn't dare take one fig cookie out of the package on the counter, until he came in and I could ask, "Papa, can I have a cookie?" One day, Papa asked, "Vat's got into you anyvay?"

I told him about the "Thou shalt not steal" commandment and how Miss Hankins said if you took one cookie without permission, it was stealing.

"Eat vhatever's around here, for Christ sake, and don't act so damn foolish."

***

Like Papa always said, "If it ain't one damn ting it's ten more." During the month of August, it turned sizzling hot. Papa didn't know how he would provide grassland for the cattle. The once lush pastures had dried up and turned brown. Even the gophers didn't pop their heads up out of their holes.

Papa mulled the situation over and talked to Jacob, his best friend and good neighbor who had immigrated to America around the same time he had, and they came up with a good plan. That was when Papa asked me, "Sissy Pie, vould jou be villing to help vit the cattle?"

I looked at Papa. "Help with the cattle, what do you mean?"

"Vell, you could ride Sally and herd da cattle in dat open acreage down by da stockyards. Jacob owns dat land, and he told me da otter day dat dere's plenty of grass out dere for da cows to eat and he ain't using it for any ting, but dere's no fence to keep da cattle in."

"Herding cattle sounds like fun! What about the hobos that hang around the stockyards? Should I be afraid of them?"

"I haven't seen any hobos hanging around dere for over a jear or more, so I vouldn't vorry about dat. Besides, Maggie vill be vit jou."

So began one of the busiest summers of my life. Every morning while Papa did the barn chores, I'd brush Sally with the currycomb until her coat was clean and smooth as silk and put on her bridle. When Papa was through milking the cows, I'd ride off, my bare legs swinging against her sides, and drive the cattle to the wide-open range.

Often times, I'd pack a bag of books and take with me. There were summer afternoons when I'd tie Sally to a fence post. She would bite off a plant full of blossoms with her teeth and munch them while I sat on the soft grass and read, "Alice's

Adventures in Wonderland," and other favorite stories of mine. I didn't have to worry about the cows getting out of hand, because Sally was a natural when it came to rounding up the cattle. If the cows did happen to go astray, she would trot up behind them, and nudge them ever so gently in the rear end with her nose, and steer them back where they belonged.

I loved herding the cattle, but the sweltering days became long and boring out on the prairie, where everything seemed so still. I very seldom saw anyone except on one hot afternoon a tiny Indian woman in a brown dress, carrying a bucket over her arm and gathering little pieces of lignite coal that had tumbled off a boxcar alongside the tracks. When she saw me watching, her small face turned red, and she picked up her bucket and took off running.

I'd think up things to do and daydream about what I'd be when I grew up. Papa told me I should be a nurse because there was always a need for nurses. I knew I could never work in a hospital—like I've said, ever since I saw Mama's bloody car accident, my stomach churned at the faintest sight of blood.

I'd imagine myself married to a nice, strong, good-looking man with dark curly hair. We'd have four children, two boys and two girls. I'd bake big batches of oatmeal-raisin cookies and have them spread out on the breadboard when my husband came home. He'd hug me and tell me how delicious they tasted, and I'd let my kids eat all the oatmeal-raisin cookies they wanted because they were wholesome.

Other times, I'd form strands of Sally's coarse black mane into thick braids, then rest my head on her warm shoulder and lie there, whiffing her nice horse smell. Or I'd play like we were coming out of the chute at a rodeo and ride Sally at a full gallop through the stockyard gates with Maggie running alongside me, playfully nipping at my ankles.

I drove the cattle down to the pond near the railroad tracks every hour or so. I loved watching them guzzle the cool water. You would think the cows would get frightened when the train smoked and clattered by, but they didn't stop drinking and hardly raised their heads.

Early one morning, out of the blue, I discovered if I hollered loud enough I could hear my echo, so just for fun I started yelling cusswords, "asshole, bitch, sonofabitch, piss, shit, pecker," and the worst one of all, "cocksucker."

Then I'd listen for the dirty words to ring back and laugh my head off.

One afternoon as I rode behind the cows, slowly herding them home with their bags so full the milk streamed out of their teats, Papa met me in front of the barn with an ornery look on his face and motioned for me to stop.

I pulled on Sally's reins. "Whoa, girl."

Papa uttered around the stem of his pipe, which as usual had gone out, "Hannah, Yacob stopped by dis afternoon and asked me, 'Did jou know dat jour daughter is sitting out dere on dat horse cussing up a storm? I can hear her vay up in my jard, jelling dem dirty cussvords.'"

Papa took the pipe out of his mouth and knocked the ashes out on a fence post. "Vat do jou got to say about dat, Hannah Marie?"

"Old ugly chicken-face Jacob told you that? Geez, I was just playing around, yelling and having some fun."

Papa walked away and led the cows into their stanchions. Looking over his shoulder, he shouted, "I don't vant to hear any more smart-talk out of jou, and jou stop dat damn cussing. Do jou hear me, Hannah Marie?"

"Yah, I hear you."

***

Early one summer morning, Mrs. Nickerson called and asked if I would be available the following Saturday to babysit Junior while she attended an all-day Ladies Aid Convention and luncheon in Grand Forks I jumped at the chance. Junior was an adorable little fellow, going on three years old, and a slow talker with dark brown eyes that sparkled with mischief.

I arrived at the Nickerson house bright and early on Saturday morning. Mrs. Nickerson greeted me at the door in her pale green housecoat, and then hurried down to her bedroom to get dressed. Before she left she handed me a list, little jobs she would like me to do—if I had the time.

She was no sooner out the door when Junior announced, "Hanners, let's go for a walk."

"Okay, sweetie, but you must wear a sweater."

I looked around for Junior's sweater, but it was nowhere to be seen. His older sister's pale yellow wool sweater hung on the coatrack in the hallway. I asked him, "Junior, would you be willing to wear Beth's sweater?"

He shook his head no, but mumbled, "Ohhhhh, OK."

I held the sweater open while Junior giggled and squirmed his way into it. We walked outdoors hand in hand and headed down the little country road that ran by the Wilson farm, where a patch of red tulips and brilliant yellow crocuses bloomed.

"Look at the pretty flowers, Junior. Can you say 'flower'?"

His dimples crinkled when he looked up at me and grinned. "Preddy flower."

"Can you smell the pretty flowers?"

"Hmmm, mm."

I felt Junior's warm hand pulling away from me and he started to squirm.

"What's the matter, sweetie?"

In a little voice, "Let's go home. Bet's sweater makes me so nerbous."

"Well, if that's the case, we'll turn around."

A bird cheeped and twittered on a thistle by the side of the road.

"Look, Hanners, bird."

"That's right, it's a bird."

Back inside, I helped Junior out of his itchy wool sweater. He scrambled over by his toy box and gathered a pile of blocks.

"Hanners, watch me build a tower."

"I'll watch you while I scrub the kitchen floor, OK?"

I pretended the black-and-white-square pattern in the linoleum was one big checkerboard, and I scrubbed the floor, square by square.

I paid no mind when Junior scurried by, carrying a baby bottle. But when I heard the refrigerator door open, I stopped what I was doing and leaned on the old mop handle to watch him. First, he grabbed the milk jug and filled his bottle to almost full. Then he slammed the refrigerator door shut, scampered to the cupboard, picked up the Karo syrup container and clumsily poured some dark syrup in with the milk.

Lastly, he stood in the middle of the kitchen, shaking the bottle as hard as he could with the happiest look on his face. When he got it mixed just right, he scrambled into the living room, plopped down on the davenport, and clutched the baby bottle in both hands. His chubby, rosy cheeks popped in and out when he sucked on the nipple. In no time his eyes slithered shut and he fell fast asleep. I picked the peach-colored afghan off the back of the davenport, covered him up, and went back to scrubbing.

Good God, he's three years old going on four, and he still sucks on a bottle.

I kept busy and felt a great sense of accomplishment when I finished each task and checked it off the list. In the middle of folding a basket of laundry, I heard Junior shout.

"Hanners, come quick. I need you."

"Did you have a good nap?" I asked as I dropped everything and ran to his rescue.

There stood Junior in the narrow, dimly lit hallway, stark naked. The walls were smudged with little red handprints.

I panicked. *Is it blood?*

I flipped on the hall light and found that Junior was smeared from head to toe with red lipstick.

"Junior, what did you do?"

"I play with Mama's lipstick."

"Where did you find the lipstick?"

"Off Mama's big dresser."

He wailed, "Look Hanners, look at my weenie."

Oh, my God. The lipstick-tube lid was stuck on the end of his little weenie.

"Take it off, Junior."

He whimpered, "Won't come off."

I said, "Take the lipstick-tube lid off your weenie, right now."

He shilly-shallied. His face crumbled like he was about to cry, and he grabbed hold of the lid. One little pluck, and he handed the messy lid to me.

He whooped, "All off, Hanners! It didn't hurt."

How will I ever get the lipstick washed off the walls before Mrs. Nickerson comes home? But first of all I have to get Junior cleaned up.

"Follow me, you silly little man. You're getting in the bathtub for a good scrubbing."

***

It had to have been the coldest day of the year. The ground was frozen hard, the birds were gone, and the wind whistled around the eves, blowing drifts over the barnyard fence. I walked outside onto the front porch that evening and discovered Maggie wasn't in her old bed. I immediately slipped into my snowshoes, rushed to the weatherworn storage shed and snatched a horse blanket off the hook. Then I took off to search for Maggie. I walked aimlessly for what seemed like forever and ever. Before long, moonlight flashed through the trees as I plowed through snow-covered fields, pulling the sled behind me, and calling, "Maggie, Maggie."

My glasses fogged up, so I stopped, yanked a handkerchief out of my snow pants pocket and wiped them off. I felt desperate as I stood in the cold of night and looked all around. I closed my eyes and said a little prayer: "Please God, help me find Maggie." And just like that, I saw the tip of Maggie's gray head sticking out of the snow bank. Her long fluffy tail swished back and forth when she heard me walking towards her. I knelt and rubbed the snow out of her once brown eyes, now turned glassy white. She whimpered and pushed on my hand with her nose.

I was shocked to feel how skinny Maggie had became when I picked her up. Why, I could even feel her ribs. I wrapped her in the brown horse blanket and lifted her on the sleigh, then tucked her in safe and sound and started for home. A north wind pushed at my back, slapping my blue wool scarf against my face. My chest ached from breathing in the cold air and my fingers stung.

As soon as we got home, I hauled her old wooden makeshift dog bed into the kitchen, warmed up a bowl of milk and plopped it down in front of Maggie. She sniffed the milk and turned away. I watched as she hobbled over and struggled to get in her bed. Her wet nose grazed my arm when I gave her a little boost. She crawled under the old sheep's-wool quilt and curled up. Heavyhearted, I walked upstairs.

Less than a week later, Papa found Maggie lying out behind the barn in the snow, lifeless. In two more weeks she would have been eighteen years old.

Papa told me, "Hannah, jou know as vell as I do dat Maggie vouldn't be vit us much longer. It's a blessing. Da poor ting couldn't see and she didn't vant to eat. Dere aren't many farm dogs dat survive da cold winters and live to be as old as Maggie did."

I blubbered, "I know, Papa, but I feel so sad. I can't believe I'll never see her again. I'm going to Grandma's right now and let her know that Maggie died."

Papa patted my head. "Run along, Sissy Pie."

I slipped into my snowshoes and skimmed over the banks. It always amazed me how a person could walk over the deep snow with snowshoes on and not sink, but without Maggie it wasn't much fun. I even imagined I saw Maggie running up ahead and looking back with her head cocked to one side, checking to see if I was still coming.

When I got to Grandma's house, she was standing out on the porch. "Hannah, I just finished feeding the chickens, and when I saw you coming without poor old Maggie, I just knew."

"It's so sad, Grandma."

Grandma pulled me into her arms. "My word, how I hate the thought of Maggie no longer with us, but just think how happy your mama will be to see Maggie scampering up those golden streets to join her in heaven."

I smiled. "Oh, Grandma, I never thought of that. I love you so much."

"I love you too, my dear. You know, Maggie became awful thin and weak towards the last. We all knew she couldn't go on much longer, but that doesn't make it any easier when the end does come. I bet your pa will get you another dog soon."

"Yeah, but there will never be a dog like Maggie. I know I can never love another dog as much as I loved my sweet Maggie."

Papa met me in the driveway when I got home. "Hannah, I vrapped Maggie's frozen body in da Indian blanket and put her inside a vooden box. She vill have to stay in da garage until da ground thaws and I can dig a grave for her."

As long as Maggie's body lay in the garage, I couldn't make myself go out there.

***

On a bright spring day, I held back the tears as I stood beside Papa and watched him dig Maggie's grave. All the happy memories of Maggie flashed through my mind. Maggie, bringing in the cows, how she climbed the ladder to the haymow and surprised everyone. How she danced out a welcome when we came home, and how upset she got if she saw me crying.

A few weeks later, Papa planted a cherry tree beside Maggie's grave, and I wrote a poem in memory of my sweet Maggie.

Old Maggie

Poor old blind dog

Lost in the field

Snowflakes falling

Seems she doesn't feel

Brush off the snow

Boost her on the sleigh

Pull her home

Hoping she won't stray

***

The fall that would change everything came nearer every day. I turned thirteen, graduated from the eighth grade and started high school in town.

The all-brick school building in Munich seemed enormous to me, but I liked the idea of walking through corridors into separate rooms for each class and having a different teacher for each subject. School started at nine a.m. and finished at four p.m. As a rule, girls were not allowed to wear pants in high school.

The sophomore class was in charge of the dreaded initiation that took place during my second week. They blindfolded me, then ordered me to take off my shoes and socks and walk straight ahead. I felt so tense I could barely move. Someone nudged me from behind, and I crept along with my arms straightened, hanging stiff at my sides.

Oh, my God! I'm walking on big fat earthworms. I can feel them wiggling between my toes and under my feet.

I stomped on the worms and screeched—the kids roared with laughter.

Will it ever end?

The sickening odor of medicine encircled me. *I can't take this for another minute.* Then a squeaky little voice said, "Hannah, you can take off your blindfold now."

I pushed the blindfold off my eyes and over my head and looked into Clay Mufferson's acne face, smeared with white salve, then busted out laughing along with the rest of the kids when I discovered I was standing on long, fat tubes of cooked macaroni.

I didn't sleep well that night, agonizing over what I would have to tough out the second and—thank God-last day of initiation. That day, I was ordered to hold hands with my social studies teacher, Mr. Clemm, and walk home with him at lunchtime. Feeling absolutely humiliated, I shuffled alongside tall Mr. Clemm. I hated the feel of his big sweaty palm in my hand.

A crowd of kids stood in front of the school, riveting their eyes on me and giggling like idiots.

The minute we approached Mr. Clemm's front doorstep, I shook my hand loose. He looked down at me and grinned. "You were a good sport, Hannah."

Oh, yeah!

Mrs. Norgaard, the music director, was special. A slim young lady with pretty green eyes and thick, curly brunet hair. She wore the most fashionable clothes, and I fantasized about dressing like her someday. I was absolutely thrilled when she asked, "Hannah, would you like to join the Girls' Choir?"

Everyone liked my singing at the Bible school program. Why not?

"I would love to."

Mrs. Norgaard had a way of making each and every one of us girls feel like we belonged, and I excelled in her music class.

That same year Clay Mufferson started following me around the corridors with his arms full of books. One day, I came back from history class to find a delicious-looking peach sitting on top of my desk. Clay sat two aisles over in study hall. I felt him looking at me, so I glanced his way. He grinned at me from ear to ear. I mouthed, "Thank you."

I cringed when he caught up to me in the hallway one afternoon and threw his arm around me. Acting all nervous-like, he sputtered, "Hannah, would you like to go to the school dance with me on Friday night?"

I felt my face getting hot. I couldn't even look at him when I shook my head no.

He burst out, "Hannah, what is it with you? You treat me like a dog. You'll be sorry someday."

I wished the nerd would leave me alone. He was a nice kid and smart, on the honor roll even, yet I couldn't force myself to go on a date with him.

***

One terrible afternoon, I stood among the girls in choir singing "Harbor Lights" when suddenly I broke out in a sweat and felt like I was about to pass out. Painful cramps came over me.

I raised my hand.

Mrs. Norgaard looked my way. "Yes, Hannah?"

In a little voice, I asked, "Mrs. Norgaard, may I be excused?"

She smiled and nodded.

I headed straight for the girls' restroom, walked into the stall, pulled down my panties and saw they were stained with blood. *Oh, my God—I've got my period.* I'd heard enough about "that time of the month" from Annabelle. Even so, I felt awkward walking down the hall with a Kotex stuffed in my underpants.

Could anyone tell?

***

Papa had finished the fall harvesting when I rode into town with him to settle up with Mr. Halverson at the grain elevator. We stopped at the Munich Mercantile afterwards.

I stood in the candy aisle with my hands jammed into my jeans pockets, looking at all the different kinds of candy bars, deciding which one I wanted while Tova helped Papa find his items.

Tova stood behind the counter, wrapping up two tins of Heinz baked beans and a box of Cream of Wheat, tying them tightly and handed the package over to Papa. Papa glanced over at me and chuckled when I hurled a candy bar onto the counter. He paid

106

for it all and tossed me my Payday. At the same time, the bell over the door rang and the door swung open. A nice-looking lady walked in, wearing a bright red-and-white-striped dress.

Tova exclaimed, "Well, hello, Lucy! I didn't expect to see you this time of day, now that you're working at the Bell Telephone Company."

Lucy laughed. "Well, here I am."

"It's always good to see you. Lucy Swan, I'd like you to meet Johan Jonesen and his daughter, Hannah."

She turned and looked at me with the sweetest smile. "Hi, Hannah."

"Hi, Miss Swan."

Papa held out his hand. Lucy glanced up at him, chewing lightly on her lower lip, and wrapped her little hands around his. In a voice as warm as butterscotch, she said, "Johan, I think I've seen you around town."

Papa cracked a smile. "And what brings you to dis neck of the voods, Lucy?"

"Well, Dr. Melvin Knightley happens to be my uncle, and since my mother passed on, Uncle Joe thought it would be good for me to live closer to family. I've wrangled a job at the telephone company as the central switchboard operator. I must say, it's quite a change after working in the burlesque business in Chicago, but I love it."

Papa smiled, listening.

"Vell, it's been a pleasure meeting jou today, Lucy Swan. Did I say dat right?"

"Yes, you sure did."

"See you around."

Lucy beamed. "I hope so."

The floorboard creaked as Papa carried the package under his arm, worked his way through the aisles of canned goods and walked out the door.

As soon as I got into the car, I unwrapped my Payday and started to eat it as the car jerked along the country road. I spun around in the seat and couldn't help but laugh when Papa began whistling, *Yankee Doodle*

CHAPTER 7

If Papa taking up with Lucy wasn't enough to keep the folks talking, the rumor that Mr. Murger was chasing after a younger woman, a nurse he met when he stayed at the Fargo Hospital with Radovan really had their tongues wagging.

Papa declared, "Venzel Murger vit anotter woman? Dat's da most foolish ting I've ever heard. Naw, Venzel's not dat stupid. Vhy he tinks da vorld of his Missus and his kids, but den again people vill do anyting."

Grandma exclaimed, "Johan, you say people will do anything, but Wenzel with a girlfriend, now, that's absurd! I can't imagine a decent man like Wenzel chasing around on his lovely wife, Dakota." She chuckled, "What young woman would want him in the first place?"

That same afternoon I rode with Papa into town. He left me off uptown, then drove to the grain elevator. I gazed wistfully at the barber pole when I walked by. I'd always got a kick out of hearing the old-timers sitting on the benches outside the barbershop, talking politics and telling stories in an animated way, but when I heard the old duffers gossiping and saying unpleasant things about Mr. Murger, I didn't like it one bit.

Does Annabelle know? If she does, she's never let on.

Shortly after Papa and I got home, Mr. Murger let Annabelle off at my house to spend the night. Later, I sidled up to Annabelle while we washed the supper dishes and whispered, "Let's sneak Papa's car and go for a ride tonight after he goes to bed."

"Oh, my God! Really?"

We finished the dishes, cleaned up the kitchen and took off upstairs to my room, and I plopped down on my bed. Annabelle stretched out beside me and rested her arm across her eyes. We lay still as could be, and as soon as I heard a loud snore coming from Papa's bedroom downstairs, I poked Annabelle.

"Papa's asleep. Let's take off, but be extra quiet going down the stairs."

We carried our shoes, tiptoed down the steps and snuck out the back door into the dark of night, then hopped into Papa's Hupmobile Skylark. Lickety-split, I stuck the key in the ignition and started up the engine, and we jackrabbited out of the yard.

I gripped the steering wheel with both hands and glanced over at Annabelle, crouched way over on the passenger's side with a big grin on her face, and I busted out laughing.

"Annabelle, can you believe it? We got out of the house without Papa waking up."

Annabelle giggled, "Isn't this a riot?"

"Oh, yeah. Where would you like to go?"

"Jeez, I don't care, into town, I guess. Maybe we'll see Trevor, but it's sort of late. Wouldn't it be something if we ran into that good-looking guy you've been telling me about?"

"You never know."

It was quiet except for a few crickets chirping. Jacob's yard light burned bright when we passed his place. Annabelle stuck her head out the window and screeched, "Trevor, where are you? I want to see you." Then, she quickly rolled up the window and settled down on the seat. "It smells like rain, Hannah."

"Don't say that."

And sure enough, just when we got into town, a heavy fall of rain with a high wind struck. Thunder cracked, lightning lit up the sky, and when I turned on the windshield wipers I found out the wiper on my side didn't work that good.

I pulled up in front of the Munich Bar and parked. A Hank Williams song, *Why Don't You Love Me*, flowed from inside, and a tipsy couple stumbled out through the swinging barroom doors, hollering and cussing at one another.

Annabelle and I huddled on the front seat, peeked through the steamy windshield and watched the two of them scuffle on the sidewalk.

The chubby gal wore a black pencil skirt with a long slit up the back. Her legs extended from ridiculous red high heels, and her long blond hair blew in her face when she spun around. She threw a cigarette butt on the sidewalk, stomped on it and struck the guy. His black Stetson flew off his baldhead and cartwheeled down the street. He hotfooted after it, snatched it up, slapped the hat against his thigh to release the water and shouted, "You drunken bitch."

The inebriated woman stood with her heels planted on the sidewalk, set her hands on her hips and scowled. "You can kiss my ass."

"Naw, I wouldn't want to do that, it looks too much like your face."

Annabelle started laughing so hard it turned into a coughing attack. She sputtered, "This is better than being at a drive-in movie."

I started up the car, put it in reverse and carefully backed out of the parking space, but it wasn't much fun driving around town with a broken windshield wiper and the rain pouring down so hard it was almost impossible to see out.

"God, I wish we'd never snuck the car in the first place," I cried.

"Things have a way of working out," Annabelle mumbled.

"Yeah, that's easy for you to say when it's not your father's car."

"Now you're getting mad."

"No, I'm scared."

I drove out of town, and just as I turned onto the main road, tick-swoosh —the windshield wiper out-and out-quit. The road grew narrow and more treacherous. I slowed way down when the front wheels began to sink and mud splashed up over the fenders and the bumper. The engine roared as the back left wheel dropped to the hub and the Humpmobile Skylark jerked to a stop in the bog.

Peering out the window, I could see the mud-caked tires spinning hopelessly in the slush.

"Annabelle, there is no way we can dig deep enough, even if we did have a shovel, or try hard enough to make it out of here. We need help to pull us out of this mess."

I switched off the engine, crossed my arms over the steering wheel, then laid my head down and shut my eyes in a desperate, pathetic attempt to pretend it wasn't really happening.

Annabelle didn't speak as the quiet sound of the rain drummed on the metal top of the car. The air smelled clean.

"What time is it, anyway?" I asked.

Annabelle wept aloud. "I don't know. I don't have a watch. Oh, Lord, sweet Jesus, help us."

Next, she jumped out of the car and started running around like a chicken with its head cut off. She tapped on my window and hollered, "Hannah, I'm going to walk to the closest farm house for help."

I shrieked above a blast of thunder, "No, Annabelle, stay with me. Please get back in the car before the lightning strikes."

"Somebody, please help us!" Annabelle screamed, then swung the car door wide open and jumped back in with globs of mud clinging on her shoes. I watched as she squirmed around, picked up an old rag off the floorboard and wiped them off.

"I absolutely hate sitting here," Annabelle cried.

"Papa always says "When there's lightning, the safest place to be is inside a car.'"

"Well, I guess we're safe then. Big deal." Annabelle scoffed.

I leaned back and closed my eyes.

Oh, God, if I could just drive the car out of here I'd be the happiest person in the whole wide world. I wonder if Papa woke up and noticed his car was gone.

We sat out in the middle of nowhere, terrorized, trying to think of what we could do, when all of a sudden Annabelle grabbed hold of my arm and pointed towards the back window, screaming, "Hannah, look."

I jumped up, threw myself over the backseat and squinted to see.

Off in the distance, it looked like headlights. Excited, Annabelle and I hung over the seat and watched, as the dim lights grew brighter and edged closer. Eventually, a big pickup with giant tires pulled up. A tall, thin man tumbled out and started walking our way.

My heart fluttered.

Who is he? What if he's a rapist?

The man plodded up to my side of the car, shoved one hand deep in his trouser pocket and tapped on the window with the other.

"Hello in dere!"

Oh, my God, it's Jacob.

My hands trembled when I rolled down the window.

"Hi, Jacob!" I screaked. "I'm so glad to see you."

"Hannah, is dat jou behind da vheel of Yohan's Skylark?"

112

"Yes, Jacob, it's me."

"Vat the heck are jou girls doing out in veather like dis, at dis hour? Dis is a bad one, ain't seen an automobile sunk this deep in my vhole life."

"I'm sure glad to see you, Jacob," I told him again.

"I bet jou are. Vell, I don't have a chain vit me, and I doubt if I could pull you out vit my truck anyvay, but I'll tell you vat, I'll drive home and come back on my tractor. I know for damn sure I can pull jou out of da mud vit my tractor."

Jacob hopped back in his truck, stuck his head out the window and shouted, "Shut jour lights off, Hannah," then sped off.

I wailed, "You can bet your boots Jacob's going to tell Papa."

Annabelle sat stoic. "Hannah, we're in deep trouble and we both know it."

"Yes, we are, but thank God, we didn't wreck Papa's car."

Rain ran off the brim of Jacob's hat when he jumped off his tractor and grabbed hold of the big log chain, then drug it around and hooked it onto our car. One whopping tug and he pulled us out of the muck.

Right away, Jacob unhooked the chain, jumped back on his tractor and shouted, "I'll follow jou girls till I see jou turn into jour driveway."

I stuck my head out the window and hollered, "Thank you, Jacob."

Sitting high on his tractor seat, he waved a big glove.

Thank God, we finally got home safe and sound. I pulled around by Papa's gas pump behind the granary and filled the tank up to three-fourths full, like the gauge read when we took off. I parked the car in its usual spot.

The screen door squeaked when I opened it, and we wormed our way inside. I heard Papa breathing softly in his little bedroom when we snuck by his door.

Early the next morning, Papa woke me when he hollered up the stairs, "Hannah Marie, did you take the car out last night?"

"No."

Clomp, clomp, up the steps Papa came and poked his head in the doorway of my bedroom.

I stuck my head out of the covers and blinked until my eyes focused. The sun shone beautifully in my bedroom window.

"Vell, how come da car is full of mud, den? I know damn vell I didn't leave it like dat."

"The car is full of mud? What are you talking about?"

"Don't act so stupid, Hannah Marie. Jou know damn vell vhat I'm talking about. Vell, I must make a quick trip to town. Jou girls try and behave jourselves, OK?"

"Yes, Papa."

We were still in bed when Papa got back from town, and he had a lot more to say.

"Don't tink you can pull da vool over my eyes, joung lady. I saw Yacob in town and he told me how he pulled you girls out of the mud last night vit his tractor. Sometimes, I vonder vat I'm going to do vit you, Hannah Marie. Jou know better den to drive into town vitout a driver's license. Jou use to be such a goot little Sissy Pie, now you lie and steal and do vatever you dam vell please."

"I'll never sneak the car again," I cried.

"Da best thing jou can do right now, Hannah Marie, is get jour butt out of dat bed, and get out dere and clean dat dirty car."

"OK, Papa."

With a weary look, Papa turned and walked back downstairs.

I bounced out of bed, ran downstairs and out the back door. Quick as a bunny, I filled the scrub bucket full of water and added some detergent, and Annabelle and I went to work. As I knelt on the ground, scrubbing the rims with a big soapy brush, I told Annabelle, "I meant it when I told Papa I'd never sneak the car again."

"I know. We're so lucky Jacob came along when he did."

Annabelle started to laugh. "Hannah, I wonder what ever happened to the drunk couple fighting on the street?"

"They're probably still fighting."

***

The summer before my junior year, on a blistering hot August day, Cindy picked us girls up and drove to the old swimming hole. As soon as she stopped on the gravelly beach, we tumbled out, screaming and racing barefoot, seeing who could be the first to dive in and swim through the cool, clear water.

We hadn't been in the water long at all when Cindy leaped out of the swimming hole and hollered, "Hold on, everybody. Stay right where you are." Then she ran to her car, flung the trunk open and pranced back, carrying a six-pack of Hamms beer. She shouted, "Girls, there's lots more where this came from," and handed us each a can or two.

It wasn't long before free-spirit Florence took a few good swigs, wiped her lips, then slipped off her bikini top and flung it on the beach, yelling, "I dare you to be next." Just like that, bikini tops of all colors flew in the air.

I had to pee something awful.

Cindy hollered, "Pee in the water."

"No, I don't want to."

Instead I ran up on the bank, stumbling behind a dogwood bush, and that was when my head started to spin. Even so, I jumped back in the water, swilled more beer, then unsnapped my blue polka-dot bikini top and swung it round and round above my head, laughing like a fool.

We ducked underwater when an old model T sped by, honking its horn.

Annabelle giggled, "I hope that wasn't Jacob."

Beer spilled from Lois's mouth when she staggered out of the water, picked up her Kodak camera and shouted, "Say 'sex,'" then snapped one picture after another of us half-naked girls.

Everything was uproariously funny until Betty doubled over and held onto her stomach with both hands, crying, "Oh, help me, God." Then she heaved her guts out. Yellow puke floated on top of the water.

Cindy bellowed," That's it, girls. No more drinking. Let's pick up the beer cans. Now, I'm warning you girls, don't any of you ever breathe a word to anyone that we stole the beer from Greske's bar. Get your tops on. We're blowing this pop stand."

Timid Olga yelled, "You stole the beer?"

"Well, how else would we get it, silly."

Olga stood on the bank fastening her bikini top, and looked at Cindy in complete shock. "How did you ever dare steal beer from Mr. Greske?"

"It was easy, on our way by Greske's last night we noticed the stockroom door was hanging wide open, so we pulled around to the back. There was loud music from the barroom full of rowdy people, and just like that, we helped ourselves to a case of Hamm's beer, then barreled out of there."

"Are you feeling better, Betty?" Cindy asked.

"Oh, yeah, I'm feeling absolutely wonderful after I threw up."

I shouted, "Let's cut out."

Later that same summer, I got a driver's permit. At long last, I could drive Papa's truck legally and help him haul wheat to the grain elevator. The good part was, the driver's permit allowed me to drive back and forth to school as well.

That fall, I registered for Miss Lois Olson's Home Economics class. Miss Olson had to have been the youngest teacher I'd ever known. The only way you could tell her from the students was her open-toed pumps and silk scarves that hung to her knees.

Home economics started out with cooking lessons. On the very first day, Miss Olson taught us how to make vegetable beef soup. I thought it was great fun cutting up vegetables on the big chopping block. While the soup simmered on the huge stove, Miss Olson talked about nutrition.

I didn't know how to set the table properly until Miss Olson taught us where the forks, knives and spoons should go beside the plates and soup bowls, and the proper place to put the glasses. After a few good cooking lessons, Miss Olson let each student make the lunch of their choice and invite the boys from our class to eat with us. When my turn came, I chose to make vegetable soup.

Henry sat at the head of the table and took a spoonful of soup with carrots, peas, parsnips and potatoes bumping together in the fragrant broth. He exclaimed, "Hannah, your vegetable soup is the best I've ever tasted, even better than my Grandma makes! And the crust on your rolls taste so good."

Home economics class wasn't like school. In the second semester we learned to sew. Our final assignment was to make a dress. The prospect of sewing my own dress excited me.

That very afternoon, I walked uptown after school to shop for the materials I needed. As I bounded down the street, I was taken aback when a good-looking guy with dark hair drove by in a blue truck. I stopped dead in my tracks to get a better view.

Jeez! He has to be the best-looking guy I've ever laid eyes on.

116

Tova helped me pick out the perfect pattern, buttons and some pretty print fabric, then wrapped it all up in one big brown package and tied it with a string.

"Please put it on Papa's tab," I said.

"I already have, my dear. I hope to see you in that dress when you're done sewing it."

"I'll wear into the store someday and show you."

"Please do."

As soon as I got home, I spread the cloth on the dining room table, pinned the pattern pieces on it and cut out the fabric. Then I eagerly sat down at Mama's old Singer sewing machine and went to work. I soon became disenchanted when the bobbin knotted up; the needle got away from me and the fabric bunched. And to top it all off, I couldn't get that good-looking guy off my mind.

I spent several nights sewing long after Papa had gone to bed. After many attempts, I got the skirt hemmed perfectly straight, and as I worked I liked the dress less and less. But Miss Olson gave me a final grade of A+ in home economics. Amazing!

***

By and by, I happened to see that handsome guy drive through town once again. Who was he? I doubted he even noticed me, but I sure wished I could get to know him. As time went on, I found out his name was Rome and his younger brother, Gilbert, who didn't look anything like him, was in my class. The next time I saw the blue truck roaring by, I gave a little wave. Oh, my God, he grinned and waved back.

***

I dreamed about Mama for the first time that night. In my dream, Mama was wearing a short purple dress. Her bare arms and legs fluttered as she floated through beautiful white clouds. A breeze blew over her shoulder-length hair hiding her face. I reached out—she disappeared.

***

On a gorgeous spring morning, I was headed out the back door when Papa hollered, "Hannah, would you pick up jour grandma's high-blood-pressure pills at the Rexall drugstore after school today and bring dem to her? She called late last night and reminded me."

"OK, Papa. Do you need anything in town?"

"No, notting I can tink of."

I drove to the Rexall drugstore first thing after school and picked up Grandma's pills, but before I went to her house, I stopped off at the Munich Café where the kids hung out. To my surprise, as soon as I walked into the café, I immediately locked eyes with Rome, who just so happened to be sitting in the front booth.

His face creased into a smile and he motioned with a sweep of his hand to come, sit down. My chest grew tight. Suddenly feeling more awkward, I slid into the booth across from him and looked into the bluest eyes I'd ever seen.

"So you're the little redhead who waves at me when I drive by. I hear your name is Hannah."

I smiled and nodded my head.

"What have you been up to, Hannah?" he asked.

I grinned. "Not much."

My face felt like it was burning up. My heart was almost beating out of my chest, and I couldn't think of a sensible thing to say. Finally, I mumbled, "Rome, I have to get going."

"What's your hurry?"

"I have to give Grandma her pills. I know she's waiting for me to get to her house."

He smiled and lowered his voice. "I hope I see more of you, Hannah."

I walked out of the café on cloud nine—I could hardly remember a thing we talked about.

Did he really say he hoped to see more of me?

I knew Papa wouldn't like the idea of me dating someone who was already out of high school, but if by some miracle Rome asked me out, I was going.

***

Grandma wasn't in her kitchen as usual when I walked into her house. Rhubarb was asleep on the back of the davenport.

The sun shone through her bedroom window into the hallway, and it was so quiet you could hear a pin drop. I peeked into Grandma's bedroom and found her asleep,

118

tucked under a patchwork quilt. I placed the pills on her dresser, then reached over and patted her on the shoulder. She made little snoring sounds. "Grandma, wake up. Are you feeling OK?"

Grandma's eyes opened and she peered at me from under the covers. "I'm fine, dear, just tired. Good thing you came by and woke me. I shouldn't be wasting my time in bed on such a sunny day. What time is it, anyway?"

"It's after five p.m., Grandma."

"My word, I came into my bedroom after I ate my dinner, lay down and the next thing I know, the day is almost gone."

I picked up her hand and held it. "Don't worry, Grandma. You must have needed the rest. I set your pills on top of your dresser, and since you're feeling alright, I'll be on my way."

"Now, don't go hurrying off, dear. I made some potato candy last evening especially for you."

I hadn't seen Grandma since the day she got crabby at me when I asked her if she ever had a boyfriend besides Grandpa. Funny thing, Grandma never apologized, but she always gave me something special after she acted ornery.

Grandma's hair hung loose from her bun as she waggled her way out of the covers and sat on the edge of the bed, rubbing her arthritic knees. I plunked down beside her as she struggled to straighten her cotton stockings and slip into her wooly bedroom slippers.

"Hannah, don't ever let yourself get fat like me. You just saw what a hard time I have when it comes to pulling on my stockings and getting up out of bed? You know, I have high blood pressure, diabetes, and weak knees, all caused from being overweight."

"I'll try not to get fat, Grandma."

Why doesn't Grandma do something about her weight and stop eating big fat sweet rolls with butter and banana cream pie? Every time she goes into town, the first thing she does is head for the Mercantile to buy candy corn; then gives me a few pieces and eats the rest herself before we even get home.

I promised myself right then and there that I'd starve myself before I let myself get fat.

Grandma hobbled into the butler's pantry, packed up the candy and handed it to me.

"Be sure to give your Pa a piece."

"I sure will. Grandma, would you give me a copy of the potato candy recipe sometime?"

"Why don't you write it down right now?"

"I guess I could do that."

Grandma turned the pages in her recipe book to the candy section. "Here it is, dear, potato candy." She gave me a sheet of notebook paper and a pencil, and I plunked down on a chair by Grandma's table and copied the recipe in my best penmanship.

POTATO CANDY

1-lb. pkg. confectioners' sugar	1/4 c peanut butter
1 7 oz. pkg. coconut	2 squares baking chocolate
1 medium potato, cooked	

Boil potato until it is cooked. Mash in a bowl and add confectioners' sugar, coconut and peanut butter. Mix with a fork until well blended. Press into a pie plate. Melt chocolate and spread evenly over mixture. Put in refrigerator and let set until chocolate is hardened. Cut and serve.

Helga Larson
Munich, ND

"Thank you, Grandma. I've never made candy before, but since I've learned to cook in home economics class, I like to try new things."

"Your mama always made potato candy at Christmas time."

"That's why I wanted the recipe." I folded the page carefully and tucked it in my jeans pocket.

"Oh, Grandma, I dreamed about Mama for the first time the other night. Do you ever dream about her?"

"Yes, I have dreams about Cajsa, but I never remember them when I wake up. Do you remember your dreams?"

"Well, about all I remember is Mama floating in the clouds."

"That's because she's in heaven, my dear."

I smiled. "I wonder if Mama remembers me?"

"Of course she does, Hannah."

"Well, I better get going. Thank you for the candy, Grandma."

"You're welcome, my dear. Come back and see me soon."

Jeez, I still couldn't help but wonder why Grandma got so upset when I asked her if she ever had a boyfriend besides Grandpa.

***

Winter had settled down over the prairie again. On a chilly Friday night in November, a bunch of us girls went to hear the big band play at the Community Hall and walked into a packed crowd on the huge dance floor.

We sank down on the wooden chairs that weren't taken against the wall and hoped some guys would ask us to dance soon.

I leaned back and listened to the beautiful sound of the big band and reveled in seeing folks of all ages out on the dance floor, cutting a rug.

Annabelle giggled and gave me a little poke. "Just look at that little old man out there in that grey pinstripe suit with the high-water pants, doing the cha-cha. Do you see any good lookers out there, Hannah?"

I laughed, "No, not really. Watch that old lady in the navy blue polka-dot dress and red pumps, with her big ass bumping into everyone."

"Oh, my God, Hannah, you always make me laugh."

"You know, there are so many people out there, I can't tell who's who."

"I wonder if anyone is ever going to ask us to dance, Hannah?" Then, all excited, Annabelle jumped up off her chair and poked me again. "Hannah, look who just came through the door."

Oh, my God, in walked Rome with a big smile on his face, strutting right towards

121

me. I could feel my heart thumping away. He held out his hand. I put my small hand in Rome's big one and he guided me onto the dance floor.

Rome taught me some jazzy new steps that night. I had a marvelous time dancing to *The Tennessee Waltz*, and rollicking to the *Chattanooga Choo Choo, Pensylvania 6-5000* and my favorite, *In The Mood*.

Rome took me home that night. It was strange how my emotions would swing suddenly from one direction to another. Here I had this beautiful, starry moment to be alone with Rome, and I felt so nervous I just wanted to get home. As soon as we got to my place, I grasped onto the door handle, and hurried to get out.

Rome grabbed my hand and pulled me towards him.

I looked up in his face.

He smiled down at me, so sweet. "What's your big hurry, Hannah?" He hopped out of the car and walked me up to my door.

What a gentleman.

Before he turned and walked away, he gave me a little hug, and asked, "How about going dancing again next Friday night?"

I grinned. "I'd love to." Needless to say, I could hardly wait for the next Friday night to come.

***

Driving by Nick's Drive-In on a warm summer day, I happened to see a HELP WANTED sign in the window. As soon as I got home, I called Nick's Drive-In. Mr. Collins answered the telephone.

"Hello, Mr. Collins, it's me, Hannah. I see you have a HELP WANTED sign in your window, and I'm looking for a summer job."

"You are? Well, why don't you come in and see me, then."

"When would be a good time?"

"Could you come in tomorrow? I'll be here all day."

"OK, I'll see you tomorrow, Mr. Collins."

When I got there the next day, Nick, a stocky man of medium height with a head of thick, dark brown hair and a kind face, stood in the kitchen in front of the grill, flipping hamburgers, when I walked in. He looked up, laid the spatula down and walked out to greet me.

I felt my heart racing.

"Hi, Hannah! Thanks for coming in."

"Hello, Mr. Collins."

He wiped his hands on his long white apron. The aroma of burgers frying wafted off of the grill.

"So, you want to work here."

"Yes, I do."

"How old are you?"

"I turned sixteen last December."

"Do you have transportation, and can I count on you to get work on time?"

"Getting to work on time will not be a problem for me, Mr. Collins. I got my driver's license when I turned sixteen and Papa will let me use his car."

"Do you know how to make change?"

I grinned. "No, but I'm willing to learn."

With a pleased look on his face, he said, "Report to work at ten tomorrow morning."

"Thank you, Mr. Collins."

"You can call me Nick."

Nick headed toward the back room, and I started walking out the front when he called, "Wait a minute, Hannah. What size dress do you wear?"

"Eight."

Out he came carrying a brand-new white uniform, trimmed in black, and handed it to me.

Grinning from ear to ear, I picked up the uniform and held it in front of me. "It looks like the perfect size. Thank you."

"Oh, I meant to ask you, how is Johan doing?"

"He's doing good, busy with haying, but since it rained last night he couldn't work in the hayfield today, so he gave me a ride. He's waiting out in the car."

"Tell him hello."

"I sure will, Thanks again, Nick. I'll see you in the morning."

Nick grinned. "See you tomorrow, Hannah."

I ran out of Nick's Drive-In, jumped into the front seat beside Papa and sat for a minute, clutching my new uniform, before I tipped my head back and busted out laughing. "Papa, I just landed a real job! I go to work in the morning."

Papa chuckled, "Jou are quite the gal, Hannah."

"You know, Papa, I've dreamed of working at Nick's Drive-In ever since Great-Aunt Hortense took us there a long time ago."

"Is dat right?"

I slipped into my new uniform as soon as I got home. It fit me perfectly and I loved it.

It's going to be so much fun to put on this uniform and carhop! Oh, my God, I can't wait.

The next day, Nick stood by the cash register with a happy smile on his face when I walked in at ten minutes to ten.

"Well, Hannah, I see you're right on time." He motioned for me to step over by the register.

"Hannah, of utmost importance in this business is to make correct change." He opened the drawer, took out a ten-dollar bill and laid it on top of the register. "Say the customer hands you this ten-dollar bill and his meal cost one dollar and ninety cents. You give him back one dime, that makes two dollars, you give him three one-dollar bills, that makes five dollars, and then you hand him a five-dollar bill, that's ten."

"Count the change out loud as you're handing it to the customer, and leave the bill the customer gave you on top of the register until he is fine with the transaction. Then you place the money in the cash register, in the correct slot and close the drawer. Always say thank you to the customer. Now, Hannah, I want you to do what I just showed you."

Nick laid a ten-dollar bill on the register, and I counted out the change exactly like he had spelled it out.

He patted my arm, "You're going to do alright, Red."

I grinned. *No one ever called me that before.*

"Red, You can eat anything you want while you're at work, except steak. And one more thing: keep an eye on the trays. They aren't cheap, you know. Don't give the customer a chance to drive off with one. If they do, I'll have to deduct the cost of the tray from your paycheck."

"I'll do my best not to let that happen, Nick."

I felt a little awkward saying "Nick" because I'd been taught to address adults by Mr. or Mrs. So and So. The only other adult I called by their first name was Elsie, and she insisted I call her by her first name.

Nick exclaimed, "Oh! Before I forget, I expect you to help out at the front counter when you have free time, Hannah."

"OK, Nick."

Believe me, I kept an eye on the customers' cars, and when somebody looked like they were anywhere near ready to take off, I bolted out there as fast as I could and snatched the tray off their car window.

Nora worked as a waitress in the dining room. She was middle-aged and overweight with varicose veins bulging out of her heavy legs, the likes of which I'd never seen before. She wore her bleached-blonde hair rolled up on top her head. Her face always looked tired and she complained about everything. The story went: she had a lazy husband and a bunch of kids at home. Her kids called her off and on during her work shift, whining about one thing or another, and she allowed it to happen.

Watching Nora, and listening to her carry on, I knew right off I wasn't going to be working in a restaurant when I got as old as her. I would go on to school, and have a real career after I graduated from high school.

Meghan and I were the only carhops. Right off, she took me under her wing and we became friends. Meghan was a cute little gal who knew her business and strutted around the restaurant with her long, dark brown ponytail bouncing on her back. Meghan started working at Nick's Drive-In right after she graduated from high school, and she'd been working there for almost two years. I thought it was funny how she never talked about going onto college or doing anything different.

One day she confided in me that her parents were divorced. Her father had run off and married a much-younger gal. She went on to say that her mother told her, "That bastard father of yours is the cause of all my problems.' Hannah, my parents hate each other."

Meghan was the first person I ever knew whose parents were divorced, and I couldn't imagine parents hating each other.

Meghan snickered, "I just broke up with my old boyfriend, Olaf, because he was getting too serious and I'm checking the guys out." We'd giggle and race out to the cars, seeing who could get there first, especially if there was a good-looking guy waiting.

CHAPTER 8

Gunda Elofson, the cook at Nick's Drive-In, had large brown eyes under oddly pointed black brows, and a pleasant-looking face. She was almost as fat as Grandma. Gunda and her husband had emigrated from Sweden, and she talked broken English just like Papa.

Gunda told me her only child, Isak, had recently moved to Louisville, Kentucky, with hopes of becoming a jockey and racing horses at Churchill Downs.

"Dat boy of mine has loved to race horses since he vas a little tyke. He knows so much about horses too; vell, his papa taught him. He's yust a little guy." She chuckled. "Not like his mama. Don't tink he weighs more den one hundred thirty pounds, yust the right veight to be a horse jockey. Knowing Isak, he vill do yust fine, but I sure do miss my boy."

Gunda made the best French fries I'd ever tasted. If I had free time, I'd sit on a little wooden stool beside a big tubful of potatoes and help Gunda peel them. The fun part was shoving the long Idaho potatoes through the slicer and seeing them turn into perfect French fries.

I must tell you, going to work at Nick's Drive-In was a real eye-opener. For instance, I was taken aback when the old Bridgeman delivery guy stuck his head through the little window between the dining area and kitchen and teased, "Hey, cutie, how would you like to go out with me? I could show you a real good time."

The dumb ass. Who the hell does he think he is? I heard he's twenty-six years old and married, with little kids at home.

I felt my face turning red. I wanted to jump up and tell him what I thought—go home and show your wife a good time, but I didn't want to create a scene at work, so I nodded without smiling and went back to peeling the potatoes.

I was surprised to see Meghan act so nonchalant when he came on to her. She just laughed it off. "Guess he wants to see if he still has it. Hannah, the first time he flirted with me, I got upset too, but then I realized how stupid he is. You should hear what some of the truck drivers say. I don't let the bullshit bother me anymore. I just pick up my tips and go on. It's part of working as a waitress, I guess."

Right then, I decided I'd be like Meghan, and wouldn't let the bullshit bother me anymore either.

Then there was the time I happened to walk past the storeroom and overheard Nora grumbling to Nick, about me. I stopped dead in my tracks and leaned against the door to listen. "Hannah works less hours than I do and she gets way more tips than any of us. Nick, why don't you make her share her tips?"

Nora never says anything good about anyone, and now she's talking about me.

I heard Nick's harsh voice loud and clear. "Nora, you start treating the customers like Red does and you'll get the tips too. Wouldn't hurt to smile more."

Nick's warm approval of me made me like my job all the more. It was fun car hopping and meeting all the different customers, but like I said I knew I wanted to have a real career someday. I didn't want to become an old lady and all I'd ever done was wait on tables in a restaurant.

LeRoy, a regular customer who worked as a mechanic's helper at Bob's Chevrolet, brightened my day when he dropped in at two thirty every afternoon and sat on a chrome stool at the front counter. He'd order a chocolate sundae every single time, and with a big grin on his face he'd watch me make it. "Hannah, would you add an extra glob of chocolate while you're at it?" He had a cute little dimple in his chin and thick, dark, curly hair. I took a liking to him.

I couldn't help but laugh the morning Gunda came running into work, huffing and puffing, with her arms full of stuff. She glanced up at the big clock on the wall. "Looks like I'm right on time." Then she set her purse down, and gave me a cheery greeting as she shrugged out of her brown corduroy jacket.

"Good morning, Gunda. It looks like you were in a real hurry getting dressed this morning."

"I'm yust fine. Vhat do jou mean, in a hurry, Hannah?"

"Well, just look at you—your blouse is on inside out."

She glanced down at her top.

"Oh, my Got, Hannah, I can't believe dis." She squeezed her eyes shut, her head shook, and she started to laugh so hard tears ran down her cheeks. Then she quickly snatched a napkin from the holder, wiped her eyes, and teetered into the bathroom to change her blouse right side out.

Gunda was still laughing when she came out of the bathroom. "Vhat a vay to start my day, huh, Hannah? But ve sure had a goot laugh, didn't ve, honey?"

Gunda called everybody honey.

One afternoon, the cars were lined up in front of Nick's Drive-In like you wouldn't believe, when Nora took it upon herself to carhop. As soon as Nora ran outside, a fat-faced man, slouched behind the wheel of a black Hudson, waved his arm out the window. I heard him shout, "Over here, lady. I've been waiting longer than any of those ding-a-lings."

Nora hurried over and took his order, then rushed back inside, shouting, "Gunda, six orders of shrimp with fries."

The big guy straightened up when Nora came bustling out, carrying six baskets of hot shrimp with fries, and hollered, "I hope you're not bringing me all those, lady. I told you, I wanted six shrimp with fries."

Nora sighed in disbelief. "I was sure you said six orders of shrimp with fries."

"You better clean your ears, lady."

Flustered, Nora carried the extra baskets back to the kitchen and plunked them on the back table. Out of breath, she plopped down on the wooden kitchen stool, brushed her forehead with the back of her hand and murmured, "I don't care how many cars are lined up out front; I'm leaving the car hopping to you kids."

"Nora, I'm sorry that guy was mean to you. After all, you were only trying to help, and it seems it all backfired."

"Backfire, it did, Hannah."

Then she stood up and glanced all around. "Thank God our boss isn't here."

Good old Gunda took charge, and arranged the shrimp and fries on the back table like a sumptuous buffet. In the end, we girls had a fine time grabbing shrimp, dipping them in cocktail sauce and eating them on the run, until every last shrimp was gone. The only fish I'd ever tasted in my life before this episode was fresh trout and salmon out of a can. That day, I discovered I absolutely loved shrimp.

But nothing could make me happier or get my heart beating faster than when Rome walked into the restaurant and plunked down on a counter stool, with his eyes fixed on me and a big smile on his face. At once, I'd stop whatever I was doing and rush to take his order.

"What brings you here this time of day?" I asked one afternoon.

"Well, I'm on my way for a long haul, and I wanted to see my favorite girl before I left town."

It was late when I got off work, and I was glad to see my workday come to an end. But going home was never the same without Maggie scampering to greet me. It seemed I'd never get over missing Maggie.

Looking around, I was surprised to see a strange vehicle parked out front. The living room shades were pulled up halfway, and I heard music playing. *Jeez, what's going on?*

I snuck up to the window, stood on my tiptoes and peeked in. Oh, my God! A record spun on the Motorola phonograph, "It's Only a Paper Moon." And Papa had his arms around Lucy as they waltzed round and round on the hardwood living room floor.

Now, I know Papa likes to go dancing at city hall when a good band's playing, but him and Lucy waltzing around in our house? They must have been dancing for some time too, because I can see Papa's rolled up his shirtsleeves, and there are big circles of dampness under each arm and down the middle of his back.

I ran inside and let the screen door slam behind me. Papa hollered, "Hello, Hannah!" Lucy chimed in, "Hi, Hannah."

Embarrassed, I shouted back, "Hi, Papa, hi, Lucy," then headed upstairs to my room, crawled into bed and pulled the covers all around me. I couldn't even explain the feeling I had after the shock of seeing Lucy dancing in our house. And Papa's unusual behavior was beginning to make me wonder what was going on with the two of them.

The window shade at my head flopped softly in a warm wind, and through the screen I heard flies buzzing. In a little while, the back door opened and shut. I could hear Papa and Lucy talking. Eager to hear what they were saying, I rolled over next to the window and leaned my elbows on the windowsill, my chin on my hands, paying close attention.

"Look up in da sky, Lucy. Jou can see da Big Dipper as plain as day."

"It's such a beautiful evening, Johan. I don't think I've ever seen so many glistening stars in my whole life. Oh, my goodness. Where did you come from? Johan, look, she's rubbing my leg and wants me to pick her up."

"Dat's Mittens, Hannah's cat. She's a friendly ting, all right. Hannah named her Mittens because she had four white paws; vell, now she has three. One foot got caught in a gopher trap, and dat was da end of dat pretty white foot."

Lucy must be holding Mittens.

I pricked up my ears, and listened to Lucy carry on. "Oh, you poor baby. My, you have such a soft, fluffy, thick coat with so many gorgeous colors. Who cares if one little foot is missing, huh? Just listen to her, Johan. She's purring. You silly kitty—now she's licking my chin. I hate to put her down."

I heard Lucy's car drive away.

If Mittens took to Lucy, she has to be a nice person.

Papa came up with all kinds of cockamamy excuses to go into town after he met Lucy, and it got so he forgot what he was supposed to do as well, like on that rainy cold morning when I hurried down to the hen house and found the eggs that Papa had not gathered, and I collected them before I left for school.

I knew Papa was very lonely without Mama, yet it never entered my mind that he might have a girlfriend someday. At times I felt jealous of Lucy, but then I liked to see Papa enjoying life again. One good thing: after he met Lucy, he wasn't fussing about what I was doing all the time. It was strange how my emotions would swing suddenly from one direction to another.

I felt envious when Annabelle and her family left in their 1952 Woodie station wagon on a family vacation to Western North Dakota and didn't ask me to go along.

It made me think of the time when Mama, Papa and I went on a short trip and drove through the pretty Peace Garden into Winnipeg, Canada. Papa hadn't taken a vacation since Mama passed away.

I asked Papa once why we never went on trips, and he told me, "I don't feel like going avay vitout Cajsa, and besides, vho vould milk da cows?"

That was then, but now I know he wants to stay close to home because of Lucy.

"You could get Jacob to help, Papa."

"Jou tink so? Vell, tings must be going goot vit Venzel and Dakota if dey are going on a wacation, den."

As soon as Annabelle got back, she came over to see me and told me all about her trip. "Hannah, we drove through the Turtle Mountains, by farmsteads, pastureland and beautiful clear blue lakes. I couldn't believe how pretty the wildflowers were. Dad told us the Turtle Mountains provided trading and trapping for the early settlers."

"I didn't know there were Turtle Mountains in North Dakota."

"Hannah, I didn't either until I saw them. When we stayed at the Knotty Pine Motel in Bismarck, my whole family went swimming in the big pool. Radovan told me his legs felt perfectly normal when he swam in the warm water."

"I'm glad Radovan learned to swim."

"He learned how when he was at therapy. I saw the capitol building too, Hannah. It's the tallest building in North Dakota."

"Really?"

"Hannah, remember when crazy Mr. Iverson taught us about the Center of North America? Well, now I've seen it. Coming back, Dad stopped in Rugby to show us the Geographical Center of North America. The center is marked with a monument shaped like a pyramid. On the plaque, it read and I copied it: The monument is twenty-one feet high, six feet wide at its base and it sets on a heart-shaped foundation."

She reached in her bag. "Hannah, I brought you a little present." She handed me a beautiful package, gift wrapped in pretty daisy flower tissue paper.

"Thank you so much!" I exclaimed.

Thrilled, I carefully unwrapped the gift. Inside was a little ceramic monument of the Center of North America.

"Annabelle, I love it, and I'll cherish it forever. I have a perfect spot in my bedroom for it. Thank you for thinking of me while you were gone."

"You're welcome, Hannah. I think of you no matter where I am."

I couldn't wait for the school day to end because I had plans to see Rome. The minute my last class was over, I walked outside into beautiful sunshine and saw him drive up in his 1950 gray Chevrolet. He sat with a big grin on his face, watching me dash down the long, open stairway, two steps at a time. Then he reached across and swung the passenger's car door wide for me to hop in.

"Hi, Hannah! How did school go today?"

"I had a great day. My last class is typing, and I'm so happy I'm learning to type. I love that class."

"How would you like to go roller-skating?"

"I'd love that too."

Rome drove us straight to the Stump Lake roller-skating rink. When we walked in, the place was almost empty.

"Where is everybody?" Rome exclaimed.

I nudged Rome's arm. "I'm glad there aren't many skaters on the rink. Since I'm new at this, I need all the space I can get."

Rome coached me, and I ended up having so much fun, skating to "Rock Around the Clock," and "The Great Pretender" by The Platters.

I laughed when Rome told me, "You're a born roller skater, Hannah."

"I love to roller-skate as much as I love to dance!"

After skating, we ate burgers at the Munich Café and drove around town to see what was going on. Too soon, I had to tell Rome, "It's time to take me home."

Rome grinned and spun the car around. He drove down by the tall grain elevators and parked in a secluded area, where he pulled me into his arms and kissed me on the mouth.

It was my first proper kiss, and I felt like electric bulbs had exploded inside my head.

I turned away. He used two fingers under my chin to bring my gaze back to his, and we kissed some more.

It was almost midnight when I finally got home. Thank the good Lord, Papa wasn't home yet. I burst through the kitchen door and peeked out the window, watching as

Rome drove away. Once Rome was out of sight, I scampered upstairs to my bedroom, flopped on my bed and thought about that kiss.

Jeez, all I wanted to do was lie there and feel the breeze through the screen of my bedroom window, while thoughts of Rome filled my mind. The way he stared at me over the top of his black sunglasses, his happy smile, his shock of dark hair. I cracked a smile when a puff of wind blew through the screen. It was a secret feeling I'd never felt before, and I wanted to kiss him some more.

I was sitting at the kitchen table reading one of my favorite novels, *Little Women,* when Annabelle's voice on the other side of the screen door caught me by surprise.

"Knock, knock, anybody alive in there?"

Delighted, I jumped up and ran to greet her. "It's so good to see you, Annabelle."

Sad to say, we didn't see each other as much as we used to, now that Annabelle was spending most of her free time with Trevor, and I was busy working at my job and going out with Rome.

"I can't stay long."

I gestured for Annabelle to follow me outside, and we plunked down on the back steps. Right off, I noticed Annabelle had Trevor's class ring hanging on a gold chain around her neck.

"Are you and Trevor going steady?"

She sat blowing dandelion puffs at me and chuckled, "Sort of. Trevor really loves me and he wants us to get married after I graduate."

"Are you in love with him?"

"I think so. Mom says I'm too young to know what love is."

"Did you realize there are three girls in our class getting married right after graduation?"

Annabelle laughed, "Well then, I'll make four."

"You know, Annabelle, the last thing I want to do is marry a farmer and end up living out in the boondocks the rest of my life. Ever since I studied about California in geography class, I've dreamed of living in San Francisco. I'd like to see what it's like to live through a whole winter without snow. Besides, I want to get out in the world and see different places before I settle down with a husband.

But I do dream of having children someday too." I've never visited a big city, so I fantasize about becoming an airline stewardess and flying all around the world, seeing places I'd never been."

Annabelle sat listening, stroking her thumb against her fingers.

"Hannah, I know you'll miss all the farm animals if you move away, and you can't keep them in the city."

"I never thought of that, but I know for sure I'll have a dog no matter where I live, and a cat too. It would be so much fun to walk on the beach with my dog whenever I felt like it. You could visit me anytime, Annabelle."

"I'd love to come and see you. I hear you've been seeing Rome a lot since you went to work at Nick's."

"Who told you that? I suppose you've heard that Papa has a girlfriend too?"

"Mm-hmm. Do you like her?"

I shrugged.

"How do you like your job, Hannah?"

"I love car hopping and the tips, and I get to eat anything I want, except steak. That's OK because I don't like steak anyway. I ate shrimp for the first time the other day and I really liked it. I'll tell you one thing I've learned working at Nick's Drive-In, and that is, after watching old Gunda standing over the hot grill all day, and Nora carrying big trays of food on her swollen legs, restaurant work isn't the kind of life I want. I'm going on to college and I'm going to have a professional career."

"Good for you, Hannah. I don't think I could ever leave my family and live away. I would miss them too much. I want to marry Trevor, and raise my own family right here on the wide open North Dakota prairie."

"I can understand, Annabelle. Maybe if I had a big family, like you do, I wouldn't want to move away either."

Just then, a loud rustling sound sprang from the direction of the vegetable garden. I turned to look and busted out laughing. Seesaw, the goat, looked absolutely hilarious, standing in the middle of the tomato patch and crunching on a big red tomato with the juice running off his chin.

Annabelle giggled. "Look at his cute little face. He looks like he's smiling, Hannah."

"Seesaw does have an adorable face, but he's a pest, and he's not supposed to get out of the barnyard. Look over there where the fence is broken. He must have knocked it down and jumped through."

"Oh, yeah, I see."

"Papa isn't going to like the idea of Seesaw tramping in his garden one bit."

I leaped off the step, ran up behind Seesaw and yelled as loud as I could, "Get out of the garden, right now."

Seesaw bellowed *baa, baa* and ran like the wind. Then he leaped through the broken fence and landed on all four legs in the barnyard, where he belonged.

Annabelle stood beside me, cracking up. "Did you see the terrified look on Seesaw's face when he was flying over the fence, Hannah? You scared the daylights out of the old goat."

"Yeah, it was funny to see how fast his little short tail wiggled when he sailed through the air."

I ran to the toolshed, picked up a hammer, and was about to mend the fence myself when Papa came rattling in, in his old truck.

"Hi, girls! Vhat's going on?"

"Seesaw jumped through the fence and got into the garden."

"Vell, it looks like dat damn billy goat ate most of our goot tomatoes. Hand me da hammer, Hannah. Dat goddamn goat. I don't know vhy ve keep him around in da first place. He's notting but a damn nuisance."

Annabelle shouted, "I got to get going, Hannah."

"Do you have to go already? It seems like you just got here."

"Trevor is coming over to my house any minute."

"OK, Annabelle, hope I see you again soon."

I felt sad at times because it seemed like all of a sudden; Annabelle and I were going our own separate ways. Yet I knew deep in my heart, Annabelle and I would remain friends and stay close no matter how far apart our paths would take us.

Papa gulped down his supper, and the next thing I knew, he was scurrying out of the steamy bathroom, all spruced up and smelling like Old Spice.

"Hannah, I won't be gone long," he shouted as he rushed out the back door, hopped into his car and drove away.

When it came time for me to go to bed, I couldn't believe that Papa wasn't home yet. I slipped into my pajamas and crawled under the covers. Alone, I felt my heartbeat quicken. I left the light on and lay there, anxiously tracing my fingernail over the red-checked and blue-flowered and yellow-swirled patches that had once been my great-grandmother's apron or Grandma's housedress in my quilt.

Finally, I turned off the light and wrapped the covers over my head, but I still couldn't fall asleep. I folded my hands together and prayed that Papa would drive in.

At long last, sunshine peeked in around my window shade. I swung myself out of bed, pulled up the blind and looked out. Thank the good Lord: my prayers were answered when I caught a glimpse of Papa climbing up the back steps.

I ran downstairs into the hallway. "Papa, where in the world have you been? I didn't sleep a wink all night, worrying about you."

Papa smiled and put a soothing hand on my shoulder. "No need to go vorrying over jour old papa, Sissy Pie."

Papa rushed into his bedroom, where he shucked his good clothes, pulled on a pair of old pants and a blue work shirt, and headed outdoors. I heard him whistling "Yankee Doodle" as he hurried to the barn, carrying a milk bucket in each hand.

I looked out the kitchen window and saw Sally galloping across the barnyard towards Papa. She swung her head over the fence to be petted. Papa rubbed her ears and stroked her neck, but I could tell his mind wasn't on Sally.

As mad as I felt at Papa for making me worry all night, I was happy to see him in such good spirits, and know he was OK. And to hear him whistle "Yankee Doodle" again made me laugh.

That night, I dreamed about Mama again. In this dream, Mama looked like an angel in a long white gown, standing beside a beautiful white horse and surrounded by clouds. A gorgeous castle sat in the background. She smiled at me, then vanished.

Strange how I never dreamed about Mama until Papa met Lucy.

What happened next was bound to make the headlines in the *Munich Recorder*. Soon after Papa's all-night date, I came tearing up the back steps and almost collided with

Papa, who stood at the top of the stairs, uneasy, straightening his suspenders.

"Hannah, get in the car and go pick up your grandma. I have sumting I vant to tell you bot."

Any time Papa had something to say, it was something we couldn't wait to hear.

"Why don't we both go to Grandma's, and you can tell us there?"

"No, vhat I vant to tell jou, I vant to say right here, in my own house."

"What's the big hurry?"

"Never mind, yust do as I tell jou, Hannah Marie."

"Ya, but I'm hungry."

"Why didn't you eat at vork?"

"Because we were too busy."

"Jou can eat someting vhen jou get back."

I saw Grandma through the lace curtain in her kitchen window when I drove into her front yard. She waved a soapy hand, motioning for me to come in.

I swung open her screen door and hollered, "Grandma, hurry, Papa wants you to come over right now, he has something important to tell us."

Grandma hung the dishtowel on the rack. "Why don't you tell him I can't come right now?" But even as she spoke, she started taking off her apron.

Grandma waddled out to the car, plunked down on the seat and sat wringing her hands. "My word. Do you suppose he bought the Dilbert McDonnell farm? It's been for sale for some time now. I overheard him talking to Jacob one day about how he wouldn't mind owning that land someday."

"No, he wouldn't have a meeting just to tell us that."

"What if he has some serious illness?"

"Oh, Grandma, don't say that."

"Well, one never knows."

"Oh, Grandma, Papa is never sick."

"I'm just trying to think of what it could be."

"Grandma, let's just wait and find out."

When Papa saw Grandma and me coming up the back steps, he walked over to the top of the stairs and held the door open, with a look on his face that I had never seen before. And boy! Was I ever surprised to see Jacob sitting at the kitchen table.

Grandma, wound up like a two-dollar watch, stood leaning on the kitchen counter and asked, "Johan, do you want us to sit in the parlor?"

"No, Lieula, vat I got to say, I can say right here in the kitchen."

The chair legs creaked when Papa pulled the chair out from under the table and sat down. He gestured for all of us to join him around the table.

Grandma limped and huffed her way across the kitchen, making a great show of rubbing her hip, and lowering herself with a pained sigh onto a high-backed chair. I plunked on the chair across from Jacob, watching him chew on a matchstick and roll it from one side of his mouth to the other.

Papa took the pipe out of his mouth and laid it in an ashtray. He leaned back in his seat and laced his fingers together. "Now, jou know as vell as I do dat I've been courtin' Lucy Swan for some time. She's a mighty fine voman."

He turned to me. "Hannah Marie, you're almost grown-up now."

I nodded.

All of a sudden, I'm grown-up?

"Vell, folks, vat I've got to tell you is: Lucy and I are getting married."

The news almost took my breath away.

I can't picture Papa married to anyone but Mama, and I really can't imagine Papa and Lucy kissing or anything like that.

"Papa, did you say that you and Lucy are getting married?"

"I've asked her and she said yes."

Grandma's mouth dropped open and her face went white. "Well, I never."

Jacob scratched his head hard and fast. "The hell jou say, Yohan."

In a faint voice, Grandma uttered, "What's this world coming to? She's half your age. Johan, you could be her father."

"Age is yust a number."

Grandma put her hands up to her face and whined, "Johan, you are going to marry a woman who has a history of working in the burlesque business. Don't you care what people will say?"

Papa rubbed his chin and looked over his bifocals at Grandma. "Jah, I care, but I care more about Lucy. I yust told you, I'm marrying her and dat's dat."

Jacob slapped the table with his big hand. "Goot for jou, Yohan."

Grandma pushed back her chair, stood up and strode right out the door.

"Come on, Hannah," she wailed.

In a hurry to leave the table, I nearly turned over my chair. Papa heaved himself from his seat and walked me to the back door with his arm across my shoulders.

As soon as we got in the car, Grandma started in, "How could he do it? Now, I'm telling you, when a woman marries a man old enough to be her father, you can bet your boots it's for what she can get out of him. Johan is a fool. Hannah, you keep your mouth shut. It may all blow over and no one will ever know. Maybe your pa just thought she said yes."

"I don't know what to think, Grandma, but the way Papa's been carrying on with Lucy, we shouldn't be all that surprised. It's wonderful to see Papa in such good spirits. And remember, Lucy is Dr. Knightley's niece. She can't be all that bad."

Grandma harrumphed, "I hear you got yourself a boyfriend, too, Hannah."

"Where did you hear that?"

"Oh, not much goes on around here without your old grandma knowing about it. I'm warning you, Hannah, don't you go letting this guy have his way with you. Do you hear me?"

Grandma lowered her voice so I had to lean towards her to hear what she said. "Guys don't respect a girl they can go all the way with."

"Oh, Grandma."

Less than a week after Papa announced he was getting married, he asked me if I would be Lucy's bridesmaid.

"Doesn't Lucy have any girlfriends?" I wanted to know.

"It isn't dat, Hannah. Lucy vants jou to be a part of our vedding, and so do I. Jou'll have to get jourself something nice to vear."

I got happy over the thought of buying a new dress.

"What color dress should I get?"

"Oh, I don't know about dat, Hannah. Maybe jou should ask Lucy."

"OK, I'll be the bridesmaid. Who will be the best man?"

"Yacob."

"Jacob and me?" I laughed. "Oh, my God, we'll sure make a sightly couple, huh, Papa?"

"Vell, he's my best friend. It vill yust be you, me, Yacob and Lucy. Ve're getting married in da Cando courthouse."

"I thought you had to get married in a church."

"Not all da time, Hannah."

For Papa's sake, I'd made up my mind I would make the best of it, and be happy for him.

On the day they were to become husband and wife, Papa, Jacob and I drove to Lucy's house and found her waiting on the front-porch swing, swaying back and forth. The minute we drove in, she jumped up and came running with a smile on her face. "Boy, don't you look dapper!" she blurted out when she saw Papa dressed in his navy three-piece suit and matching tie.

"Vell, you're looking pretty goot yourself, my dear," Papa told Lucy.

Lucy had on a pretty off-white dress with a matching jacket, and her hair was done up so cute.

"Did you do your own hair?" I asked Lucy.

"Oh, yes, I did."

"It looks nice."

"Thank you, Hannah. You look quite lovely in your pretty pink dress. I'm very happy you agreed to be my bridesmaid."

"Thank you."

I had to admit, Jacob looked spiffy as well, dressed up in a tan suit. He sat beside me in the backseat, looking first at Papa, then Lucy, with a silly grin on his face. And off we went, barreling down the familiar road to the Cando courthouse.

Judge Crankpin was bent over behind his big oak desk, rummaging through a drawer, when we walked into his chambers. He looked up when he saw us. His round, chubby face broke into a smile. He glanced at the gold watch that fit snugly on his wrist. "Mm-hmm, looks like you're right on time, folks."

Judge Crankpin picked up the wire-ring notebook that lay on his desk, flipped it open and gestured for all of us to move up to the front of the chambers.

Lucy looked like a nervous wreck, standing alongside Papa and gripping the fancy red purse that matched her pumps. The hands on the big clock behind the judge's desk read eleven a.m.

Judge Crankpin stuck his feet into his loafers and lifted his obese body off the soft-cushioned chair. Holding the notebook in one hand and leaning on his cane with the other, he didn't waste any time getting to the nuptials and spoke with a voice of authority:

"Do you, Johan Jonesen, offer yourself wholly and joyfully, and do you choose Lucy Swan as the person with whom you will share your life, in laughter and in tears, in conflict and tranquility, loving what you know of her and trusting what you do not know yet?"

Papa gazed at Lucy adoringly. "I do."

Judge Crankpin looked into Lucy's eyes. "Do you, Lucy Swan, offer yourself wholly and joyfully, and do you choose Johan Jonesen as the person with whom you will share your life, in laughter and in tears, in conflict and tranquility, loving what you know of him and trusting what you do not know yet?"

Lucy said sweetly, with tears in her eyes, "I do."

Papa fumbled in his vest pocket for the gold wedding band and slipped it on Lucy's finger.

Judge Crankpin nodded his head and smiled. "You may kiss the bride."

Papa placed his hands on either side of Lucy's face and rested his lips on hers for only a second.

Even after witnessing the whole ceremony, it's hard to believe Papa is married. It'll take some getting used to, that's for sure.

Judge Crankpin plunked back down in his chair and smiled approvingly. Then Jacob and I followed Lucy and Papa as they walked out hand in hand. Boy! Were we surprised to see tin cans tied on the rear bumper of Papa's car and JUST MARRIED chalked across the rear window.

Papa chuckled. "Who do jou tink did dat?"

Jacob chimed in, "Jou know as vell as I do, jou can't get avay vit notting around here, Yohan."

142

From the courthouse, Papa drove us to the Cando Café for a wedding-dinner celebration. Mr. Carlson, the proprietor and a jovial soul, met us at the door. He shook Papa's hand, and showed us to a special table set with a bouquet of daisies placed in the center. Papa grinned. "Mr. Carlson, I see jou vent all out for us today."

"I'm glad you think so, Johan."

Papa sat down and blurted out, "Order vhatever jou vant, folks."

I picked up the big menu and studied it over real good. I couldn't believe all the choices: chicken, Swiss steak, pork chops, roast beef and all kinds of salads. When the waitress came around, I looked up and smiled. "I'll have the shrimp and French fries, please."

Jacob ordered a T-bone steak, rare.

Lucy was tickled when Betty, our waitress, rounded the corner from the kitchen, carrying a little wedding cake with a hand-painted bride-and-groom ornament placed on top. "It's carrot cake," she told us.

"Oh, Betty, how did you know carrot cake was my favorite?"

"A little birdie told me."

There was ice cream too.

When it came time to pay, Mr. Carlson bustled over to our table, patted Papa on the back and declared, "It's all on me, Johan. I want to wish you and Lucy a long, happy life together." He turned to Lucy. "The daisies are for you, my dear."

"Oh, thank you, thank you, Mr. Carlson. Daisies are my best-loved flower."

Lucy picked up the bouquet, and we left the restaurant. When Papa stopped in front of Jacob's house, Jacob immediately jumped out of the car and hustled around to Papa's half-open window, then stood bent over with his hands grasping the glass. "Tanks for everyting. It vas a real honor to be your best man, Yohan." He reached his long arm through the window and patted Papa on the shoulder. "Jou know, Yohan, I tink dat vas da best T-bone steak I've ever tasted. Tanks again, and I vant to vish jou and Lucy a happy life togetter."

"Jou are velcome, Yacob. Glad jou liked da steak."

Lucy had already quit her boring job at the telephone company after Papa made it clear, "No wife of mine is going to vork outside da house." And that very day, Papa started moving Lucy's belongings into our house.

I couldn't imagine, and I didn't even want to think about Lucy living with Papa and me in our house. But the good part was, I wouldn't be leaving Papa all alone when I went away.

I hadn't felt like talking about Papa getting married, until it really happened. Now I could hardly wait to tell Grandma all about the wedding. As soon as I got home, I changed into my jeans and took off on my bike as fast as I could to Grandma's house.

Sure enough, when I told Grandma the news, she grabbed her chest like she was having a heart attack. "Married by a judge? What's this world coming to? I'm sick over the whole thing, just plain sick."

"Grandma, we went to the Cando Café after Judge Crankpin married Papa and Lucy, and I ate shrimp and fries. Mr. Carlson wouldn't let Papa pay for anything. And we had carrot wedding cake and ice cream for dessert."

"My word, that does sound lovely."

"There were daisies on the table, and when it was time to leave, Mr. Carlson gave them to Lucy. Grandma, Lucy was so happy and she looked pretty. Papa looked handsome too."

"I hope your pa knows what he's doing."

"Papa's moving Lucy's things into our house right now."

"Is that right?"

"It looked like all Lucy has is a small dresser, and a rocking chair from her grandma, no other furniture, but I saw lots of purses and shoes. Oh, and she has a portable radio, a cute little thing, sort of pinkish-beige with red trim. Papa set it on the little shelf in the kitchen above the cook stove."

I had heard Lucy tell Papa, "It's too quiet without a radio playing."

"Oh, Hannah, I don't like the idea of Lucy sleeping in my daughter's beautiful brass four-poster bed that I gave Johan and Cajsa for a wedding gift, but you know it's really none of my business what Johan does."

Papa had left Mama's stuff as it was, and it really bothered me when, right off, Lucy started clearing out Mama's personal belongings to make room for her own things in the dresser drawers. She cleaned rooms, closets and cupboards, and threw out stuff without asking. She went right ahead and moved the furniture from one place to another like she owned the whole place.

There were many troublesome changes after Lucy moved in. I shuddered at the thought of suppertime with Lucy's dreadful cooking. I couldn't help but long for the nice meals Papa used to cook for us. And I really missed the times when Papa and I would sit at the supper table and talk about everything. With Lucy's smug little face looking at me from across the table, I didn't feel like telling Papa nothing.

I wished for the good old days. Thank God I would be through high school and leaving home soon.

One evening while Lucy, Papa and I were gathered around the supper table, I looked over at Papa grappling with a piece of tough steak on his plate, his expression woeful, and I burst out laughing. It only got funnier when Lucy put her hand on Papa's hand that held the knife and asked him, "Do you like the way I cooked your steak, sweetheart?"

Oh, my God. I tried to swallow my giggles, but I couldn't quit laughing.

"What's so funny?" Lucy asked. I couldn't answer, couldn't stop laughing. Papa paused with a biscuit halfway to his mouth, and stared at me with a threatening scowl. I glanced down at my watery potatoes, leathery meat and mushy peas, and began stirring them round on my plate, hoping it would all disappear.

CHAPTER 9

I smelled the aroma of coffee brewing on the stovetop. *Arthur Godfrey Time* blazed from Lucy's little radio when I plunked down on the kitchen chair to slip on my winter boots. At the same time, Lucy walked in, reached up and turned the volume down.

She put two fingers to her lips. "Shsssh, Hannah, I think I hear a kitty meowing."

I sat still and listened. "It's Mittens at the back door. She has a habit of wandering up to the house every now and again, but Papa doesn't want her in the house. He says cats belong in the barn."

MEOW, MEOW. Lucy wiped her hands on her apron and hurried to the back door.

"Oh, Mittens, just look at you, sitting on the cold stoop with those big, forlorn green eyes looking up at me. You poor baby. I guess it wouldn't hurt anything if you came in for a spell."

"I told you, Papa doesn't want cats in the house, Lucy."

Lucy swung the door open with her foot and Mittens scampered by.

OK, if Lucy allows Mittens in the house, then I'll feed my kitty a special treat, something she really likes.

Mittens scampered right behind me when I jumped up and ran to the pantry. I snatched a can of tuna off the pantry shelf, then cranked it open with the old metal can opener and dumped into a bowl, and set it on the floor in front of her.

Mittens gobbled it up, then flopped down on the braided oval rug in front of the cookstove, stretched every muscle in her fat body and purred so loud it rattled the windows.

As the day wore on, I heard Lucy talking sweet to Mittens. "My goodness, Kitty, I hate to disturb you when you're sleeping so peacefully, but it's about time for Johan to come home, and we better get you back where you belong before he walks in the door."

I shouted, "Don't bother, I'll take her, Lucy." I ran over, scooped Mittens into my arms and carried her back to the barn.

It made me happy that she liked Mittens, but it irritated me when Lucy acted like Mittens was her cat.

It happened all over again a few days later. I was sitting at the kitchen table, tearing my toast in half and dunking it into my egg; Lucy was sipping a cup of coffee when Mittens's cry was heard from the back.

Lucy opened the door, and Mittens scampered in. Right off, Mittens leaped on my lap and began kneading her way into a circle, then curled up and shut her eyes.

"How can I eat my breakfast with you on my lap? You silly kitty."

The next thing I knew, Mittens was living in the house full-time. It really rubbed me the wrong way when I thought about the times I'd wished I could bring Mittens in, and Papa said, "No, cats belong in da barn." Now, it was just fine when it was Lucy's idea. Aw well, my wish had finally come true! I loved it when I'd walk into my bedroom and find Mittens sprawled on the foot of my bed. It cracked me up to see the shocked look on Lucy's face when she'd open the back door and discover a dead mouse or fat gopher lying dead on the step that Mittens proudly deposited for all of us to see.

***

When harvest ended in the fall, neighbors and friends threw a wedding party for Papa and Lucy. In the back of the Community Hall stood a good-sized kitchen table, filled high with hams, fried chicken, baked beans, potato salad, deviled eggs, assorted vegetables, rolls, salads, and lemonade; off to one side, desserts of all kinds filled a table of their own.

"Fit for a king," I heard Papa say.

A whopping band started up early in the evening, with Mr. Murger playing the fiddle, Jacob exhaling and inhaling on the harmonica (another surprising side to that old man) and Lars Larson strumming the guitar and singing.

I danced the butterfly with a young man on either side, twirling me around, and I jitterbugged with every guy who asked me. The little kids had fun too, laughing and scooting around on the slippery dance floor.

It looked like Grandma was enjoying herself, sitting at one of the many card tables against the wall, draped with hand-stitched, heirloom linen tablecloths. I overheard one of the old women say, "I never dreamed Johan would find a lady to marry, but a fine one he did."

A scrawny-looking woman with freshly permed gray hair, sitting at the far end of the table, chimed in, "Lucy is just what Johan needed, someone to warm up his life."

I watched Tova whirl around the dance floor with several different gentlemen. And boy, could that gal dance! Good old Tova, she loved to drink beer and party. Several young men stood near the beer kegs, growing loud-voiced and boastful as the night wore on.

Lucy was taken by surprise, and so was I, when Mr. Murger broke away from the band, swayed through the crowd on the slick dance floor and tapped Lucy on the shoulder. "May I have your slipper, please?"

Surprised, Lucy giggled, "You're asking me to take off my shoe?"

Mr. Murger nodded and held out his hand. "Please?" Lucy looked up at Papa with a puzzled look. Papa chuckled and shrugged his shoulders.

Lucy hesitated before she slipped off her pretty red pump and handed it to Mr. Murger, who snatched it up and reeled his way around the dance floor, collecting gift donations. Folks threw in coins and a bill or two until the shoe spilled over with money.

The people were so nice and friendly and jolly—at that moment I loved the whole world.

The best part happened when Jacob set down his harmonica, crossed the dance floor and crouched in front of Grandma. "Lieula, may I have dis dance?"

Grandma got to her feet, and they started in hippety-hopping to a two-step, followed by a polka—enough to make anyone feel out of breath.

When Grandma and I left the party together, she put her arm around me and whispered, "Hannah, Lucy really is good for Johan."

I grinned. "She makes him happy, that's for sure."

I wanted so bad to include Lucy, and for all three of us to get along, but there were many times I wished she wasn't around. Life was so good when it was just Papa and me. I'll never forget the evening Papa and I headed to the barn, and she ran up behind us, grabbed Papa's arm, and whined, "Johan, I want to learn how to milk a cow."

Papa guffawed. "Are jou sure jou vant to milk a cow, Lucy?"

"Yes, I'm sure."

"Vell, come along vit us, den."

Lucy's jealous when Papa and I are together without her.

I felt the warmth of the cows and horses flowing through the barn when we walked in. Papa picked up the three-legged milk stool and motioned for Lucy to come sit down. He stood by and watched as Lucy plunked down on the stool and leaned against the flank of Elsie the cow.

Lucy giggled like a little kid at the sound of the ping when the first streams of milk hit the bottom of the bucket. When it turned into the slush, slush of a filling pail, Papa shouted, "By Got, Lucy, jou're catching on fast!"—BOOM! Elsie kicked and her shitty foot stuck in the bucket. Lucy flew off the stool, and warm, sticky milk flew every which way, splattering Lucy in the face and soaking her pretty yellow polka-dot shirt.

Lucy pulled herself up from the dirty floor and took off running down the middle of the barn, screaming, "I'm never going to milk another cow as long as I live."

Papa laughed through his nose. "See jou up at da house vhen ve are done vit da chores, Lucy."

The aroma of rosemary chicken baking in the oven brought a big smile to Papa's face when he walked into the house after making hay in the hot sun all day. He hurried over to the kitchen sink where Lucy was drying dishes and washed his hands.

Lucy threw the dishtowel over her shoulder, reached up and brushed Papa's forehead. "Johan, I worry about you having a sunstroke."

"Jou don't have to vorry about me, Lucy."

As tired as Papa was, he perked up when he looked at the supper Lucy had put together. "Uff da, yust look at da nice table jou got dere, every ting smells so goot too. Yust vhat a man needs after a hard day."

Papa sat down at the kitchen table, filled his plate with chicken, potatoes and carrots from the garden, and took a mouthful. Immediately, a most peculiar expression crossed his face, and he slammed his fork down. The chair legs screeched when he pushed himself back from the table.

"Och da leba," he muttered.

"Whatever is the matter?" Lucy cried.

"Uff da, Vhat in da vorld do you call dis?" It's vay too salty for my taste, and so lumpy it's a fright."

"It's mashed potatoes, my dear."

Papa shook his head. "No, I'll yust eat da carrots. Thank you. Vat did jou do, Lucy, pour a vhole shaker of salt in the potato pot?"

"Well, I remember watching my mother cook. She threw in a pinch of this and a pinch of that. Maybe I tossed in too big of a pinch."

"Jou tink so, huh? Vell, I'll tell you vat, Lucy. To be on da safe side, don't even bodder adding salt to anyting."

Holy cow! Papa finally said something about Lucy's awful cooking.

Disheartened, Lucy sat at the table, wringing her slim hands. "Yah, I know I don't know much about cooking. I never cooked a thing until I married you, sweetheart, but I dream of cooking scrumptious meals someday."

I couldn't help but feel sorry for her. "Lucy, I learned to cook in home economics. Maybe I could help you."

Irritated, she responded, "Hannah, I don't need you telling me how to cook."

"Well, Grandma is the best cook in the world." I turned and looked at Papa. "Isn't she, Papa? I know she would be willing to help you, Lucy."

"Jes, Lieula is a goot cook."

I heard Papa holler, "Come on, jump down, jou're home."

Who's Papa talking to?

I ran outside, and to my surprise, there was a shaggy pup hovering by Papa's legs.

Excited, I shouted, "Papa, where did you get the dog?"

"Vell, vhen I drove out of town, I saw dis dog standing by da side of da road, shivering, so I pulled over and stopped. She vasn't vearing a collar of any kind; she looked like a poor, starving critter that someone dropped off. She's really no more than a big puppy, and she reminded me of Maggie."

"Can we keep her?"

151

"Jah, I doubt if anyvon vill ever claim her."

I plopped down on the ground beside the puppy and stroked her back, her head. "She does have a pretty, soft coat like Maggie." She lifted her paw for me to hold. "Papa, her paws are big like Maggie's too. The poor puppy is trembling."

"Give it time and she'll be OK. I tink she's part collie like Maggie vas. She'll get big and I bet jou anyting she'll make a damn goot cattle dog."

Just then, a truck drove into the yard, and two deliverymen wearing white shirts with the Gamble logo on their pockets jumped out.

Papa ran over and directed the guys through the back door. Excited, I watched the men carry the television up the back steps, ascending the wooden stairs sideways. I shouted, "Papa, I had no idea you were going to buy a television."

"Vell, Lucy has hinted how she vould like a television, and it's about time ve got von. All da neighbors have television."

Now, isn't that just wonderful, whatever Lucy wants, Papa goes out and buys.

I ran inside and watched the men uncrate and set the television on one side of the living room. Just as they were twisting the buttons to get a clear picture, Lucy came dancing out of the bedroom in her red furry bedroom slippers, pushing her hair back and placing rhinestone combs on either side. With a big smile on her face, she looked up at Papa. "Sweetheart, you finally broke down and bought us a television."

When I ran back outside, the puppy was nowhere in sight.

"Oh, my God, why was I so stupid to go and leave the frightened puppy alone?" I cried. "Where in the world could she be?"

I took off running like a chicken with its head cut off, searching everywhere. At long last, I spotted the puppy's little terrified face peeking through the spokes of a wooden wagon wheel out behind the barn, and when she saw me, she came running. Bless her heart. I felt her body shake when she pushed her shaggy head against my leg and licked my ankle.

I scratched her ears. She rubbed her wet nose against my arm and looked up at me with her sad eyes, one blue and one brown. I held her against my chest, and she snuggled in like she belonged there.

I whispered, "You never, ever have to worry about not having a home again, and we'll get you fattened up in no time."

She whimpered and licked my chin.

Papa stood with his hands hooked under his suspenders and chuckled. "Jah, she's a dandy."

"Papa, did you notice she has one blue eye and one brown eye?"

"No, I guess I didn't look at her eyes dat goot. Vell, I'll be darned. My fatter had a horse one time with one brown eye and one blue eye."

It took time to settle on a good name for the puppy. In the end, I dubbed her Pooker. She was a shy dog, yet brave as could be. Once she had grown familiar with her new home, if she thought she spied an intruder, she barked like crazy and ran after whoever it was.

I took Pooker for long walks no matter what the weather. When she ran in the snow, she looked more like a big rabbit than a dog. She made me laugh when tiny snowflakes dropped on her eyelashes and made her blink.

Lucy got so she loved watching television. She'd stop in the middle of her housework to watch her favorite program, *Queen for a Day*. Sometimes I watched it with her. We'd sit together on the davenport and listen to the women tell their heartbreaking stories. Some had little children crippled by polio; some told about their houses burning to the ground, and death and divorce. The one with the saddest life, that received the loudest clapping from the audience, got to trade her troubles for a red velvet cape and roses and all kinds of modern appliances. Some women broke down and cried in the middle of their sad tales, and Lucy cried right along with them.

It surprised me when out of the blue, Lucy asked if I would go with her to Grandma's house, sometime soon."

The very next day, Lucy and I drove to Grandma's. Lucy surprised me when the minute we walked into Grandma's kitchen, she blurted out, "Lieula, would you be willing to teach me how to become a good cook?"

A big smile crossed Grandma's face. "Why, the idea. I'd be delighted to teach you what little I know about cooking."

Lucy brushed a lock of hair off her forehead with her wrist and grinned. "What little you know about cooking. I hope someday I can cook like you, Lieula. When would be the best time for you to help me?"

"Thursday mornings are good after I get all the eggs gathered, so why don't we plan on you coming over next Thursday?"

"That sounds perfect to me."

Grandma hobbled into the butler's pantry and came out with a copy of the cookbook, *A Tribute to North Dakota Families.*

"This is for you to keep, Lucy."

"My goodness, are you sure, Lieula? Maybe Hannah would like to have it."

"The church sold them last fall and I bought six them. I have one for Hannah, too, whenever she wants it."

Lucy sat by the kitchen table and began to thumb through the pages.

"Why, there are recipes for everything in this cookbook, Lieula. Thank you."

Grandma chuckled. "You're welcome, Lucy. I'll look forward to seeing you gals on Thursday. Have you given any thought as to what you'd like to cook?"

"Not really, but it'll be something Johan likes for sure."

Lucy and I got to Grandma's house early on a cloudy Thursday morning. When Grandma heard us walk in, she shouted from her bathroom, "Come on in, girls. I'll be out in a minute."

I pulled a chair away from Grandma's kitchen table and motioned for Lucy to sit down, then plunked down on a kitchen stool beside her. I loved the clean, soapy smell that always filled Grandma's kitchen.

Soon, Grandma shuffled out of her bathroom, smoothing her hair and sticking big gray hairpins into the bun on top of her head.

"Hi, girls! I just came in from gathering the eggs, and was waiting for you to get here."

"Lieula, I decided the Amber Rice Pork Chop Casserole recipe on page forty-two is what I'd like to cook. I brought all the ingredients with me."

"That's a good choice. I know how fond Johan is of pork chops. I got the Amber Rice Pork Chop Casserole recipe from an old friend of mine, Cindy Outen, and I submitted it to the *A Tribute to North Dakota Families* cookbook. Cindy's passed away since then, I hear. All my friends are dying, it seems."

Grandma paused, then continued, "First off, I gather all the ingredients the recipe calls for and set them on the counter. Here, girls, put these on." Grandma handed us both flour-sack aprons. "A good cook always wears an apron."

Lucy read the recipe out loud:

AMBER RICE PORK CHOP CASSEROLE

1 1/3 cups Minute Rice

1 1/2 cups orange juice

6 pork chops, seasoned and browned

1 can chicken gumbo soup

Put rice in bottom of casserole. Add orange juice. Top with pork chops. Pour soup over all. Bake at 350 degrees for 1 hour.

"It doesn't sound too difficult," Lucy said.

Grandma set the cast iron skillet on the burner, added a big glob of butter and stood in front of the stove, watching it melt. Then she turned and looked at Lucy. "I like to cook with butter, it adds a good flavor. Now, I'm going to sit down and watch you cook, Lucy."

Grandma leaned back against the counter and crossed her arms. You could hear the pork chops sizzle when Lucy plopped them in the cast iron skillet. In a bit, she dangled a chop from the big meat fork.

"Does this look brown enough to you, Lieula?"

"The chops look mouthwatering. You're doing a great job, Lucy."

Lucy poured the Minute Rice in the dish, added the orange juice and the pork chops, then carefully poured one can of Campbell's chicken gumbo soup on top of it all and popped it into the oven.

While it baked, Grandma poured cups of fresh-brewed Folgers, and we gathered at the kitchen table, sipping coffee and flipping through pages of the cookbook. Excited, Lucy said, "Look here," and she pointed to "HINTS" in the back of the book. "Listen to this: 'When going to a child's party and you don't have gift wrapping, use a funny paper as wrapping for the gift.'"

When it was time to remove the bubbly pork rice casserole from the oven, Lucy got up from the table, quickly opened the oven door, and with a big smile on her face, she took it out and set it on a hot pad on top of the counter. "Hmmm, I didn't know pork chops could smell so good."

"Lucy, your pork chop dish looks scrumptious. What's the funny look? Is something stuck on my face?"

Lucy laughed. "No, no, Lieula." She laid a hand on Grandma's arm. "I can't believe how good my pork chops turned out. Cooking isn't that hard after all when you have a good teacher."

Grandma chuckled, "I bet Johan is going to love his supper tonight. It sure beats his old standby, sardines and crackers."

I chimed in, "I loved the times when Papa and I ate sardines with crackers for supper."

Grandma handed Lucy the dish inside an insulated casserole carrier. "Lucy, you should be very proud of yourself."

Lucy beamed. "I can't thank you enough for all your help, Lieula," she said, and started out the door; looking back, she thanked Grandma once more.

Lucy talked nonstop all the way home. "Today was so much fun, Hannah. Thank you for going with me. Now, if I simply follow the recipe and do as it says, I can make anything in the cookbook Lieula gave me."

"You're welcome. It was fun for me too, and I learned some new things as well. All we ever made in home economics class was soup."

Sally and I galloped into the yard and stopped in front of the blacksmith shop where Papa stood, slipping the neck loop of his canvas apron over his head and knotting the ties behind his back.

"Hi, Sissy Pie! Vhat jou been up to?"

"Oh, I just took Sally for a ride through the pasture for something to do."

I jumped down and tied Sally to a fence post by Papa's shop. Right off, Pooker came running and dropped her red ball by my feet. I picked up the ball and threw it, and

Pooker retrieved it over and over again.

I laughed. "Pooker, you never get tired of chasing the ball, do you?"

Papa chuckled, "Pooker catches onto tings real fast. I don't know how jou came up vit da name, Pooker, but she's a Pooker, alright."

The band quit playing—it was time to leave after dancing the night away. Rome grabbed hold of my hand, and we walked out of the Stump Lake Pavilion into clean, fresh air. As we sauntered down the narrow pathway to his car, I looked up at his face, and belted out, "Put your arms around me, honey."

Rome threw his arms around me. "Hold me tight."

Together we sang, "Huddle up and cuddle up with all your might."

That's the way it was with us—just plain fun!

"Vell, what do jou know?" Papa guffawed, when Jacob pulled up into the yard and came to a screeching stop in his old dilapidated pickup. Papa walked over and kicked a front tire. "Looks like jou have a tire going flat, Yacob."

Jacob jumped out of his truck. "By Got, it sure looks dat vay. No vonder da truck vas so hard to steer. I'll have to dake care of dat right avay. Vhat jou vorking on, Yohan?"

"I'm fixing some old horseshoes."

Jacob looked over at me. "I see jou're having fun throwing da ball to jour dog, Hannah."

"Oh, yah, Pooker loves to play ball."

Jacob pulled the bill of his cap down over his eyes to keep the sun out. In a loud voice, he said, "Yohan, I see Hannah is her old happy self again since she got a new dog."

"Jah, dat's for damn sure. I vish I'd got anotter dog sooner."

"Jah, I bet jou do. Yohan, I got a favor to ask of jou."

"Vat vould dat be?"

Jacob looked at Papa through his thick wire-framed glasses that made his eyes look tiny. "Yohan, I hate to botter jou, now dat jou have a missus and all, but I vas vondering if jou could give me a lift to the eye doctor in Grand Forks next veek? It vould be a big help. I'll pay for da gas."

"Don't vorry about dat, Yacob. Vat day do jou have to be dere?"

"Vednesday, at eleven a.m."

Papa nodded, his head wreathed in pipe smoke. "Jah, I tink I can vork dat out. Ve'll have to get up before the chickens if ve vant to be dere by eleven, Yacob."

When it came time to go, Lucy decided she'd rather stay home. "I want to catch up on some things around the house," she told Papa.

She doesn't want to miss Queen for a Day.

That's when Papa asked me, "Why don't jou ride along and keep me company Sissy Pie?"

Wednesday morning, Papa and I took off bright and early, but when Papa drove up in front of Jacob's little white house, Jacob was nowhere to be seen.

Disgusted, Papa mumbled, "I get up and rush my ass off to get over here, now goddamn it, vhere da hell is he?"

Papa waited for a little bit before he honked the horn and started to get out of the car. At the same time, Jacob came stumbling out of his back door, carrying his black dress shoes and a pair of navy blue socks. The screen door slammed shut behind him.

I hopped in the backseat so Jacob could sit up front.

I noticed Jacob's cap hung sideways on his head. Out of breath, he grabbed hold of the door handle and eased himself onto the seat; then he straightened his cap and looked over at Papa. "Goddamn it, Yohan, as vound up as I vas vhen I vent to bed last night, tinking about going to da doc and all, I can't believe I vent and overslept."

"Jah, I vondered vhat da hell vas going on vit jou vhen jou veren't out front vaiting for me. It ain't like jou to be late for anyting, Yacob."

Jacob sat slouched over, putting on his socks and shoes, when Papa rammed the car in gear and took off like a bat out of hell.

"Take it easy over dem damn potholes, Yohan. Jou could wreck jour car going so goddamn fast."

I reached over the seat and patted Jacob's shoulder. "Can you see OK?"

"Jah, I can see as goot as alvays, but it feels like someting in my eye all da time."

Jacob looked at Papa. "Yohan, I vas surprised da otter day vhen I saw da REA truck in jour jard." REA stood for the Rural Electric Association. "I daught jou were one of dose who'd never get rid of your 32-volt Delco and wind charger system."

"Vell, I didn't really vant to, but I had to vhen I bought da television."

"Oh, jah. I sure like having da REA. So does da missus. No more lights going dim and charging up the batteries eidder."

I fell back against the seat and gazed out the window at the sky, thinking about Rome. I liked Rome's funny way of saying things. I loved that he liked to dance too. Sometimes he was gone on long hauls with his truck, and I wouldn't see him for weeks at a time. He was a hard worker. I wondered if he thought of me while he was gone. I thought about him all the time. I had an aching crush on that guy.

When we got to the Grand Forks Clinic, Papa drove slow into the big lot and parked. He inched himself out from behind the wheel and shrugged into his tan dress jacket that he'd thrown in the backseat. The three of us hurried into the clinic and plunked down on the hard chairs in the waiting room. We didn't have to wait long at all before the receptionist called, "Jacob Jenson."

"Yacob, if jou don't see me out here when jou're done, I vill be vaiting in the car."

"OK, Yohan."

I couldn't help but notice the large woman sitting across from me. Her rump hung over on both sides of her chair, and she kept staring at me through Coke-bottle lenses. When I'd look at her, she'd quickly turn away.

Dear God, don't ever let my eyes get that bad.

The old man sitting beside her wore a cardigan that used to be a woman's. I could tell because the buttons were backward.

Papa picked up a *Look* magazine and thumbed through it. He pointed out an article about Jack Benny making his TV debut.

"Hannah, listen to dis, it says here, 'Eight million homes in the US now own televisions.' Isn't that someting?"

"I'm glad we have a television, Papa."

It wasn't long before Papa tossed the magazine on the end table. "Come on, Hannah, let's go. I'm tired of sitting on dis hard chair."

I followed him down the hallway as he mumbled to himself, "Boy, dis sure is a hell of a big place. A man could get lost avful damn easy around here."

Suddenly, Papa jabbed my arm with his elbow and motioned for me to look across the way. I peered through the big glass window, and oh, my God. There sat Mr. Murger

159

next to a strange, attractive, dark-haired young lady.

A sheepish look came over his face and he glanced down at the floor when he saw us.

Papa mumbled under his breath, "It can't be Venzel. It's gotta be somebody dat looks like him."

"Papa, it's Wenzel Murger."

"Come on, Hannah, let's go to da car."

Soon, Jacob came traipsing through the parking lot, wearing a black patch over his left eye. He climbed into the car. "Ja, Yohan, dat vasn't so damn bad after all."

"Da hell jou say."

Papa shoved the car in reverse and started to back up. "How is it on jour side, Yacob? Jou know, da damn cars have me so yammed in here it's a goddamn fright."

Jacob patted the patch over his eye, and twisted around in the seat. "Ja, Yohan, go ahead, yust back her straight out."

Papa laughed when I hollered, "Goose it, Papa."

Papa drove through the busy city streets at a slow pace, but when he got out on the highway he tromped on the old gas pedal and let her rip.

"Jah, I'm glad dat's all over, Yohan."

"Jah, I bet jou are. Hey, jou're not going to believe dis, but I saw Venzel sitting dere at the clinic vit a joung woman, not bad-looking, eidder."

"Jou saw Venzel vit a woman jou didn't know?"

"Jah, he yust sat dere, running his fingers through his hair, and looking down at the floor."

"Da hell you say, maybe dere's some trut to vat de're saying about him chasing around."

"It could be he's dere seeing da doctor about his hemorrhoids too. Jou know how he's alvays complaining about his goddamn piles, alvays reaching around scratching his ass."

"Yohan, maybe it was a patient sitting next to him too, yah?"

"No, I doubt dat vary much, not da vay dey vere perched."

I laughed. Papa chuckled and blew a puff of smoke. "Jah, vho da hell knows for sure? But like I alvays say, people will do anyting. I'm not gonna say a damn vord to nobody, and don't you eidder. Dakota is having a bad enough time, da vay it is."

"Jah, Johan, you can bet I von't say a goddamn vord to nobody. Vhat joung girl vould vant anyting to do vit dat old fart anyvay? Den, again it coult be some relation too, yah never know."

"Jah, Dakota has her hands full, alright. How's Radovan doing anyvay, do you hear anyting?"

"Radovan is doing yust great. Last I heard, he's going to the North Dakota State University, vants to be an attorney someday. It's a damn shame about his shriveled-up legs, but dat kid has a good head on his shoulders, and he's learned to get around damn goot on dose crutches of his. He'll show us all, yust vait and see."

I lay on the seat, and swung my arm over my eyes.

How in the world will I ever face Annabelle after seeing her father sitting there with a strange woman?

"Yacob, vat da hell is dat patch doing over jour eye anyvay?"

"Oh, da doc put some drops of some kind in dat eye. It stung like a sonofabitch, but it'll be OK, notting to vorry about."

We were coming up on Greske's Gas Station and Saloon when Jacob shouted, "Pull in here, Yohan. Like I told jou, I vant to pay to fill up jour gas tank, and I'll buy jou a cool von vhile ve're dere."

"Jah, dat sounds like a damn goot idea, Yacob. Vat time is it, anyvay?"

Jacob pulled his gold pocket watch out of his white shirt pocket. "Don't vorry, you got a couple hours or more before milking time."

"Yah, I could sure go for a cool von about now, myself."

The place was empty when we walked in and bellied up to the bar. Right away, Mr. Greske brought over an Orange Crush and plunked it down in front of me. "Hannah, I haven't seen you in a coon's age. How are you, anyway?"

"I'm doing good, Mr. Greske. It won't be long until I graduate from high school. Thanks for the pop."

"You're welcome. So you're a senior already. My goodness, it seems just like yesterday when Johan came rushing in on his way home from the Devils Lake Hospital, the day you were born, proud as punch and handing out the biggest cigars I'd ever

161

seen."

After a beer or two, Jacob nudged Papa on the shoulder. "Hey, Yohan. Did jou hear da von about Ole buying life insurance?"

Papa grinned. "I don't believe I have. Go aheat, tell me."

"Ole tells Lena: 'I yust had my life insured for $25,000.'

"Lena: 'Dere jou go again—alvays tinking of jourself.'"

Papa slapped the bar. "Ja, leave it up to Lena. Hey, tinking of life insurance, I got von for jou, Yacob.

"As Ole lay dying, he asked his wife, Lena, 'Vould jou get me some of dat lutefisk you got cooking on da stove?'

"'I'm sorry,' said Lena, 'I'm saving dat for after da funeral.'"

Jacob slapped the bar and let out a hell of a laugh.

They made me laugh.

They downed one more cool one each before Papa announced, "Jah, vell, hell, ve better hit da road."

We left Jacob off, and stopped at Grandma's house on our way home. Papa stuck his head in the back door and hollered, "Hellooo, Lieula."

"Come on in."

Grandma sat in her easy chair with a book on her lap.

"How's jour day treating jou?"

"Oh, Johan, my hips hurt, so I sit a lot. I really don't like to complain. Like you always say, 'It doesn't do any good to complain anyway.'"

"Jah, dat's for damn sure."

Grandma looked over her bifocals and smiled at me. "Well, hello, Hannah! How are you?"

"I'm doing good, Grandma. Papa and I are on our way home from driving Jacob to the eye doctor in Grand Forks."

"Did you go clothes shopping?"

"No, we waited for Jacob at the clinic and that was about it. What you been doing?"

Grandma held up her book. "I've had my nose stuck in this book all morning. I haven't even got around to reading today's newspaper."

"What you reading?"

"*The Catcher in the Rye*, by J. D. Salinger."

Papa broke in, "Vell, ve yust stopped in to see how jou vere, Lieula. Guess ve'll be on our vay."

"That's very good of you, and I appreciate it."

When Papa and I got home, we walked into the living room—the television was blaring, and Lucy was dusting an end table and straightening out the doily on the back of the davenport. It shocked me when Papa started in hollering, "Uff da, vere da hell is my easy chair? Vat da hell is it doing vay over dere in da corner, anyvay? I can't even see da TV from dere."

"Go ahead, move your chair wherever it suits you best, honeybunch, but you don't have to shout. Aren't you even happy to see me?"

Papa uttered with a laugh, "I'm alvays happy to see jou, Lucy, but dis moving stuff around like jou do gets on my nerves after avhile. Can't jou just leave tings da vay day vere?"

It struck me as comical when Lucy called Papa honeybunch.

CHAPTER 10

Papa was on his way to the barn when he called and asked me if I would drive Lucy to the train depot. Lucy's friend and past coworker, Andrea Sue Clifford, was soon to become Mrs. Chester Thornapple, and Lucy was going away to attend her wedding in Chicago.

While I waited with Lucy at the train station, she confided in me that after reading Andrea's recent letters, she wasn't that crazy about going. "Hannah, I liked working with Andrea and we became good friends, but since she's met Chester, all she writes about is how brilliant Chester is, the fancy restaurants he takes her to, and how he's not afraid to spend money on her. It sounds to me like he's made of money."

"How did he become so rich?" I asked.

"Family business, why, there was one whole page in Andrea's last letter, telling about the fabulous house Chester lives in that'll soon become hers. She bragged about his fancy cars. He has a pilot's license and owns his own airplane."

"She wrote, 'P.S. I hope after you read about Chester it won't make you jealous.'"

"Really, she wrote all that?"

"Yes, she did. I don't think Chester inheriting the Thornapple Brokerage Firm from his father means he's one bit smarter than any of the rest of us."

"Do you think she's in love with him?"

"Well, knowing Andrea the way I do, she wouldn't get married if she weren't in love. I believe the reason she's so impressed with Chester's riches is because she came from a poor family, and she didn't have fancy things growing up."

I stood beside Lucy on the depot platform, holding her little brown satchel. "After what you've just told me about Chester, I'm curious to hear what you'll think of him when you get the chance to see him."

When the train came in sight, Lucy shrugged her shoulders and glanced over at me. "Yah, I'm anxious to meet Chester myself."

I can't explain what came over me, but when I got home and walked into the quiet house, I headed straight to Papa's bedroom and started snooping through Lucy's top dresser drawer. I didn't feel comfortable digging in Lucy's stuff, but maybe I'd get to know more about her.

There were perhaps twenty letters, some unfolded and filed flat, and others still in their envelopes. There were love letters. One letter was from an Albert, begging her not to leave him. He would make it up to her. "Stay with me and we'll have the baby you always wanted."

I found a note; it must have come with flowers or a gift. It said simply, "Lucy, my wife." Oh, my God, that was the first I knew of Lucy ever being married to someone besides Papa. In another letter, I learned Albert had begged Lucy to forgive him for his infidelities, or for the one infidelity in particular that seemed to have caused their separation. I was very careful to put things back exactly as they were.

A couple of days later, I happened to answer the phone when Lucy called. "Hannah, my plans have changed, I'm coming home sooner than I thought I would. Could you pick me up on Wednesday?"

The Great Northern ran late the day Lucy returned. I was on edge all morning, thinking about seeing Lucy after I'd snooped through her stuff. Would it show on my face or how I behaved? I felt a sense of shame the minute Lucy stepped off the train and walked towards me with a big smile on her face.

Right away, I asked, "How did the big wedding go?"

"Oh, it was really something, Hannah. It took place in a beautiful, historic Baptist church. There were fragrant flowers, roses, tulips, calla lilies and pink peonies everywhere. Andrea looked absolutely beautiful in spite of the fact that she's gained a lot of weight." Lucy reached up and smoothed the hair back from her eyes. "I bet that wedding cost a pretty penny."

"Do you suppose Chester paid for it?"

"I bet he paid for most of it. He seemed to be a very nice fellow, down-to-earth. I noticed when Andrea and Chester were on the dance floor, Chester's head barely reached her shoulder, but boy, could he cut the rug!"

166

I laughed, "Sounds like they were having fun!"

"We all had a good time and I'm glad I went."

I picked up Lucy's largest piece of luggage and headed towards the car. Someone passing by was whistling. Lucy ran alongside me, carrying the rest of her bags, and we tossed them into the trunk, hopped in the car and headed home. Lucy leaned against the passenger door, digging in her pocketbook, and pulled out a compact, then applied fresh powder to her nose.

"I'm so glad to be home. It's hard to believe I ever lived in the bustling city of Chicago."

"Papa was really happy to hear you were coming back sooner than you intended, Lucy."

Lucy snickered, "You know, I missed that man of mine something awful."

I was upstairs lying on my bed, studying for my final history exam, when all hell broke loose.

"No, jou ain't taking my daughter out dis time of night."

Boom! The front door slammed shut.

Papa talked loud, "Vat da hell das Rome tink? He can come around dere any time of da day or night and Hannah is going out vit him? Vell, he's got anodder tink a-comin. I hope da Christ she gets him out of her system and damn soon."

"Johan, I understand how you feel, but please try to calm down."

When I walked out of my bedroom the next morning, Papa met me at the top of the stairwell. "Hannah, jou let that boyfriend of jours know he can't come around dere any damn time he feels like it and tink jour going out vit him. Oh, no. I'm not going to allow my daughter to run out late at night and ruin her goot reputation, dat's for damn sure."

"It wasn't that late."

"I said it vas. He's too damn old for jou anyvay."

"Too old? What about you and Lucy?"

"Never mind about me and Lucy."

Later, when I was with Rome, he told me he was coming back from the Twin Cities that Friday night, driving on the main road that ran by our house when he decided to stop by. It wasn't like there was a pay phone around to call me before he got there, but try and explain that to Papa.

Sun streamed down on Annabelle's light brown hair and her tanned arms when she rode into our yard and jumped off her bike. Her face looked sad, and she blurted out, "Hannah, I got so much to tell you."

"Leave your bike on the porch, Annabelle, and we'll go up to my room where we can be by ourselves, and you can tell me everything."

Annabelle stomped up the steps behind me, then sunk down on the edge of my bed with her arms wrapped around her knees.

I sat down in the rocking chair, facing her. "What's troubling you, Annabelle?"

Tears started rolling down her cheeks.

I handed her a tissue from the box on my nightstand.

She blew her nose and took a deep breath. "It's so terrible."

"It can't be that bad."

Sobbing, she cried, "But it is. Hannah, remember when you told me about Meghan's father leaving her mother and marrying a younger girl?"

"Yes, I sure do."

"Well, I think that's what's happening to my parents."

I was at a loss for words. I leaped out of the chair and threw my arms around her.

Grandma asked me to walk with her to pick up her mail. Her face broke into a smile when she reached into her big mailbox and took out the letter she'd been waiting for from her sister, Hortense, 1550 Glen Ayr Drive, Fox Lake, Wisconsin.

Her chubby little hands trembled as she stood, bent over beside the mailbox, and carefully opened the envelope. I watched as her eyes danced over the beautiful blue-ink lettering. I tried to look at the flourishes and curlicues, but Grandma turned the other way and held the letter so I couldn't see it.

All of a sudden, Grandma's face lost its color, her lips quivered and her eyes grew teary. In a shaky voice, she wailed, "Why, the idea." She quickly crumpled the letter in her fist, stomped around to the back of the house and threw it into the burning barrel.

I couldn't believe my eyes. "Grandma, what did it say?"

"Oh, never mind what it said."

Grandma hobbled back to the house as fast as she could go. Out of breath, she flopped on the davenport, and reached for the white hankie in her apron pocket and swiped her face with it. I sank down beside her, and didn't know what to say. Grandma didn't talk either. We just sat in the silence of the afternoon. When I finally glanced up at the clock on Grandma's mantel, I saw it was time to start chores.

"Grandma, I hate leaving you, but I have to get going and help Papa milk the cows."

"You run along, dear, and don't you go worrying your pretty little head about your old Grandma. I'll be just fine."

I gave Grandma a little kiss on her chubby cheek. "Good-bye, Grandma."

"Good-bye, dear."

What in the world did that letter say?

I snuck around to the side of the house by the burning barrel. Oh, my God! I could see the letter lying in the bottom of the barrel—it hadn't burned after all. I jumped up and hung over the side, then stretched out my arms as far as they could go, and dug around in the ashes and debris until I got ahold of it and snatched it up. The tip of the envelope was scorched a little, but other than that, it was all in one piece. I shoved it into my pocket and ran out of Grandma's driveway. When I got to the curve in the roadway, where Grandma couldn't see me and no one was around, I opened the letter.

> Dear Lieula,
>
> I don't quite understand what you're getting at, but it's a little too late to come back home if that's what you're thinking. Father always said you were impulsive and headstrong, running off to North Dakota and marrying that shiftless farmhand, then raising little Cajsa to believe he was her father. You must stick to your chosen life.
>
> Love, Hortense

What in the world was that all about? Well, I'm certainly not going to allow Great-Aunt Hortense's spiteful ways to affect how I feel about Grandma. That's for sure.

I felt sick and guilty as I stood in the middle of the road, holding onto the letter. I didn't want to take it home with me, but oh, God, what was I to do?

Then, out of the blue, I started ripping the letter into a million tiny pieces and watched the fragments fly away in the wind.

It was late when I got to Grandma's house the next day. The lights beneath the living room door shone. I opened the back door and hollered, "Hi, Grandma, it's me."

No answer.

I don't know why I snoop through other people's business. Something just comes over me, and then I feel awful afterwards.

I yelled once more, "Hi, Grandma."

She must be sleeping.

I swung the door open and walked in. Oh, my God! I found Grandma lying down on the davenport, fully clothed, with her hands folded on her chest as though she were arranged for viewing at a funeral home. My chest grew tight. I bent over and carefully removed her eyeglasses and set them on the coffee table.

I bet reading Great-Aunt Hortense's dreadful letter made her sick.

I whispered, "Grandma, say something."

Is this the beginning of Grandma's downhill slide? This isn't supposed to happen. Grandma's supposed to live forever.

I plunked down beside her and grasped her hand. Grandma murmured, "Some orange juice, please, dear. Could you?"

I raced to the kitchen, grabbed a glass from the high wooden cabinet, then hurried to the refrigerator and poured it full of orange juice. With a trembling hand, Grandma grasped the tumbler and sipped the sweet juice. Over the rim of her glass, she sighed, "It's my diabetes."

She lay back and rested for a bit. "Hannah, I'd feel much better if I could get to my own bed. Would you help me, dear?"

I took hold of Grandma's arm and helped her off the davenport. She leaned heavily on me as she shuffled through the hallway into her bedroom. She wiggled out of her dress, slipped into a long flannel nightgown and slowly crawled under the covers, into her wrought iron bed.

I tucked a comforter around Grandma. I walked over by her bedroom window and stood for a minute before I lifted one lace panel and looked out. The moon was bright. I gazed down the field and saw cows and sheep. The stars seemed close enough to touch. When I glanced over at Grandma, she seemed to be resting peacefully. I tiptoed out of her bedroom, down the hallway into the kitchen and gave Papa a ring.

"Hello."

"Hi, Papa, it's me. I stopped at Grandma's and got the scare of my life when I found her lying limp on the davenport. She seems to be feeling much better now, but I think it would be best if I spend the night with her."

"Jou sure jour not vit Rome some place or otter?"

"Geez, Papa, if you don't believe me, come over and see for yourself. It's lucky I got here when I did or maybe Grandma would have never made it."

"It vas dat bad? OK, den, dake goot care of jour grandma, and ve'll see jou sometime tomorrow, jah."

I wrapped up in Grandma's bulky chenille bathrobe and went to bed on the cot in the back hall. I could hear Grandma making little snoring sounds before I fell asleep.

The ringing of the telephone pulled me out of a horrible dream. I sat up blinking. In my dream, Grandma lay passed out on the floor and I was bent over her body. I jumped up and elbowed my way through a crowd of oddball people crouched in the hallway, staring at me and laughing as I struggled to reach the phone. Desperate, I yelled—so loud I woke myself up.

I pressed both hands to my face and waited while the images in my head went away. Outside the window, a rooster crowed. I heard Grandma's voice coming from the kitchen, and I smelled the strong aroma of coffee brewing.

I threw back the covers and scrambled off the cot, hastily dressing in yesterday's clothes, which I'd shaken out of the night before. I hurried down the hallway and into the kitchen, where Grandma stood in front of the phone. She hung up the receiver, quickly turned around and looked at me with a big smile. Her cheeks looked rosy, and she looked healthy.

I exclaimed, "Grandma, you look beautiful. You'd never guess you'd been so ill just a few hours ago." I whispered under my breath, "Thank you, God."

"That was Lucy on the phone. She's on her way, and she thinks I should see Dr. Knightley, but I'm feeling so good I don't think it's necessary to see a doctor now."

It took some coaxing from Lucy and me to convince Grandma to visit the doctor. When we finally got to Dr. Knightley's office, Grandma nudged my arm and whispered, "Hannah, please come with me into the examining room."

Dr. Knightley checked Grandma over good. Looking at her from under his bushy eyebrows, he declared, "Your blood sugar count is not good, Lieula. I'm going to have to prescribe a stronger dose of insulin. It's important that you stick to your diet and make sure you get proper rest. I would like to see you in three weeks. I'll have Ruth schedule an appointment for you at that time."

Grandma blushed. "Thank you, Dr. Knightley."

Dr. Knightley patted Grandma's shoulder and smiled. "I hope to see an improvement when you come back." He turned and walked out of the room.

I couldn't shake my miserable feeling all day, thinking about Annabelle, and worrying about Grandma as well. Thank God, Rome was waiting outside for me when I got off work.

The minute I slid into his car, he blurted out, "I've never seen you looking so down in the dumps. Hannah, what can I do?"

"Just take me home."

Rome playfully tapped my knee. "Oh, come on, baby, let's try and be a little bit happy."

I snuggled up beside him, put my fingers on his cheek and looked into his sexy blue eyes. "You make me happy."

We drove around town for awhile, and ended up having the time of our lives at the Stump Lake roller rink, skating to some of my favorite tunes, "Ain't Misbehavin'" and "Dream a Little Dream of Me." Later on, when I happened to look at my watch, I was surprised to see how late it was, and I cried out, "Rome, I have to get home."

When we pulled up and stopped in front of my house, I reached for the door handle and fought to get the door open.

"What's your hurry, Hannah? Wait a minute, I want to walk my girl to the door."

He gave me a little hug on the doorstep before I went inside.

I would never understand my crazy emotions. One minute, I wanted to be with Rome, and the next minute, I couldn't wait to get home to my own cozy bedroom.

I ran down the stairs to find Lucy sitting by the kitchen table, writing a grocery list. She looked up. "Hannah, would you like to ride into town with me?"

"Sure, if I can drive."

"That's fine with me."

When we drove up, Jacob came walking out of the Mercantile, carrying a brown bag full of groceries. He stopped where he was and grinned when he saw me get out of the car. "Hannah, looks like jou've come a long vay vit jour driving since I pulled jou out vit my tractor dat night."

I shook my head and made a silly face. "I try not to think about that night, Jacob."

Jacob looked at Lucy. "Vat's Yohan up to?"

"We left him working in a patch of garden, planting lettuce, radishes, carrots, and a row of sweet peas."

"Da heck jou say. Sounds like jou von't have to buy any wegetables next vinter. Jou know something, Lucy, jou've turned dat man around, and let me tell jou someting, stopping at Greske's bar and tipping a cool von or two vitout him yust ain't the same."

Lucy chuckled, "I'll tell him you said that."

We walked into the Mercantile and saw Sandy Tinsley standing in front of the counter along with her identical twin girls. Lucy carried on: "Sandy, my goodness, how your little girls have grown since I last seen them. How old are the little cuties? You know, I can't tell one from the other."

"I know it's hard to know who's Jessica or who's Serenidy, but Jessica has a tiny mole on her cheek that gives her away. We plan to celebrate their third birthday next month."

Lucy greeted the little girls, "Hi, Serenidy! Hi, Jessica!"

Serenidy grinned from ear to ear and held out a little rubber doll. "See my new doll."

"My, what an adorable baby you have there."

Jessica hung onto her mother's skirt, grinned and waved her hand.

Sandy explained, "Jessica is the shy one—she lets Serenidy do all the talking."

"Well, you certainly have some beautiful girls. It's so good to see you, Sandy."

"It's good to see you too, Lucy. How's married life?"

Lucy beamed. "Just great."

Sandy looked over at me. "How are you, Hannah? I hear you'll be graduating soon."

"Oh, yeah, and I plan on going to college."

"Good for you."

On our way home, Lucy reached over and poked my arm. "Hannah, I would love to have a baby of my own someday."

"You gotta be kidding."

"No, Hannah, I mean it."

I just couldn't imagine Papa packing a baby around.

I put on my sleeveless white blouse and my new blue jeans with the cuffs rolled up, then pulled my hair back in a ponytail and plunked down on the kitchen stool by the window to wait for Rome.

The minute I saw him drive up, I ran for my jacket and bolted out the door. Rome jumped out of his car. His face broke into a happy smile when I slithered in around him and plopped down on the seat. Rome drew me close and whispered, "I'm taking you to the drive-in movies to see *Singin' in the Rain*, starring Gene Kelly."

My heart leapt and raced and even danced a little—I loved musicals.

I could hear the gravel crunching underneath the tires when Rome drove very slowly into the drive-in movie theater and all around. The aroma of popcorn and hot dogs coming from the snack bar filled the air.

Rome found the perfect spot in front of the big screen. I watched Gene Kelly with my head resting on Rome's muscular chest. He smelled so nice. I laughed when I saw Gene Kelly dressed in a yellow slicker, hanging from a lamppost and swinging his umbrella in the wild joy of new love. I loved seeing him stomp through the puddles in the gutters, making big wet splashes.

As the night wore on, I rolled the window down and peeked out to see who was in the cars next to us, but I couldn't tell because their windows were steamed up just like ours.

The news took everyone by surprise. Tova Johnson had turned her business over to her brother, Julius, and joined the Sisters of Mercy Order.

"Why, the idea!" Grandma exclaimed. "The Munich Mercantile will never be the same without Tova. Hannah, I'd like for you to give me a ride into town as soon as possible so I can have a face-to-face talk with that lady friend of mine."

"OK, Grandma." And the next thing I knew, I was headed back to town on a beautiful, crisp, brilliantly sunny day with my grandma. When we pulled up in front of the Mercantile, Grandma looked out and said, "I see Standing Bear's kids are in town, Hannah."

I hopped out of the car and put my hand to my forehead to block the sun, in an attempt to watch the little boys in tattered overalls running barefoot up and down the street. The littlest guy had a slingshot stuck in his back pocket and a scruffy-looking dog nipping at his heels.

Standing Bear stuck his head out of the barbershop door with a big white towel hung around his shoulders. "Hey, you boys, all three of you, pipe down out there. I told you to quit your running before one of you gets hurt and I'm not telling you again. As soon as Alvard gets done cutting my hair, you come in here for your much-needed haircut, Holy Track. Then I'll buy you boys an ice-cream cone at the creamery."

Holy Track yelled back, "Papa, I don't want to sit in the barber chair all day."

The biggest boy spun around and gawked at the woodpecker hammering away in a nearby tree. He started to sing really loud: "The woodpecker pecked on the schoolhouse door. He pecked and he pecked until his pecker got sore." And, silly me, I stood, leaning on the car, laughing my head off.

Oops: at the same time, Grandma stumbled on the steps leading into the store— her pocketbook slid off her arm and stuff spilled all over. She shouted, "Hannah, stop that foolish giggling and come help me."

175

I ran over. Snatched up her coin purse, a compact of powder, her rosary and all her valuable things, and shoved them all inside her pocketbook.

"Thank you, dear."

"You're welcome, Grandma. Nothing got broke, not even your little pocket mirror."

When Grandma and I walked in, Tova stood behind the counter, stooped over the open cash register, counting the bills. Looking up with a solemn expression, she slammed the drawer shut, rearranged the big pickled pigs' feet jar on the counter and smiled.

"Hi, Lieula! Hi, Hannah!"

I grinned and waved.

Grandma shouted, "Hello, Tova! What's this I hear about you joining a convent, of all things?"

Tova chuckled, "You heard it right, Lieula. It's something I've dreamed of doing all my life."

"Are you sure you want to live in a Catholic community and follow their orders?"

"Oh, yes, I'm ready for a big change. You know, Lieula, to be honest, I'm sick and tired of coming into the store day in and day out and seeing the same old faces. To tell you the truth, there are days when I can hardly stand the foul smell coming from the back room when Bjor is butchering and cutting up a steer or pig. Oh, God help me. Well, I guess he has."

"Why, the idea. Tova, it'll be different for all of us, and I sure hate to think of coming into the store without you here to wait on me. I'm going to miss you something awful, but I do want to wish you the best. You know, there was a time in my life when I thought of joining a Catholic order. My father wanted me to."

I stood by the big wooden barrels full of all kinds of different candies.

Grandma—a nun?

"I'll miss you too, Lieula. But I'm really excited and looking forward to a change, something that will give me a real heartfelt purpose in life—serving people who suffer from poverty and sickness."

Tova pushed her curly hair out of her eyes and gestured for Grandma to move up closer. Grandma shuffled over, leaned her hands on the counter and shook her head in disbelief.

Tova spoke softly, "Lieula, taking the vow of celibacy won't be a big deal like some folks seem to think. You know, you don't miss something you've never had." Tova snickered, "Not that I haven't had plenty of chances."

Grandma's face turned red, and she looked up at the door to see if anyone was coming in.

And silly me, I got the giggles all over again. I tucked my chin down and covered my mouth with my hand, but I was laughing so helplessly I made a honking sound.

Tova slapped the counter and guffawed.

"My word, I've heard it all," Grandma cried. "I don't know if I should laugh or cry. Come on, Hannah, we better be on our way."

I looked over my shoulder as we were going out the door, and Tova was still laughing.

Grandma was laughing too when we got in the car. "Just when you think you've heard it all, Tova up and joins a convent. Like I just told Tova, I hate the thought of going into the Mercantile with her not there, but change is what life is all about, whether you like it or not."

I shifted the car into second gear. "I don't like to think about Tova leaving either. I wonder if we'll ever get to see her after she joins the order."

Grandma leaned against the headrest and looked straight ahead, her pocketbook in her lap.

"We'll just have to wait and see, I guess."

Grandma's kitchen was filled with that heavenly scent only Thanksgiving can bring, and she was in the kitchen preparing the corn pudding when we got to her house.

GRANDMA'S CORN PUDDING

5 eggs	4 tablespoons cornstarch
1/3 cup butter, melted	1 (15.25 ounce) can whole kernel corn
1/4 cup white sugar	2 (14.75 ounce) cans cream corn
1/2 cup milk	

Preheat oven to 400 degrees F (200 degrees C). Grease a 2-quart casserole dish. In a large bowl, lightly beat eggs. Add melted butter, sugar and milk. Whisk in cornstarch. Stir in corn and creamed corn. Blend well. Pour mixture into prepared casserole dish. Bake for 1 hour.

I got the potatoes ready. Lucy shut herself in the butler's pantry to make the lettuce salad and whip the cream for the pumpkin dessert.

PUMPKIN DESSERT

Crust:

1 cup flour	1/2 cup oatmeal
1/2 cup brown sugar	1/2 cup butter

Mix together and press into greased 9" x 13" pan. Bake at 350 degrees for 20 minutes.

Custard:

4 eggs, well-beaten	1/2 tsp. vanilla
1 large can pumpkin (30 oz.)	1 tsp. cinnamon
1 can evaporated milk	1/2 tsp. ginger
1/4 cup sugar	1/2 tsp. cloves
1/2 tsp. salt	

Mix well and pour over crust. Bake at 350 degrees for 35 minutes.

Topping:

1/2 cup chopped nuts	2 tbsp. butter

1/2 cup brown sugar

Sprinkle on topping and bake 15 minutes more.

Elsie Hall

Munich, ND

I stood beside Grandma at her kitchen counter, mashing the potatoes. Grandma sighed and whispered, "I miss your mother more than ever during the Thanksgiving holiday, Hannah."

"I miss her, too."

"You know, Thanksgiving was Cajsa's favorite holiday. She loved turkey, especially the white meat, and that's about the only time we had turkey at our house. She didn't like pie crust that much, so I always baked her favorite pumpkin dessert rather than the traditional pumpkin pie."

"I love pumpkin dessert too, Grandma."

"I know you do, dear."

The table was set in the dining room with Grandma's finest linen and best china, glass and silver.

I loved when my family gathered around Grandma's big dining room table; before we started eating dinner, it was custom for everyone to tell what we were most thankful for that year.

I shouted, "I'll be first. I'm thankful that my family is together today and for all the good food on the table, and I'm very thankful that I'll be graduating from high school soon and going away to college."

It was Grandma's turn. "I feel just like Hannah does, thankful that we're together today, and for all the good food and for our good health, and for everything."

Papa was thankful for the good wheat crop, and to know he could provide for his family. Lucy looked right at Papa, then turned and looked at Grandma and me, and her face turned red, "I'm thankful for the delicious Thanksgiving meal before us, and I'm thankful that Lieula took the time to teach me to cook and everything, but most of all I feel blessed that you've accepted me as part of your family."

Grandma chimed in, "You should be mighty proud of your cooking, Lucy."

After dinner, when the dishes were done and things cleaned up and put away, we played canasta. Lucy had never played canasta before, but she caught on quickly and seemed to enjoy the game as much as I did.

I always felt melancholy when the long Thanksgiving weekend came to an end; yet I looked forward to going back to school on Monday. I missed seeing the other kids more than anything. I wouldn't have been so anxious to get back if I'd known what was in store. Life's next development caught me totally by surprise.

The little snow crystals blowing in my face and all around me felt good on my way to school Monday morning. I strolled through the corridor, feeling pretty smart in my new pale blue sweater (Rome's favorite) and carrying an armful of books. When Gilbert caught up to me and nudged my elbow. In a hushed tone, he asked, "Hannah, did you know that Rome left town last night?"

I spun around and looked Gilbert in the face. "What? Are you kidding me?"

"No, it's true, Rome and the Gunderson brothers are on their way to Wallace, Idaho, with the promise of good jobs working in the silver mines. Rome said he was sick and tired of not having steady work around here."

I was so overcome with emotion, I couldn't speak.

Gilbert walked beside me all the way to our classroom. I quickly slid into my desk and hid my face behind my big notebook. My head felt like ants were crawling inside it.

Rome *is gone and he didn't even tell me good-bye.*

I rested my head on my palm, stared out the window and barely listened as the teacher drew triangles and parallelograms on the board during geometry class.

I tried not to think about it, but on our way out of school that afternoon, I told Annabelle.

"You'll never believe what Gilbert told me as soon as I walked in this morning— Rome left town on Friday for Wallace, Idaho. Annabelle, he never told me he was leaving."

"I don't know what to say except I'm sorry, Hannah. It's hard to believe he would go away and not even say good-bye."

"Please, don't tell a soul."

"Of course I won't tell anyone. But, you know, the whole town knows by now. I mean they know he left, not that he didn't say good-bye."

It wasn't like Rome and I made any promises to each other, but some how, deep down, I had always imagined we would be together. Weren't there promises without words? To me they were the strongest kind. Promises made with silent kisses, touches of our hearts. I was too embarrassed to tell him how my heart raced just thinking about him. He was my first love—I just knew deep in my heart he cared for me, too.

We walked along the street with Annabelle's arm wrapped over my shoulder. "I guess I wasn't the country gal he truly wanted. I'll be OK."

My classmates and I had a ball creating cool posters for the upcoming Sock Hop. Munich High put on three Sock Hops a year, and the last dance for the school year was scheduled on the following Friday night.

You didn't have to have a date. Sock Hops were informal get-togethers where students often came alone or in groups.

The rules were simple:

- No shoes on the gym floor, socks only, and that included chaperones
- No smoking in the gym
- No drinking alcohol
- Respect the chaperones
- Everyone in school was invited

When I dug around in my closet looking for my poodle skirt, it wasn't there.

I ran down the stairs and hollered, "Lucy, do you know what happened to my poodle skirt?"

"I took it to the cleaners, dear."

"I took it to the cleaners, dear," I mocked.

"Hannah, why are you acting so spiteful?"

"Because you have no business digging through my closet, or even going into my bedroom, for that matter."

"Hannah, I heard you talking about the Sock Hop coming up, and I was only trying to help. I noticed when you came home wearing your poodle skirt the last time, there were some pretty big spots on the front of it. You wouldn't want to wear it like that, would you?"

Papa stood leaning against the kitchen counter. "Hannah, Lucy just told jou, she vas only trying to help jou."

"Well, why didn't she tell me she stole it out of my closet? Lucy, you better have it back by tomorrow night or else."

Papa stuck out his lip in a thoughtful way and said, "Hannah Marie, jou know damn vell Lucy didn't steal jour skirt, for Christ's sake."

Lucy chimed in, "Hannah, I'll pick your skirt up in the morning."

"Lucy, please stay out of my bedroom and my closet from now on, OK?"

Lucy raised her voice, "You're acting like a spoiled brat, Hannah."

"Oh, yah. Let me tell you something, Lucy. My life was much happier before you ever moved in. Papa, will you tell her to stay out of my room?"

Papa stood there with a befuddled look on his face and didn't say a word.

CHAPTER 11

I hated how Papa always took Lucy's side. Sometimes they both drove me crazy. *Aw, well, it won't be too long until graduation and I'll be out of here.*

I thought obsessively about what I'd wear to the Sock Hop. When the night finally got there, I put on my poodle skirt and my pink angora sweater, pulled my hair back in a ponytail and tied it with a pretty pink ribbon, and I was ready to hop! But before I left to meet Annabelle, I snatched up my Elvis Presley record and took it with me.

I was really surprised to see Mr. and Mrs. Murger standing amongst the crowd of teenagers when we walked through the balloon-arch entryway into the Sock Hop,

"Annabelle, you didn't tell me your parents were chaperoning tonight."

"You didn't ask. You know how the parents take turns chaperoning. Well, tonight happened to be Mom and Dad's assigned duty to watch that we behave properly."

"Oh, OK."

"You know, some parents don't approve of Elvis Presley's type of music and won't chaperone or even allow their kids to come. I like that my parents are in favor of the Sock Hops."

"Your parents are hep, Annabelle."

Annabelle busted out laughing, "Oh, yeah, real cool cats!"

The varnished gymnasium floor was cleared for dancing, and the turntable sat on a wrought iron stand. A huge banner hanging on one wall read, "Rock 'n' Roll Is Here To Stay." Posters of Elvis Presley and Marilyn Monroe were on display.

A long table sat against one side of the gymnasium with a warmer of hot dogs, along with potato chips, bottles of Coke and a big pan of brownies for dessert.

Cy Bergstrom and Bobby Atkinson rushed in, carrying their favorite records, hits by Bill Haley and Chuck Berry.

"Fat City!" Cy shouted, after eyeballing the place.

Bobby grinned. "It's cook, cookin'!"

Bobby looked hip with his hair slicked back in a duck's tail. I watched him shrug out of his black leather jacket, dressed in blue jeans and a white T-shirt with a pack of Camel cigarettes rolled up in the sleeve. All the girls liked to dance with Bobby because he could really jitterbug.

A bunch of us ran out on the gymnasium floor and started to bunny-hop when "Glow-Worm" started playing. I loved to dance the Hokey Pokey as well, and you didn't need a partner.

Annabelle and I stood by the record player, drinking bottles of Coke and checking out the guys. The lights were turned down for a brief period. That's when I saw Gilbert and Olga way over in the corner, necking up a storm.

I grinned when Bobby sauntered my way with a big smile on his face and reached for my hand. "Come on, snake, let's rattle." I jumped up and we hit the dance floor, jitterbugging to "Rock Around the Clock." Every time the record stopped, Bobby dashed over to the turntable and played it over again.

I watched Annabelle and Trevor rollicking on the dance floor to Annabelle's favorite Connie Francis songs, "Who's Sorry Now?" and "Stupid Cupid." The whole crowd seemed to be having a good time!

I sat in Papa's favorite chair, listening to the kitchen sounds of water running and pans clanking. The sweet smell of cookies baking filled the air. When I heard Papa holler, "Jah, come on in, Yacob, and have a seat." I jumped up, walked out to the kitchen, and plunked down on a chair next to Papa. Jacob grinned and seated himself across from us. Lucy poured Jacob a cup of steaming hot coffee, and Papa handed him a plate of oatmeal-raisin cookies.

Jacob tossed four sugar lumps into his coffee before he dipped his cookie into the hot brew. He chewed as he talked, and coffee dribbled down his chin. Embarrassed-like, he pulled a big red farmer's handkerchief out of his back pocket and wiped his face.

Lucy's flour-sack apron was smudged with flour. She stood in front of the stove holding a spatula, waiting patiently for the next batch of cookies to get done baking. I noticed old Jacob eyeing the neat row of fresh-baked cookies on the breadboard.

"Boy, do dese cookies taste like more," Jacob muttered.

Papa picked up his coffee cup, set it down. "Go ahead, Yacob, help yourself. It's goot to see jou. Vhat have jou been up to anyvay?"

"Not much of anyting. Vaiting for the parts on my broken-down plow to get in so I could vork on it. I picked da parts up today at da John Deere shop, and on my vay home I stopped in at Greske's bar."

"Vhat's going on dere?"

"Not much of anyting."

"Vho all vas dere?"

"Two truck drivers and me, dat's all."

"Da hell jou say."

"Jah, vell, hell, I better get going and get to vork."

Jacob scooted his chair away from the table, stood up and started out the door. Papa followed him. Jacob lowered his voice, but I still overheard him say, "Yohan, Mr. Greske vas telling me dat he heard Venzel is in some big trouble on account of dat girlfriend of his."

"I daught dat had blown over, for Christ's sake."

"Not from vhat I heard today. Dat joung gal has hired an attorney and is daking him to court."

"Vhat for?"

"Damned if I know vhat it's all about."

It came as a surprise when Mr. Browten met up with me as I walked out of the home economics classroom and told me that he would like to see me in his office as soon as possible.

My heart started pounding out of my chest.

Why would Mr. Browten want to see me? I liked him as a teacher and I did well in his class.

I blushed and stammered, "Do—do you want me to come right now?"

"That'd be fine. I'm heading back to my office now. You can meet me there."

"OK, Mr. Browten."

I hurried into the girls' restroom and looked in the mirror. I splashed my face with cold water and smoothed back my ponytail.

I grabbed the bar of soap off the bathroom sink and scrubbed at the ugly stain on my gray skirt—of all days for me to spill tomato soup. I tried not to worry about it and take care of it when I got home, but, now that I was going to meet with Mr. Browten, I decided to run into the bathroom and see if I could snuff out the disgusting spot. Oh, my God, it turned into a gigantic watermark when I scrubbed on it. —I blotted it with a paper towel, rushed out of the bathroom and headed towards Mr. Browten's office.

Mr. Browten, a sweet-faced man, sat behind his big desk. He looked up and smiled when I walked in and motioned for me to take a seat. I sat rigid on the leather guest chair and placed my notebook over the damp spot on my skirt.

His office smelled of radiator dust. A big jar of candy root beer barrels sat on top of his desk. He shuffled through some papers, cleared his throat and pushed his glasses up off his nose.

"Hannah, I'm sure you've given a lot of thought as to what you'd like to do after you graduate."

I nodded.

"Your typing skills are exceptional. You are not only a fast typist, but accurate as well. I recommend that you think about attending ERTI, the Electronic Radio Television Institute in Omaha, Nebraska. It's a superb school. A one-year course, and when you graduate, ERTI will assist you in seeking a clerk typist or teletype operator position."

"Really?" I sat on the edge of my chair, speechless. Finally, I asked, "Where would my job be?"

"I really couldn't tell you at this time. Please give it some serious thought, talk it over with your family and get back to me."

Bowled over, I sat for a moment. "Thank you, Mr. Browten." I stood up and was about to leave when he gestured for me to stay seated. I flounced back down on the chair.

"Hannah, I want to commend you on your excellent grades. I was quite concerned when I noticed a decline in your marks last semester, but I'm happy to see you've brought them back up again."

"Thank you."

It's true. My grades dipped a little after Rome left.

"You are one smart girl with a dynamic personality and lots of potential. You can achieve whatever you decide to do with your life."

"Thank you, Mr. Browten."

"You're welcome, now do as I suggested, OK?"

"I sure will, Mr. Browten."

Mr. Browten reached into the candy jar and handed me two root beer barrels. Grinning from ear to ear, I thanked him once more and walked out the door. Oops! I almost bumped into Deanna, leaning against Mr. Browten's office door. In her sweet phony voice, she asked, "Why did Mr. Browten want to see you, Hannah?"

With a candy in my mouth, I looked right through her and kept on walking. Nothing was going to burst my bubble. I couldn't wait to get home and tell Papa.

"Dat's my girl, Hannah, go on to school. I'll help jou as much as I can, jou know dat. Den get a goot job. Don't depend on any man to dake care of jou."

Papa was wise before his time.

All I thought about after my meeting with Mr. Browten was going away to school. I counted the days off on my calendar until I would graduate from high school. I dreamed about where I would eventually live and work. I hoped it would be California.

Grandma told me one time, "You should learn how to make lefse, Hannah. It's a real good Scandinavian treat, and I'd like to teach you. Later, on a rainy Saturday afternoon, I called Grandma, and asked if it would be OK for me to come over and make lefse.

"Today would be fine." Grandma answered.

"I'm bringing Lucy too."

"OK, my dear, see you soon."

As soon as we got to Grandma's house, Lucy chimed in, Johan told me the tricky part to making lefse is rolling the dough. Is that right, Lieula?"

"That's a big part of it for sure."

"From what I've heard, Grandma made the best lefse. It sounds like whatever Johan's mother cooked or baked tasted good. If I could learn to cook half as good as she did, I'd be happy."

"Just give it time and you'll be a good cook too, Lucy."

Lucy sighed. "You think so?"

"OK, girls, the lefse recipe we will use today is special. Grandma Jonesen copied it from her mother's recipe book before she left Sweden to come to America, and Cajsa passed it onto me."

PERFECT SOFT LEFSE

3 cups mashed potatoes	1/2 tsp. salt
1/2 cup butter	1/2 cup cream
1 tbsp. sugar	1 1/2 cups flour

Prepare mashed potatoes; add butter, sugar, salt and cream. Beat well. Cool very well. Add flour and form into balls about 2 1/2 inches in diameter. Roll very thin and bake on lefse grill. Turn only once. When cool, put them in plastic bags, folding each lefse into quarters.

Olga Jardine
Stockholm, Sweden

Grandma looked on as Lucy carefully measured the ingredients and I whisked it all together in a big mixing bowl. "You're doing a good job, girls," she reassured us.

Lunchtime was special when we gathered around Grandma's kitchen table: buttering and daubing the lefse with Grandma's delicious homemade rhubarb-strawberry jam and eating one round after another.

"Hmmm, I'll bet you anything Papa is going to like our lefse, Lucy."

"It does taste yummy. It was fun making it, too."

The sun was going down. Time to help Papa with the chores when Lucy and I finished wrapping the lefse into little packages and packing them into a brown grocery bag. Grandma sat in her easy chair, looking quite pleased. "You girls ought to be proud of yourselves. You did a good job of making lefse for the first time."

I dashed over and gave her a little good-bye hug before I ran out to the car. Then I sat in the car, and waited and waited and waited for Lucy to come.

What in the world is keeping her? She knows I have to help Papa. A sick feeling came over me.

I bounded out of the car and ran back inside. Right off, Lucy screeched, "Hurry, Hannah, call Uncle Melvin."

Oh, my God. Grandma lay sprawled on the living room floor with Lucy crouched by her side. Grandma's face was expressionless, and her eyes were wide open with an intent stare.

I dashed to the telephone and rang Dr. Knightley.

Thank God, he answered on the first ring.

I shouted into the receiver, "Dr. Knightley, it's me, Hannah. I'm at Grandma's house. She's passed out on the living room floor. We can't wake her up. Please come as fast as you can."

"I'll be right dere, Hannah."

I covered my face with my hands and mumbled, "I can't believe what's happening. When I said good-bye to Grandma a few minutes ago, she looked content, sitting snug in her chair. Now look. Oh, my God. This is the worst."

"Let's try to stay calm," Lucy wailed. She went on to tell me, "Hannah, I was on my way out the door when I happened to look back. Lucia smiled at me. Then, just like that, she leapt from her armchair and grabbed onto the mantelpiece, gasped and fell to the floor."

My arms turned to gooseflesh.

Oh, my God, I hope Dr. Knightley gets here soon.

Lucy rushed to the bathroom. I watched her grab a washcloth that hung over the side of the tub and dampen it under the sink faucet, all the while talking under her breath: "It's going to be OK. Dr. Knightley will be here any minute and everything will be OK."

"Here, let me help," I cried.

I snatched the damp cloth out of Lucy's hand, bent over and wiped Grandma's forehead.

"Does this feel good, Grandma?"

No response.

"Grandma, do you know me?"

Still no answer.

I felt helpless.

Lucy ran to the phone and called Papa.

I heard Papa shout into the telephone receiver, "I'm on my vay."

Drenched with sweat, Papa struggled to lift Grandma off the floor. I helped him ease her onto the davenport, and I grabbed the soft wool blanket that lay on the ottoman and covered her.

In a low voice, I asked Papa, "Do you think it's another diabetes attack?"

Papa upset me all the more when he didn't say nothing—just shook his head and started pacing the floor and puffing on his pipe.

Shortly, Dr. Knightley bustled in with his black doctor's bag hung over one arm. An antiseptic smell filled the room when he opened his case.

Rhubarb lay sprawled out on the arm of the davenport, with her eyes fixed on Dr. Knightley.

Suddenly, Dr. Knightley stood up straight, pulled a white, neatly folded handkerchief out of his back pants pocket and took several deep breaths. He clutched Papa's arm and looked Papa in the eye. He spoke barely above a whisper. "Johan, she's gone."

Lucy screeched, "Uncle Melvin, are you telling us Lieula is dead?"

"I'm afraid so."

Grandma had died without any warning from a heart attack.

Dr. Knightley went on to say, "I hope it gives you peace of mind to know when one dies suddenly, as Lieula did, there is little time for suffering."

Immediately, Dr. Knightley walked over and rang up the coroner's office.

I stood with my arms crossed over my chest, stunned. My chin dropped onto my soft blue sweater. I couldn't take my eyes off Grandma. It was hard to believe that my grandma, whose enormous presence took away every fear, was this same pallid creature lying there. I wanted to turn and run, yet I didn't. How could I ever go on living without my Grandma?

Papa walked over and put his hand around my shoulder. The tick of the ancestral clock on the mantel sounded loud in my ears, ticktock, ticktock, ticking off the seconds. Seconds became minutes before Mr. Pierce, the undertaker, arrived.

Grandma's body was moved to the Pierce Brothers Mortuary in Munich.

The sadness overwhelmed me. It was heartbreaking to see Rhubarb roaming from room to room, looking for Grandma. I picked her up and took her with us when Papa and I went home.

Three days later, Grandma's funeral took place at St. Joseph's Catholic Church in Devils Lake. Melancholy music flowed from the organ as Papa, Lucy and I entered the church. The highly polished oak pews were full of folks dressed in dark clothing, wearing long faces and holding handkerchiefs to their sniffling noses. Boughs of white lilies filled vases and pots, sending out a soft fragrance as we made our way down the aisle and slid into the hard wooden pew.

Oh, how Grandma loved the North Dakota rose. There were lovely roses everywhere, just like how I remembered Mama's memorial service.

Great-Aunt Hortense traveled alone and arrived just on time. I watched her bustle into the church, dressed in a black silk sheath with a matching wide-brimmed hat. She stood with her hands on her hips and a puckered look on her face, gawking around. When she spotted Papa, she bolted over and squeezed into the pew beside him. She sat fumbling in her big black pocketbook and pulled out a white lace hankie.

The service proceeded. My throat choked up on the hymns so badly I could hardly sing, and from the sounds of the standing-room-only congregation, they were doing no better than me.

Knowing Great-Aunt Cassie was in the hospital recovering from gallbladder surgery and couldn't be there only added to my sadness. Uncle Dudley was back in jail for bootlegging moonshine, so he couldn't make it either; it was all hush-hush.

After the benediction, we followed Pastor Nelson out the side door and into the cemetery. Overhead, a meadowlark trilled and another answered. Pallbearers carried the coffin to its final resting place under the spreading boughs of an ancient maple. Folks gathered together as the pine box disappeared into the ground.

I wandered off by myself and plopped down on a nearby concrete bench. I wiped my eyes with the backs of my hands as I watched two ants carrying bits of something, maybe crumbs dropped by a mourning guest.

Oh, Grandma, why did you have to die?

I overheard a high-pitched voice: "I wonder what will happen to Lucia's chickens? I always bought my eggs from her, you know."

I thought about the times when Papa and I visited the Memorial Park Cemetery. It was interesting and peaceful, strolling around the cemetery. Papa pointed out where his parents were buried. I'd step softly and read the dead people's names, their birth dates and when they passed on, on the various burial sites. Some had huge monuments while others had just a little headstone, depending on what they could afford, I guess.

I found it hard to believe that of all the times Papa and I dropped by the Memorial Park Cemetery, I hadn't noticed nor did Papa point out that Grandpa Bamford was buried there. Now, they laid Grandma to rest next to Elis Bamford's grave site. I set my hands on my hips and examined the little stones. The letters were so faint I could hardly read them. ELIS BAMFORD 1878–1934, LIEULA BAMFORD 1871–1954. I called for Papa and motioned for him to come.

"Vhat is it, Sissy Pie?"

"Papa, look at the dates on Grandma and Grandpa's stones. According to what it says, Grandpa was seven years younger than Grandma. Grandma always said she and Grandpa were the same age."

Papa frowned as he pinched the bridge of his nose. "I never gave dere age much taught."

Old Great-Aunt Hortense left the cemetery in a big hurry. I saw her car going down the old country lane, picking up dust, and heading straight to Grandma's place.

Papa barely got the car stopped before I jumped out and bolted inside. I didn't get any farther than the kitchen when I pulled a chair out from the table, and plopped down on it, and buried my face in my arms and sobbed my heart out.

Papa walked over and put his hand on my shoulder. "Oh, Sissy Pie, jou alvays dake tings so hard. I know its yust awful to lose jour Grandma too, jah."

I looked up and blubbered, "I'll be OK, Papa."

The next day, as much as I dreaded going into Grandma's house with her not there, I had to check things out. I was eager to find out what Great-Aunt Hortense was doing in Grandma's house by herself

As soon as I got there, I asked Great-Aunt Hortense, "How come you didn't come to our house after the funeral service yesterday? Papa thought you'd come over and visit for a little bit."

"Oh, I wanted to find some important papers that I want to take home with me. I'm sure they're in your grandma's attic. But I ended up with such a headache, so I went straight to bed. Hannah, I'm heading up there right now." She took it upon herself to climb the crooked stairs to the attic.

"I'm hoping to find the deed for the old Fox Lake homestead," she hollered over her shoulder as I followed her up the stairs.

"Why did Grandma have the deed to the family homestead?"

"Well, Lucia made the mortgage payments when Dad was sick with tuberculosis and couldn't work. Dad gave her the deed in exchange. You know, Dad never did get back to his old self after his bout with tuberculosis."

"So, what you're saying is Grandma owned the Fox Lake family home?"

Annoyed, Great-Aunt Hortense answered, "Oh, I don't know for sure who owned what, but I do know there sure are a lot of cobwebs up here." She bent over and began to delve through Grandma's musty black trunk, crammed full of old photographs and papers.

That's when I noticed Band-Aids on all her fingertips. I asked her, "Great-Aunt Hortense, how come you have your fingers covered with Band-Aids?"

Growing more irritated, she explained, "Oh, it's from a nasty habit of biting my nails that I can't seem to quit."

The sound of Great-Aunt Hortense digging in Grandma's stuff really bugged me.

"Hannah, look at all the old certificates I've found." She handed me a bunch of documents. The mildew aroma went up my nose as I leaned against the sloped attic wall with my head bowed, fanning out the papers.

My heart sank when I pulled out Mama's birth certificate and read, FATHER UNKNOWN. So, who was my grandpa?

Great-Aunt Hortense rose to a standing position, showing excitement in her eyes when she waved the crinkly deed in the air, shouting, "Hannah, I've found it," and bolted down the steps.

I plopped down on the wooden floor, crossed my legs and studied the papers, trying to make sense of it all.

Well, then, the whole time, Mama grew up with a pretend father, but a decent man, so what did it matter?

I stood up, leaned over the old trunk and began digging out the old black-and-white photographs that I'd happened to see stuck in the bottom. Dust motes floated around me like ash. I grabbed a handful before I plunked down on an old broken-back chair and looked them over. I saw Grandma smiling. One photo showed her lots thinner with dark hair, standing amongst a group of students in front of an old country schoolhouse. Many photos were faded, with a colony of brown spots creeping across the surface.

As time went by, I found myself thinking of my grandma and grandpa a lot. Papa and I were in the barn one afternoon when I asked him, "Papa, did you know that the man who I thought was my grandpa wasn't my real grandpa?"

Papa looked over his shoulder at me and went right back to pitching hay to the cattle.

I guess he doesn't want to talk about it. I never brought it up again.

Oh, my God, I can only imagine the anguish Grandma kept bottled up inside. It certainly isn't going to change how much I love her. That's for sure.

I made up my mind then and there that I would be up front with my children and grandchildren. No surprises when I passed on.

When Papa and I walked to the house after finishing the chores, I thought of something else. "Papa, did you know that Grandma had the deed to the family homestead in Fox Lake hidden in her trunk in the attic?"

"I remember dere vas some talk about jour Grandma paying the mortgage. To tell jou da trut dat whole bunch vas so damn closed mout, I don't really know notting, Hannah."

The community settled back to its affairs and into its old groove; work was done

194

and duties fulfilled. I thought it sad, how it could go on in the old way when I felt such an aching sense of loss.

Annabelle and I were up in my bedroom when she told me, "Hannah, Trevor and I drove to Fargo last Wednesday." She held out her left hand and pointed to her ring finger. "And guess what? We looked at diamond engagement rings in Shaffer's jewelry store."

"Did Trevor buy you a ring?"

"No, let me tell you what happened."

Annabelle choked up. Her face looked like she was about to cry." It's so awful, Hannah."

"What in the world happened?"

"Well, we were in Shaffer's jewelry store, Trevor stood by me, looking on as I tried to decide which one I liked best of all the pretty rings the saleslady placed on top of the counter. Trevor nudged me and whispered, 'Which one will it be, sweetheart?' I threw my arm around him, 'They're all gorgeous.' At the same time, I happened to look out the big plate glass window, and right before my eyes, I saw my father driving down Fourth Street, lickety-split, with a strange lady sitting next to him."

"My hands started to shake. I thought I was going to pass out right there. I wished Trevor hadn't seen what I saw, but I knew he did when he told the saleslady, 'we must go, thank you so much. We'll be back another time.'"

"Oh, my God, This is awful."

"You know, I'd absolutely refused to believe the rumors about my father. I mean, how could my father do such a thing? I haven't said anything to my brothers, and they've never said a word to me. Mother looks sad most of the time, but she goes on like everything is just fine. I'm certainly not going to tell her. I have this sick feeling that something horrendous is about to happen."

"Oh, Annabelle, don't say that."

Annabelle whispered, "I feel like I hate my father."

I gave Annabelle a hug. "Try not to hate him."

"Oh, that's easy for you to say when it's not your father. I wonder, why so many bad things happen in life?"

We both sat there, not saying a word for the longest time.

Finally, Annabelle spoke up, "Hannah, let's try and think of some good things."

"OK. One good thing, Radovan is about to graduate from college. I know your father—well, your whole family is very proud of him. Radovan is so smart."

"I wish I had his brain."

"You're smart too, Annabelle."

Annabelle giggled. "You think so? Another good thing is, Trevor loves me, and I love him. Now, you tell me something good, Hannah."

"I'm going away to college soon and getting away from Lucy—that's a really good thing."

"Lucy isn't that bad, is she?"

"I guess not, but it's so different having her around after Papa and I were alone for so long."

"Actually, if you think about it, there are more good things than bad, huh?"

"That's for sure, but it's hard to think of the good when things are bad. I do feel lots better now after we talked."

Fall was the favorite season for many North Dakotans because the days became pleasantly warm—the ideal time to prepare gardens and fields for the next year. The fall of 1955 was extraordinary. Not only were we getting ready for next year's flowers and crops, but that was when Papa told me a crew of men were coming to test for oil on our property.

One sunny September morning, shortly after the oil rigs were operating on our land, I walked outside and stood beside Papa. We watched the contractors and workers hustling around in hard hats and black fire-retardant coveralls, invading our yard. Papa drove his hands into his pockets, jiggling them about a moment, and chuckled, "I tink it's all a lost cause."

"Yah, but wouldn't it be something if they did strike oil on our farm! Just think, we'd be rich, Papa."

"Naw, I doubt very much if dere's oil in dis part of da country. It's da Western side of da state, Tioga, vhere da oil is, but den again, jou never know."

The sad part of oil drilling on our farm was watching the wildlife, frightened and scurrying out of their familiar environment to get away from the noisy oil rigs.

After weeks of hard drilling, the operators came up with dry holes and moved on.

Thank God, the commotion came to an end, and we could get back to some sort of normalcy. It was absolutely delightful to see the wild ducks back, quacking and tramping through our farmyard once again.

Annabelle sat up in bed and hugged her knees to her chest. "This could be the last time you stay over at my house, Hannah."

"Oh, don't say that."

"Well, soon you'll be going off to school and I'll be a married woman."

"I know, but I don't want to think that we'll never stay with each other again."

"No more Sock Hops, Hannah."

"Now, that's something I'll really miss. Are you excited about your wedding?"

"I sure am, and I know Trevor is the only guy for me."

"Well, I thought for awhile Rome would be the guy for me. Then, look what happened."

"Yah, I know, Hannah, but you always said you wanted to travel around and see different places."

"It wasn't meant to be. I'm excited about going away to school, and I plan to ride to Omaha on the Jack Rabbit Lines. I've never traveled on a big bus before."

"I heard that it can get so crowded on buses that you may not even get a seat, Hannah."

I laughed, "I think that's on city buses, not the Jack Rabbit Lines. Wouldn't it be something if I had to stand up all the way to Omaha?"

I always attended Sunday services at the Zion Lutheran church when I happened to stay at the Murgers' house on a Saturday night. Mrs. Murger would be the first one up on Sunday mornings, calling for everyone to wake up and get ready for church, but on that particular Sunday morning Mr. Murger didn't get out of bed.

I watched Mrs. Murger wipe her forehead with the jerk of her handkerchief and trudge back into their bedroom once again. When she opened the bedroom door, from where I sat, I could see Mr. Murger lying on his bed with his hands joined under his head.

Mrs. Murger moved silently out of the bedroom and spoke barely above a whisper: "Annabelle, your father just told me we should go on without him. I do think it's best that he gets his rest. I've been worried about him, you know, he hasn't been sleeping well and there are times when he becomes agitated over the least little thing. To tell you the truth, he's been working too hard, doing the job for two since Alex up and quit."

Annabelle glanced at me and rolled her eyes.

Mrs. Murger looked around at all her children. "Kids, you know as well as I do that your father has never been the same since Radovan came down with polio."

She walked back to the bedroom, and plumped his pillow once more before we left for church. "He seems to be resting peacefully."

I sat in the long wooden pew surrounded by the Murger family, and listened to Reverend Nelson preach:

"What is authority in Christianity?

"It is Christ within you, which is love. Not the Bible, not the pope in Rome, but love. If I would go to Germany and speak in English, no matter how loud and how long I talked, the people would not understand me. But if I struck four chords of music everyone could understand the emotion which I am attempting to convey. As we set out in life we must strike the chord of God's eternal sound, which is love, and it will be understood by all people."

Grandma would have loved to hear Reverend Nelson's sermon.

As soon as we got home from church, Dakota slipped an apron over her pretty navy-blue dress and started to prepare a late breakfast.

I overheard Mrs. Murger tell Annabelle, "When I finish stirring up the pancake batter, I'll check on your father and see if he feels like eating. Honey, would you run down to the cellar and get a jar of maple syrup, please?"

"OK, Mother, do you want anything else?"

"No, just the syrup. Don't forget to take the flashlight with you."

Annabelle looked at me. "Hannah, wait for me at the head of the stairwell. Will you? It's scary going down in the cellar." Then she bustled down the rickety steps into

198

the dark.

I walked over to the top of the cellar stairs. "Annabelle, I'll be right here, OK?"

"OK."

I hung over the wobbly wooden rail and watched as she braced her hands against the dirt wall and wormed her way towards the shelf where the maple syrup was stored.

"Hannah, there's a strange, sickening stench down here that's making my nose twitch."

"I think all cellars stink."

"Hannah, what if a rat bites me? Or what if a bat flies down from the ceiling and gets caught in my hair?"

"Annabelle, just grab the syrup and hurry back."

"Oh, my God, I just bumped into something weird with my bare foot."

"What is it?"

"That's what I'm trying to figure out. Hold on a minute while I get the flashlight shone on it."

Annabelle screamed bloody murder.

"I'm coming down, Annabelle." At the same time Annabelle's mother shouted, "Annabelle, what's going on down there?"

"Mother, please come quick, it's Dad. He's lying in a pool of blood—his hemorrhoids are bleeding all over the place."

Dakota scrambled alongside me down the steps, yelling, "Why in the world would your father come down here in the first place, for God's sake?"

I thought my heart was going to beat right out of my chest.

Mrs. Murger knelt and felt her husband's rigid body. "Oh, my God, there's a shotgun lying at his side. He's dead, Annabelle, your father is dead. He shot himself."

Mrs. Murger whispered under her breath, "That's why he wanted to stay in bed this morning. He had it all planned—the spineless bastard."

Annabelle clasped her hands, gave a piercing shriek and flung herself face down on the cellar floor.

Beside herself, Mrs. Murger stood up and screamed hysterically. "Annabelle, get up off that dirt floor and help me."

Wenzel Murger had tied a length of twine around the trigger of the shotgun, passed it round the stock, put the barrel in his mouth and pulled.

Oh, mercy, it was more than I could take.

Dakota Murger let it be known that she had found her husband's suicide note on top of the dresser in their bedroom, requesting there be no funeral. He wasn't worthy of a memorial service, he wrote. Mrs. Murger honored his plea.

The headlines in the local paper read, "Mr. Wenzel Murger Commits Suicide." Below, in smaller print: "His daughter, Annabelle, discovers his body lying in a pool of blood on the cellar floor."

Grief stricken and ashamed, Mrs. Murger cried, "I don't know how I'll ever face the townsfolk or anyone for that matter. God help us."

Mr. Wenzel Murger's body was buried at the Memorial Park Cemetery alongside his father.

CHAPTER 12

On May 23, 1956, Annabelle and I stood onstage in the city auditorium, dressed in black caps and gowns. When my name was called, I marched right up and accepted my diploma from Mr. Hogwood. He looked into my face, smiled real nice, then shook my hand and congratulated me.

As I passed by Annabelle, she poked me and whispered, "Just think, next month I'll be Mrs. Halvorson."

Holding onto my diploma, I grinned. "Oh, yeah, and in less than two months I'll be on my way to Omaha, Nebraska."

There were ten boys and ten girls in my senior class.

The summer after graduation, I landed a job as a flagman working for Mr. Holland. Mr. Holland owned a Piper J-3 Cub airplane and hired me to help crop dust his cornfields. I could see his portly face out the plane's small window, smiling down at me as he swooped low over the field. He raced along at one hundred forty miles per hour, only a few feet above the cornstalks, before releasing the chemicals and leaving behind a swath of insecticides. Then he'd pull back into the sky.

My job was to run through the field and wave a white flag in the air, indicating the outside limit of the last swath, so Mr. Holland would know just where to turn the plane around for the next sweep.

If I didn't watch what I was doing and make sure to stay out of the way of the low-flying airplane, I could have been killed. Mr. Holland told me one time that he remembered hearing about a flagman who was cut down on the job. Even so, I loved working for Mr. Holland and being outside.

By this time, Dakota had sold the family home, bought a smallish house in Devils Lake, and had gone back to nursing at Mercy Hospital, the same hospital where Annabelle and I were born.

Annabelle told me that as painful as things had been, she had put the memory of her father's philandering and tragic death behind. "I don't feel like I hate my dad anymore, and I try to think of all the good things."

"I'll never forget the day your father came along and saved my life when I tried to pick cattails in the swamp waters and fell in."

"Oh, yeah, I remember that day. You were so scared, lying on our davenport, and my mom was washing off your foot. I'm going to tell you something else Mom told me?"

"What is it?"

"You have to promise you'll never tell a soul."

"Of course I'll never tell."

"She said Dad had a nervous breakdown before us kids were born, and he suffered from depression."

"Oh, really? The poor man. I wonder what a nervous breakdown really is?"

"All I know is nervous breakdowns are looked upon with such a sense of shame— like don't tell anybody. Mom told me that Mrs. Jensen had a nervous breakdown on the ship coming over from the old country. That's why she stays to herself like she does."

"Really? I never heard that before. Do you want to hear what Gilbert told me?"

"Sure, tell me."

"Rome got married."

"He did! I wonder what she looks like?"

"Me too. I still think of him every now and again."

I was overjoyed to be maid of honor in Annabelle and Trevor's charming old-fashioned country wedding on June 20, 1956. Trevor's oldest brother, Bruce, was best man. The nuptials took place outside on the Halvorson farm, encircled by sunshine and cornfields. Cindy arrived early and filled the terra-cotta pots with flowers she thought Annabelle would like.

I overheard Dakota say, "I'm happy Annabelle chose to wear my vintage wedding gown. It fits her perfectly, too." She chuckled, "It's hard to believe I was ever that small."

Annabelle beamed when she looked into Trevor's ruggedly handsome face and whispered, "I do."

A pig cooked in the ground. The dinner menu consisted of homemade buns, potato salad, pasta salad and all kinds of garden vegetables, served on long wooden picnic tables. Slices of lemon wedding cake, Annabelle's favorite, were served for dessert. All the flowers on the tables came from neighbors' gardens.

When the party ended, guests showered Annabelle and Trevor with rice as they ran to Trevor's new shiny black Ford pickup, a wedding gift from Grandpa Halvorson, and headed to the Wisconsin Wonder Spot in Lake Delton. Annabelle told me that after they'd read an article in a *Mobile Life* magazine about Wisconsin Dells, she and Trevor decided to honeymoon near Mirror Lake where they could swim, canoe, and see the unique rock formations.

They planned to move into the historic guest cottage behind the big house on the Halvorsons' third-generation farm when they returned from their honeymoon.

On a hot August day, Papa drove me to Grand Forks, North Dakota, to catch the Jack Rabbit Lines to Omaha, Nebraska. As much as I looked forward to going away to school, when it came time to tell Papa good-bye, a big lump formed in my throat, and tears started rolling down my cheeks.

"Now, now, Sissy Pie, ve'll have none of dat."

"I hate good-byes."

"Jou'll be yust fine."

I reached for Papa's hand. "I'll call you, Papa."

"No, talking on da phone cost too much. Vrite me a letter, Hannah. I daught of a couple more tings I vant to tell jou before jou yump on dat big bus. Now, vhen jou get into da big city, alvays valk on da outside of da street, not close to the alley because some lunatic could be hiding in dere, yust waiting to grab you. Another ting, vhen jou use da ladies' room, alvays hang jour purse on da hook, don't let it lay on da floor. A mugger could reach under da toilet door, grab it, and dake off vit jour money and everyting."

A blast from the loudspeaker—"Jack Rabbit Lines to Omaha, Nebraska, is now boarding."

With butterflies in my stomach, I jerked loose of Papa's hand and cried out, "Papa, I gotta go."

Papa picked up my grip off the ground and handed it to me, and I dashed towards the big blue bus. Looking over my shoulder, I shouted, "Papa, I'll always walk on the outside of the street when I get to Omaha. Don't worry."

I scampered through the narrow aisle, plunked down on a window seat and peered out the grimy window, hoping I'd see Papa. I dug a tissue out of my pocketbook and wiped at the glass, but the crud was on the outside. Finally, I caught a glimpse of Papa standing in front of the bus station, lighting his pipe. His shoulders sagged as he walked slowly towards the parking lot. I wiped my eyes on the sleeve of my sweater. Suddenly, everything in my life was different.

The engine started, and the blue monster eased slowly away from the curb and roared out of town. I waved at Papa until I couldn't see him anymore, but he didn't see me.

Finally, the big bus slowed and pulled into the Omaha terminal. Excited, I bounded from my seat, scooted through the crowd and jumped out onto the paved platform. I'd imagined the bus station to be like the Munich train depot. Boy, was I surprised to see it was five times the size or more. There were people everywhere. I snatched my letter of instructions out of my pocketbook, hailed a yellow cab and hopped in.

"Where will it be?" the elderly cabdriver asked. I glanced at my paper and gave him the address.

The way the cabdriver took off and zipped through town startled me. I saw nothing more than a short, hurried view of churches with steeples, three-story buildings, a park, a huge creamery, schools and shops of all kinds. Tall trees lined the streets.

Gawking at the cabdriver from the backseat, I noticed he had a bald spot the size of a grapefruit right in the middle of his big square head. A huge cigar hung out of the side of his mouth. I hollered over the noise of the engine, "How come it smells like a barnyard around here?"

He chuckled, "Young lady, you're in cattle country. Omaha's Union Stockyards is practically a city unto itself."

"Really? I didn't expect to smell manure in a big city."

"You'll get used to it. Won't be long until you don't even notice it."

"I hope so."

I guess I should be used to the smell, coming from the farm and all, but this isn't like the barnyard smell back home.

The cabdriver pulled up at the Hotel Fontenelle. He reached around, and I handed him the fare before I slid off the upholstered cushion and bounded out of the cab. Flabbergasted, I stood in front of the hotel openmouthed. I'd never seen such a towering establishment in my entire life.

I entered the busy front lobby with its gleaming black tile floor and brass fixtures, potted ferns, ornamental chandeliers and mirrors. Cozy sitting areas done in bright rainbow colors were welcome to any visitor. Off to the side was a black marble reception desk with a neatly dressed middle-aged woman pecking away at a red Royal Quiet Deluxe portable typewriter.

As I checked out the different brochures displayed on a rack, the women stopped what she was doing and told me, "Take whatever you like, dear."

"Oh, thank you." I picked up a Fontenelle brochure and flipped through it. Hotel Fontenelle: Heart of business, financial and theater districts. Civic, commercial and social center. Headquarters all civic clubs. Home of National Aeronautic Association. Four hundred luxurious rooms (two hundred fifty rooms air-conditioned). Fine restaurants, coffee shop and garage.

It had to be the largest interior space I'd ever been in and certainly the most impressive.

It was dark by the time I hopped into the huge elevator on my way to my room. I fumbled with the key until I got the door open and walked into a spacious, beautifully furnished bedroom with a cream-colored spread. I rushed over to the window, grabbed hold of the heavy cord and opened the brocade draw drapes. Oh, my God, I couldn't believe my eyes. Why, there were lanes of cars with their headlights on, moving through the city bumper-to-bumper.

How does anyone dare to drive in traffic like that?

On our first half-day of school, we met with Mrs. Salisbury, the administrator, for orientation. Mrs. Salisbury was a tall, horsey-looking woman with large black-rimmed glasses. You wouldn't say she was homely, but the way she was dressed, in a baggy skirt and big shirt, was not flattering. She looked like she meant business.

"Welcome to ERTI. I expect you to benefit from your time here, and I want you to enjoy it as well. You'll have to work hard and apply yourself in order to get through all I have planned for us to cover."

She pushed her long brunet hair away from her face and made a so-so gesture with her hands. "Our all-girl school has been known to have weird men drive up and park out front when classes are dismissed, and offer the girls a ride."

Her voice got louder. "Don't ever get in a car with a stranger. There is a strict regulation requiring that you be off the streets and in your room by ten p.m. Try to write a letter home at least once a week, and keep your parents informed as to how you're doing ."

Wow, sounds like I'm in for lots of studying.

Mrs. Salisbury assisted me in finding a room at Mrs. Beloi's boardinghouse, and I moved in that very afternoon. The minute I walked up to Mrs. Beloi's historic home, I fell in love with the big wooden swing on her front porch.

When she was showing me around her well kept home, I noticed Mrs. Beloi wore black chunky-heeled oxfords just like Grandma did. I peeked into the bathroom and saw a claw-foot tub just like we had at home. Mrs. Beloi shuffled up behind me and blurted out, "Always clean up after yourself when using the bathroom. Notice I have towel racks on all the walls for you girls. Don't ever leave wet towels lying on the floor."

She has no idea how tidy I kept things for Papa and me. I wonder why Mrs. Beloi walks with such a serious limp.

I turned away when she caught me staring at her legs.

"An old ankle injury where surgery went awry."

"I'm sorry, Mrs. Beloi."

"I forget I have a limp, dear."

"Hmmmm, I smell cinnamon."

"There's an apple pie baking. Come on, Hannah, I'll show you your room."

Oh, my goodness, the sun shone through the white lace curtains onto walls covered with flowered wallpaper, and over in one corner stood an antique oak desk.

Delighted, I told Mrs. Beloi, "I love my room."

"I want you to feel as comfortable as you can during your stay at my house."

I couldn't get over how pretty everything was—the porch was like a picture in a magazine, with the wicker chairs and tables, the swing and all the colorful clay pots full of flowers.

When Mrs. Beloi walked out of my room, I immediately unpacked my suitcase, hung my clothes in the little closet and put aside what I planned to wear the next day. I could hardly wait to start classes.

Next, I sat down at the little desk and wrote a letter to Papa.

> August 30, 1956
>
> 193 Superior Drive
>
> Omaha, Nebraska
>
> Dear Papa,
>
> How are you?
>
> The bus ride was long, but I arrived in Omaha safe and sound. School is everything I expected. I met a lot of nice girls during orientation this morning. The students come from all over. One girl is from Tioga, ND.
>
> Mrs. Salisbury, the school administrator, helped me find a room at Mrs. Beloi's boardinghouse. Mrs. Beloi seems to be a very kind and caring person. She reminds me of Mrs. Murger. There is a big wooden swing on the front porch.
>
> Papa, I can't get over how bad Omaha stinks from the cattle stockyards.
>
> Are you managing the chores OK without me? I miss you a lot.
>
> Love always,
>
> Hannah

XXX/OOO

PS: Tell Lucy hello.

I didn't feel like writing, "Dear Papa and Lucy." Enclosed in my first letter from Papa was a big sheet of three-cent stamps.

I was happy to know that Mrs. Beloi's place was far enough away from downtown so you couldn't smell the foul odor of the stockyards. I loved to sit on the porch swing and study. And it was fun watching all the strange vehicles drive by. I liked the convenience of city life right off. If you needed paper, pencils, soap or anything, you could just walk to the store and buy it.

Every morning on my way to school, I passed by a little hole-in-the-wall shop, stocked with newspapers, magazines, candy bars, and every brand of cigarette imaginable. The slim young man who managed the store wore large, black-framed glasses with Coke-bottle lenses, way too big for his face. I was told he was legally blind. He'd stand out front on his tiptoes and shout, "Buy your newspaper here, folks. *Omaha World-Herald* sold here!"

Miss Fontaine, a high-waisted, paunchy woman, taught our advanced typing class. Her ample bosom heaved with the effort of walking across the room. She spoke in a high-pitched tone, stressing how important good posture was when sitting in front of a keyboard. "Sit up straight, pull your shoulders back and keep your feet flat on the floor."

The gal next to me poked my arm and whispered, "A real drill sergeant."

I'd just walked into school on a beautiful crisp November morning when Mrs. Salisbury asked me to come and see her in her office. She got right to the point. "Hannah, the Navy department has a great need for civilian clerk typists at this time. And, with your exceptionally good typing skills, you are an excellent candidate. Would you like to accept a position in Washington, DC at this time?"

I sat for a moment, lost for words. Mrs. Salisbury smiled at me from behind her big orderly desk.

"Really? I would love to go to Washington, DC."

"Hannah, with your adeptness, you'll do just fine."

Oh, my God, this is more than I ever dreamed possible.

Thank God, I got control of myself and asked, "Mrs. Salisbury, when could I start work?"

"Well, you can't go to work for the government until you turn eighteen."

Two weeks later, I was once again on the Jack Rabbit Lines, headed home to North Dakota to spend Thanksgiving with Papa before I left for Washington.

On a cold, blustery Thursday morning at the very tail end of November, I walked up the steps of the Great Northern train and entered the railroad car—with an "all a-b-o-a-r-d" the train lunched forward.

I kept my nose glued to the window, looking out and enjoying all the magnificent sights. When it grew dark, I switched on the little light above me and grabbed a book out of my grip, curled my stocking feet under me, and began reading *The Grapes of Wrath*. John Steinbeck was one of my favorite authors.

The aroma of cooking circulating from the railroad kitchen made me hungry. I slithered off the red velvet cushion, slipped into my shoes and traipsed through the chain of cars on my way to the dining car.

A tall, black porter dressed in a starched white uniform greeted me with a big smile, showing perfect white teeth. He summoned me to follow him and seated me at a table near the kitchen. He handed me a huge menu.

"I'll be right back to take your order," he called over his shoulder as he swayed through the train's passageway. I sat for a minute or two, looking things over. The table was covered with a white linen cloth, set with perfectly folded cloth napkins and pretty silverware. It reminded me of a scene in an old movie: people dining in Trader Vic's restaurant, in San Francisco. Hanging on one wall was a lamp with a pretty red shade. From where I sat, I could see the cooks preparing salads and getting great big potatoes ready to bake. An adorable poster with a cartoon drawing of a fat chef caught my attention.

Fresh Bread

The Chef's an earnest, busy man

As we will try to show

He needs fresh bread for every meal

That's why he kneads the dough

Three men were loud, playing poker at one table. A young mother with two small children was reading them a story, and two ladies were chatting in the seat across from me. One of the women reminded me so much of Grandma, the way she wore her gray hair pulled back in a bun. She smiled at me when she caught my gaze.

I glanced back at the menu and took my time poring over the list of dishes available: Hearty cream of lima bean soup? Filet mignon, no thanks. Twice-baked potatoes? Hot strawberry sundae? I'd never heard of some of the items listed.

When the porter returned, I still hadn't decided; there were just too many unusual choices.

"Take your time, young lady. I'll be back."

When I finally told the porter what I wanted, he looked at me in surprise. "A Danish, please, oh, make that two."

In no time he returned, carrying my pastry on a big round tray and set it down in front of me. I levered myself upright on the dining car seat as the train tottered to and fro, and savored every bite. The porter made me laugh when he walked by and said, "You eat like that, you're gonna get fat."

I'd never tasted such delicious sweet rolls in my entire life.

After three days of riding on the train, I felt a strong, pleasant feeling of excitement when the conductor announced, "Next stop, Washington, DC." He repeated his call several times as he tottered down the aisle. One of the workers in uniform hurried off the train and set a metal stool on the ground for the passengers to step on. I thanked him when he grabbed hold of my hand and guided me to the wide plank platform. I immediately hailed a cab to take me to the Meridian Hill Hotel for women.

I started my clerk typist job in the Pentagon building on my eighteenth birthday, December 4, 1956. The office space was small. Metal file cabinets separated one work area from another.

Mr. Joseph Somby, a stout black man, was my supervisor. He was a compassionate soul who made me feel welcome and needed right from the start. He wore beautiful white starched shirts and colorful ties with stylish suits every single day.

I loved getting ready for work in the mornings and dressing in business attire. I felt quite chic wearing high-heeled shoes and nylon stockings with the black seams running up the back. I looked forward to my morning bus ride as well. I saw some of the most interesting things on my way to work, and when the cherry blossoms were in bloom, it was a sight to behold.

One particular morning, I was taken by surprise when a big balloon-shaped airship flew right by my window! I'd never seen anything like it in my life. Excited, I jumped up to get a better look, and accidently bumped into the big feet of the woman on the aisle seat next to me.

"Excuse me," I said, and riveted my eyes on the large object. I turned and asked the women, "What is that?"

"It's a blimp," she snapped, and went right back to reading the *Washington Star* newspaper.

"Thank you." I plunked back down beside the woman, who kept her face hidden behind the newspaper.

She sure is an unhappy soul.

At work, I sat at a large wooden desk and typed letters to congressmen on a Smith-Corona typewriter. If one mistake was made—one little stroke too much, a strikeover—the whole letter had to be retyped. No using erasures. Excellence was what we strove for.

I was amazed at the diversity of people who lived in the city of Washington, and found it interesting to meet and work with people from different walks of life.

On one of my first visits to the ladies' room, I happened to look out the little narrow window in the restroom and was absolutely astonished to see a beautiful view of the Lincoln Memorial and the Washington Monument. I made it a habit to peek out that window every time I went to the restroom.

211

My new friend Aretha and I stood out in front of the Meridian Hill Hotel on a Saturday evening. We hailed a yellow cab, hopped in, slid across the slippery seat and gave the cabdriver the address. He shifted into gear and took off through the city. It seemed every time I rode in a cab or bus, I saw things I'd never seen before. The city lights reminded me of Christmas time.

When we got to our destination, the driver gave a snort, pulled up to the curb and pointed to the neon sign that read "Starlight Lounge."

Excited, we handed him the fare, got out of the cab, and walked into a carefree crowd. It surprised me to see young folks sitting at the little tables, drinking longneck bottles of beer. Others were out on the crowded dance floor.

We made our way through the dimly lit lounge and squeezed into the first empty booth we happened to find. Right off, a waiter came to take our order.

Aretha spoke up, "Two Cokes, please."

"This place is really something, huh, Hannah?"

"There're lots of kids here, that's for sure."

The minute I sat down, I felt someone looking at me. I could see him out of the corner of my eye. I slowly turned my head. He smiled—I smiled back. The next thing I knew, he was walking across the dance floor and approaching me with his hand extended.

On the dance floor, I learned his name was Roger. He was an airman, stationed at Andrews Air Force Base in Maryland. He was a native of San Francisco, born and raised in California. He and his buddies were out on the town celebrating his eighteenth birthday.

I was taken by his sweet, shy manner.

"San Francisco? I dream of going to California someday."

"You do?"

Aretha turned up when the band quit playing at closing time, but before I took off, Roger nudged my arm and asked me for my phone number. I didn't waste any time rummaging through my pocketbook to find a pen. I quickly wrote it on a napkin and gave it to him.

As soon as I got into the taxicab, I plopped down on the seat, kicked off my high heels and leaned back. My feet ached from dancing. The meter ticked away as the cabdriver sped through Washington.

Aretha poked me and whispered, "Hannah, I noticed you danced with the same guy all night. What was that all about?"

"Well, there was something about that shy guy that attracted me, plus he was a good dancer."

"Oh, yeah, it looked like you were having fun."

"I always go for handsome, dark curly-headed guys."

"You do? I like blond guys with blue eyes myself."

"You can find lots of blond guys in North Dakota."

"Really? North Dakota is too cold for me. I danced with a bunch of different guys. Some real creeps, like Rex from Texas who talked with a stupid drawl." Then she busted out laughing—the kind of laugh that turns into a loud burp.

"Excuse me. Not bad manners, just good beer."

"Did you drink more than Coke?"

"Well, Rex bought me a couple of beers."

"A couple?"

"Oh, I guess I drank three beers. He asked me a hundred times over, 'Are you sure you wouldn't like me to give you a ride home?' He wasn't a good dancer either. You know, I was really surprised that they served alcohol to eighteen-year-olds. You have to be twenty-one in Iowa."

"North Dakota, too."

"What was the guy's name you were dancing with?"

"Roger, he's from San Francisco, California. Imagine me, meeting someone from California the very first time I go out at night in Washington DC. He was a real nice guy, soft-spoken. He asked me for my phone number."

"I know, I was there when you gave it to him."

"I hope he calls me."

"Let me know if he does."

"I sure will."

"The Starlight is a fun place. Let's go back there again."

"I'd love to."

Roger did call before the week was over. On our first real date, we visited the Washington Monument, the most prominent structure in the city. We climbed the eight hundred ninety-seven steps along with a crowd of eager tourists.

There was something about Roger's subdued demeanor, his gentleness and concern for others that attracted me. He was easy to be around, and I liked the way he dressed.

To live near Washington was a new and exciting experience for both Roger and me. We enjoyed visiting all the different spectacular places. Before long, we were together almost every weekend, visiting places of interest. Warren G. Harding's silk pajamas were on display at the Smithsonian Institution. There were locks of hair arranged behind a glass frame, cut from the heads of the first fourteen presidents, starting with George Washington and going all the way up to Franklin Pierce.

The top hat that Abraham Lincoln allegedly wore when he was assassinated at Ford's Theatre was on exhibit. The original Wright brothers' flyer suspended in the Smithsonian's Arts and Industries Building made a profound impression on me.

The phone was ringing off the hook when I walked in from work. It was Roger, asking if I'd like to go to the Glen Echo Amusement Park on Sunday.

Of course I would.

Listening to the screams and laughter when we rode the roller coaster made me think about the time Papa, Grandma, Annabelle and I went to the County Fair. I started feeling a little melancholy, but I snapped right out of it when Roger suggested we go to Crystal Pool. Roger was an excellent swimmer and loved to swim. I had a good time playing and splashing in the water.

We walked all around the park, stopped to watch the extraordinary carousel go round, and ate hot dogs. I talked Roger into having our picture taken in the photo booth. And when I got home, I picked out the best picture on the strip and sent it to Papa. I couldn't help but wonder what he'd think of my new boyfriend.

I felt myself growing romantically attracted to that kind, striking young man, and I looked forward to the weekends more than ever.

When I'd asked Roger about his family, he told me, "I have no memory of my mom and dad. They both drowned in a freak accident near Alcatraz when their sailboat overturned in the ocean waters. I was nine months old. I ended up being bounced around from one of my aunts—my mother's sisters—to another."

"I'm sorry."

"Don't be sorry, you don't miss what you never had."

"My mother was killed in a car accident when I was a little girl, but I had my papa and grandma who took good care of me."

It was interesting to learn how similar our backgrounds were, except for the fact that Roger grew up in a big city and I grew up in rural North Dakota. We were both born in December of the same year. Our mothers were killed in tragic accidents. And I was very happy to learn that Roger was an animal lover.

I was thrilled when I heard the news that Roger would march in Eisenhower's inaugural parade! On January 20, 1957, Aretha and I sat in the grandstand with a perfect view and watched the procession. President Eisenhower, along with Mamie, reached out and waved to the crowd as they led the motorcade. Branches of the armed forces, civilian bands and several floats followed.

Even though it was impossible to pinpoint Roger in that troop of men dressed in Air Force blues, marching down Pennsylvania Avenue, it was exciting to know he was part of it.

The following Valentine's Day, while Roger and I sat side by side on the davenport in my apartment, looking over a Washington, DC, brochure and discussing the sites we'd already visited and where we'd like to go next—out of the blue Roger tossed the brochure onto the coffee table and got down on his knees in front of me.

He quickly reached into his pocket and took out a pretty, tiny diamond ring, and he asked me to marry him. I felt a nervous shaking in my body and got all choked up before I nodded and whispered, "I'd love to."

Roger had picked out the lovely ring without my knowing, put it on layaway at the

Andrews Air Force Base commissary and made payments every payday until it was paid in full. I couldn't wait to show my diamond off to everyone. When we agreed on a wedding date, I handed out beautiful wedding invitations to my boss, Mr. Somby, and all my friends at work.

I was taken aback when Mr. Somby approached me a few days later as I walked in after lunch. In his soft-spoken manner, he said, "Hannah, my wife and I felt honored that you invited us to your wedding, and we would like to attend, but black folks are not allowed at the all-white Christian church in Arlington, Virginia."

I looked into Mr. Somby's serious face. "Really?"

Little did this country gal from North Dakota know about segregation.

On July 20, 1957, our teenage wedding took place in Arlington. I wore a simple white wedding gown and carried a tiny bouquet of pretty red roses. My heart felt like it would pound right out of my chest when I walked down the aisle on Chief Master Sergeant Woten's arm and gazed up at Roger, who was beaming broadly and looking handsome as ever in a white sport coat with a pink carnation.

When Pastor Aldren declared, "You may kiss the bride," it felt so right when Roger pulled me into his arms.

I thought of Papa the whole time and wished he could have been there, but it was out of the question for him to make a trip all the way to Virginia. For something old I had mama's pearl earring tucked away in my pretty little bride's purse.

As much as I didn't want to get married so soon after my high school graduation, that's just what I ended up doing.

Our first home was a makeshift, furnished apartment with a shared bathroom in Mrs. Ammon's house in Arlington, VA. Rent was eighty-five dollars a month, including utilities, with strict orders from Mrs. Ammon to leave the 60-watt lightbulbs be. If they happened to burn out, we were to let her know, and she'd take care of it.

The bus stop was a couple of blocks down the street. In the mornings, Roger would head to Maryland, and I'd commute to Washington, and after work, we'd come home to our cozy little apartment in Virginia.

Too soon, Roger was transferred to Scott Air Force Base in Belleville, Illinois. He went on ahead while I stayed at my job and worked as long as doctor's orders would allow me to before the birth of our baby. When the time was right, I boarded an airplane to join Roger—another first for me.

When I purchased my airline ticket, the clerk took one look at me and said, "We'll have to have a written statement from your doctor stating that you won't deliver your baby during flight."

"Really?" I turned around and hurried back to the doctor's office.

On the jet plane, I was assigned an aisle seat, but when the sweet elderly lady sitting next to me learned that it was my first airplane ride, she insisted that we trade seats. The view out the little window was breathtaking. Soaring over the clouds reminded me of fresh, soft snow.

Anxious to see my husband again, I had to force myself to sit tight until the plane landed. Roger was right there to meet me at the St. Louis airport. When he spotted me in the crowd, his face broke into a happy smile, and he busted out laughing. He'd never given it any thought that I would look so different with my belly sticking way out there.

Roger and I were filled with joy over the birth of our firstborn, exactly two weeks after I'd moved to Belleville. A smallish baby, weighing six pounds, one ounce and measuring eighteen inches long, with a fuzzy head of reddish hair and pretty blue eyes. Douglas came into the world on April 4, 1958, in St. Elizabeth's Hospital, Belleville.

Giving birth was the most beautiful, magical experience of my life. And seeing the happiness in Roger's face as he watched me bent over the hospital bed, carefully pinning a diaper on my adorable baby and dressing him up in his brand-new take-home outfit, thrilled me through and through.

"Sweets," (Roger's nickname for me), "as soon as we get home, let's lay him on our big bed and just look at him."

"Can't I walk out by myself?" I asked when a nurse came into my room with an old, ugly-looking wheelchair.

"It's hospital rules, dear."

Dr. Davis happened to walk by as the nurse pushed me through the corridor; I was cradling my baby in my arms. His face lit up. "Hannah, you must remember babies aren't made of glass."

When Roger's hitch in the Air Force ended, we packed up and headed for California via North Dakota in our new car, a 1951 green Oldsmobile we'd just purchased for three hundred dollars.

Papa ran out to greet us when we drove into the familiar farmyard, and he walked alongside me on the way to the house with his eyes fixed on his grandson. When we got inside, I laid Doug on the kitchen table and removed his blanket so Papa could get a good look.

Lucy came running out of the bedroom. She sucked in her breath, then exhaled in a loud swoosh. She took a second deep breath as she leaned over the table. "Oh, look at those little rosy cheeks, isn't he adorable? Hannah, can I hold him?"

"Of course."

Papa kept his eye on the baby swung over Lucy's shoulder. "Vhat color are da little fella's eyes anyvay?"

"Blue."

He chuckled, "Dey sure are pretty."

After visiting Papa and Lucy and showing off my baby to Annabelle and her family, we were once again on our way. Roger was happy to be going home, and I was excited to see California and places unknown.

CHAPTER 13

"Just think, sweets, we'll go through Yellowstone on our way."

"Really! I'd love to see Old Faithful."

Was I ever surprised to see brown bears running freely in Yellowstone Park when we got there, and they weren't scared of nothing. Why, they would grab onto the cars with their big paws and run right alongside the moving vehicles.

Their furry brown faces looked adorable, but it wasn't any fun when out of the blue, a cub climbed through the window on my side, scrambled over the seat and sniffed baby Doug as he lay sleeping in his bassinet.

I screamed bloody murder, "Roger, the bear is going to get our baby."

Just like that, Roger spun around and punched the baby bear on his snoot and knocked him right out the window. The cub landed on all fours and scampered into the woods.

I quickly rolled up the window and felt nothing but relief. And would you believe? Doug never even woke up.

As I reached around to pick up my baby, Roger pulled me to him in a big warm bear hug. "Sweets, I don't think the bear meant any harm, he was just sniffing for food. By the way, I overheard a park visitor say the geyser is ready to erupt any minute. Let's go before it's too late."

I held Doug tight against my chest while Roger and I stood side by side, watching magnificent Old Faithful bubble and spurt.

In California, I thought it was great fun when our route led us through the passageway of a gigantic redwood tree. I loved the smell of the redwoods, and I was absolutely amazed at how tall they grew.

Roger certainly hadn't forgotten his way around San Francisco, the city he'd been born in, and where he'd lived most of his life. He zipped through the metropolis and pulled right up in front of his uncle's beautiful Victorian home in Daly City.

Roger laughed when I asked him, "How do people know whose house is whose? The homes are built tight against each other and they all look alike."

Uncle Hoyt chuckled when I said I was disappointed that the Golden Gate Bridge wasn't gold. "A lot of people expect to see gold," he told me, then explained how consulting architect Irving F. Morrow selected Golden Gate Bridge International Orange because it blended well with the nearby hills and contrasted with the ocean and sky.

Uncle Hoyt picked up an encyclopedia from his tall oak bookcase and handed it to me.

"You'll discover all you want to know about the Golden Gate in here." I sat down beside Roger and read out loud: "The Golden Gate Strait is the entrance to the San Francisco Bay from the Pacific Ocean. The strait is approximately three miles long by one mile wide with currents ranging from 4.5 to 7.5 knots. It is generally accepted that the strait was named 'Chrysopylae,' or Golden Gate, by John C. Fremont, Captain, Topographical Engineers of the US Army, circa 1846. It reminded him of a harbor in Istanbul named Chrysoceras or Golden Horn."

Roger said, "Well, I just learned things about the Golden Gate that I never knew before."

It was extraordinary how comfortable Uncle Hoyt and Aunt Maisie made me feel. I didn't feel like leaving when it came time to go.

Roger got a job working at a Mobil service station on Eighteenth Avenue near Golden Gate Park. We rented a cute little one-bedroom house with a wooden icebox in the kitchen, where I stored Doug's baby bottles full of fresh formula. We had to keep an eye on the ice block and when it melted, we'd rush to the corner store and buy a new chunk.

I loved the beautiful sunshiny California days, and I was absolutely amazed at how fast Doug's diapers dried on the clothesline. The first diaper would be dry by the time I fastened the big wooden clothespins on the last diaper.

I loved it when Uncle Hoyt called early one Sunday morning and invited us to go with them for a drive up Highway One, along the California coast to Mendocino. A beautiful Sunday, perfect weather to go sightseeing.

I'd seen the Pacific Ocean when we drove over the Golden Gate Bridge, but this would be the first time I would visit a California beach.

Uncle Hoyt pulled up and parked at Mendocino Bay Overlook and announced, "Look, everyone, you can see a spectacular view of the village of Mendocino from here." Aunt Maisie nudged my arm and said, "Honey, you go with the guys and have a good time. The ocean breeze is too cold for the little babe. Give him to me, honey." She took sleepy Doug out of my arms. I jumped out of the car and darted towards the sea, leaving Roger and Uncle Hoyt behind.

In awe, I stood barefoot on the beach with the warm sand seeping between my toes, staring at the unbelievable views of the Mendocino Bay and the ever-changing Pacific Ocean. I was caught off guard when Uncle Hoyt scooped me up high over the waves that frothed around his ankles, and counted, one, two, three—as though he would throw me into the ocean on the count of ten.

On our way home, we stopped at The Cliff House for dinner, one of Roger's favorite restaurants. It was a busy place; even so, we got a table by the window with a beautiful view of Ocean Beach, on the western side of San Francisco. That was the first time Doug went "out to dinner" at a fancy restaurant. Roger and I took turns holding him while we ate delicious seafood and crusty popovers. I'd never eaten a popover before and they were mouth-watering. What a fun day!

As much as we loved living in California, things didn't work out like we expected. Taking Papa's advice, we headed to Minnesota for better school and job opportunities. I was happy to know I'd be near Papa again and Doug would get to know his grandpa. It seemed I missed Papa more than ever since I had my own family.

On a beautiful spring day, exactly two years and twenty-four days after Doug was born, we were filled with joy and happiness all over again when our second son came kicking and screaming into the world at the Memorial Hospital in Mankato, Minnesota.

Roger didn't get to see our newborn until after a considerable length of time, when the nurse carried him into my hospital room. The happy part was when the nurse left us alone with our baby. I unwrapped him, and we counted his tiny fingers and little toes. Roger named him Spencer.

"Sweets, I wonder what Doug will think when he sees his baby brother?"

"Honey, I can't wait to bring our baby home. I've never been away from my sweet Doug for so long, and I'm missing him something terrible."

I was surprised when the same nurse came back a little bit later and asked, "Hannah, since your baby's belly button and circumcision have healed so nicely, would it be alright with you if we used your baby for our new mothers' bath session today?"

I smiled. "Really? I would love that."

"The presentation will be held in Room 103, just down the hall."

I immediately jumped out of the high hospital bed, threw on my bathrobe and hurried down the corridor to Room 103.

It felt like my heart would burst out of my chest when I sat on the soft cushioned chair amongst the new mothers, watching my baby's tiny arms and legs flailing in the air while the nurse gently bathed him.

He's a perfect, precious baby and he's all mine—another miracle.

I nudged the older mother next to me. "That's my baby the nurse is bathing."

"I thought so by the way you kept looking at him. He's a robust little guy. I bet he'll roll over all by himself before you know it. I just had baby number six."

"Really?"

She seemed almost embarrassed when she told me she was forty-one.

Wow! She could actually be my mother.

Doug stood in the middle of the living room with a shocked look on his face when I walked in carrying our new baby. I immediately lay the baby on our big bed and gathered Doug in my arms. He wrapped his arms around my neck and grinned from ear to ear when I whispered, "I'll need you to help me take care of your baby brother."

A few days later, I happened to be in the bedroom changing Spencer's diaper when Doug scampered in. "Here, Mommy." He handed me the big bottle of Baby Magic lotion. "This is for Teber." Doug stood and giggled when I rubbed the lotion on Teber's butt. From the start, Doug called Spencer "Teber." So, that became our new baby's name. I loved my babies more than anything in the world.

The kids were young when Roger took the time to teach them our telephone number. "It's important that you know your phone number when you're out and about and need to call home in case of an emergency," he told them.

Ring, ring. Teber hollered, "Mom, can I answer it?"

"Go ahead."

"Hello."

I could hear Roger on the other end.

"Hello, who's speaking?"

"You know who I is, you is my Daddy."

"Teber, what's your phone number?"

Spencer shouted into the phone: "Hickory 7-2739."

"That's my boy. Tell Mom I'll be late."

"OK." And he plunked the phone down into the receiver.

"What's going on?" I asked.

"Don't know, all he said was tell Mom I'll be late."

It wasn't long before Roger walked in with a beautiful all-black cat in his arms. It had the prettiest green eyes I'd ever seen.

"Aw, honey, where did you get the pretty kitty?"

"A customer asked me if I would like a cat he wanted to get rid of, so I drove by his place on my way home and picked him up. His name is Midnight."

"The name sure fits him. I wonder why they didn't want him anymore?"

"I didn't ask, but you know how some people are. They get a pet and soon they're tired of taking care of it."

Spencer ran up to his dad's outstretched arms, and Roger handed Midnight to him. The doting cat snuggled against Spencer's chest and rubbed his face on his chin.

"Look, Mom, he likes me. He's purring too."

"My goodness, he is a precious kitty. He sure does like you."

"I know."

Doug chimed in, "Let me hold him."

Spencer handed the cat to Doug, and Midnight licked his chin.

"Aw, look at that, I've never seen a cat give kisses."

Roger spoke up, "He's an affectionate cat, alright. He insisted on sitting on my lap while I drove, and purred all the way home."

Midnight had no problem adjusting to his new home, and we were delighted to have him.

Roger thought it was important for kids to grow up owning pets. "Teaches them compassion," he said, and I couldn't have agreed more.

On a chilly, cloudy fall afternoon, I reached into the oven to take out my perfect apple pie when I felt Spencer's little hand on my arm.

"What's the matter, Teber?"

"Mommy, I wish that I could die."

I spun around, looked into his little face, and almost dropped the pie.

"My goodness, Teber, what would make you say such a thing?"

"So I could see if angels in the sky go barefoot or wear shoes."

That inspired me to write a poem.

Three-Year-Old's Wish

Mommy,
I wish that I could die
So I could plainly choose
If angels in the sky
Go barefoot or wear shoes

Doug got just what he wanted that Christmas, a telescope, and when the weather turned warm, we would gather in the front yard and take turns looking through the scope.

One beautiful spring evening, I sat on a lawn chair, listening to Roger describe to

Doug all about the heavenly body of stars. "Doug, there are stars in the sky both day and night. The sun is our daystar and makes our sky bright. At night, when the sky is dark, the light of all the stars can be seen. Look up in the sky at the Big Dipper. The dipper is made up of seven stars. Can you see it?"

Excited, Doug shouted, "Yes, I see the Big Dipper, Dad." He counted out loud, one, two, three, four, five, six, and seven. Tickled, Doug turned round and looked at me. "Dad explains everything so good, Mom."

On a beautiful summer Saturday, my family and I picnicked and played in the Prior Lake Park until it turned dark. The night was clear with beautiful stars shining bright when Roger took the "fun way home." That's what we called it when we drove through the forest on the narrow, crooked country road.

All of a sudden, Doug shouted from the backseat, "Hey, Dad—stop the car right here! Let's all get out and look up at the pots and pans."

Once more I was inspired to write a poem, a haiku in honor of Doug.

> Summer moonlight
> Pots and pans
> In the sky

Being a mother was my greatest and most joyous role. I loved being surrounded by my boys: the busyness, the mealtimes. I loved being the one who had all the answers.

During the fall of 1965, the dream of owning our own home became a reality when we were approved for a GI loan and hired contractors to custom build our first house on an acre of land in Prior Lake, Minnesota, right across the road from where we lived in our apartment.

We'd go on family bike rides almost every evening and check on the construction progress. Spencer rode up beside me on one of our outings and told me, "I wish Dad would quit talking about our new house, it makes me so 'cited!" We were all excited.

225

It felt surreal the day our house was completed and ready to move in. Our new home had two Swedish fireplaces, a beautiful foyer and a circle driveway, plus much more. I couldn't wait to move out of our apartment and live in it.

The morning we loaded up the truck, Midnight was in the front yard, tossing a live mouse in the air and letting it plunk back down on the hard ground. When the poor mouse tried to get away, he'd snatch it up again and throw it around some more. When Midnight tired of playing cat and mouse, he disappeared.

Later, when I walked into my new home carrying an armful of stuff, was I ever surprised to find wise old Midnight stretched out on the windowsill in the front room, soaking up the sun like he belonged there.

I'd just gotten home from work and began to fix a huge salad after pulling several kinds of lettuce out of the refrigerator, all the while straining to hear newscaster Skip Loesnerthe over the hubbub of the boys playing Monopoly in the living room. They rescued the little girl who had fallen in the well, thank God. The weather forecast predicted more rain.

"I got Broadway!" I heard Spencer exclaim. At the same time, Roger walked in. Looking over his shoulder as he hung his jacket on the coatrack in the foyer, he announced, "I want you all to be ready to go when I come home from work on Friday night."

Doug ran into the foyer. "Why, Dad?"

"It's a surprise!"

I spoke up, "Can't you tell me?"

"No, sweets, I want you and the kids to all be surprised."

Spencer broke in, "Dad, I hope it's a new dog so Ralf has a friend to play with."

"No, it's not a dog."

Doug, Spencer and I anxiously waited for Friday night to come around. As soon as we heard Dad's car drive up, we ran out and piled in. First off, Roger drove us all to Bob's Big Boy restaurant, our family's favorite place to eat out. "Order whatever you want, kids."

Spencer said, "I don't have to look at a menu, I know I want a hamburger, French fries and a chocolate malt."

I always saved room for Bob's Big Boy's delicious strawberry shortcake.

From the restaurant, Roger drove to the Mann Southtown Theatre. Doug shouted from the backseat, "Oh, good, we're going to a movie, huh, Dad?"

Spencer hollered, "Is it a Don Knotts movie, Dad?"

"Yes, it is. I overheard you telling your mother how you wished you could see *The Incredible Mr. Limpet*. Well, here we are."

Doug and Spencer thought Don Knotts was hilarious. Walking into the theatre, Spencer grabbed hold of my hand. "Isn't this fun, Mom?"

"It sure is."

Roger's family surprises made me love him all the more.

We'd lived in our beautiful home less than five years when Roger's job as a district manager transferred him to Denver, Colorado. Doug and Spencer liked adventure and they were excited to move. Roger couldn't wait to live where the winters weren't so nippy. But an awful sadness came over me at the thought of moving away from our home and our friends. And the kids and I had grown accustomed to visiting Papa whenever we felt like it. The idea of leaving Papa behind during his advancing years broke my heart.

"Jour place is vit jour husband, don't go vorrying about jour old papa," Papa said when I told him I hated the thought of not being able to get in the car and go to see him whenever I wanted.

I declared, "I don't like changes anymore."

"Sweets, that's what life is all about."

The morning we were to leave, I stood by the packed truck and busted out bawling—Midnight was nowhere to be found.

I called, "Middy, Kitty, Middy, Kitty, where are you?" Roger's eyes were laughing when I looked at him and announced, "I'm not leaving without Midnight."

"Try to stop crying and listen."

Oh, my God! The sweetest meow came from deep inside the packed truck. Roger swung the back panel open, I peeked in and saw Midnight sitting snug on one of the boxes. Once more, Midnight was not going to be left behind.

After some serious research to find good public schools in the Denver area, we were told Jefferson County rated the best. We ended up purchasing an older home that I immediately fell in love with in Lakewood, Colorado. I was surprised to learn the residential area was zoned for horses. Memories of good old Sally came back when I looked at the horse stall in the backyard. That was the first I'd ever heard of keeping a horse in the city?

There were daffodils growing all the way down the long driveway, and other beautiful flowers sprouted up wherever you looked.

I'd lugged my old trunk from Papa's house wherever I moved—years passed by before I even looked inside it. I'd forgotten what I had hidden away in there. When I opened the lid, oh, my God, was I ever surprised to find old notebook papers, yellowed from age, with Rome's handwriting on them from when he'd helped me with my history homework. I dug out an old photo of him as well. A tiny piece of my heart never quit loving that guy. I wondered if he ever thought of me.

Shortly after we moved into our Lakewood home, Doug got a job delivering newspapers for *The Denver Post*.

I went job hunting as soon as the kids got settled in their new schools. Not long into an interview with a Mr. Kelly, he suggested the best thing I could do for myself was to join the typographical union. I took his advice and served a four-year apprenticeship at Publisher's Press, then became a journeyman typographer in the Denver Typographical Union No. 49. I loved the sound of the presses running, and I looked forward to seeing my next finished project. My foreman always brought me a copy of my most recent work—hot off the press.

I ran outside to see what was going on when I heard Roger drive into our driveway and honk the horn. There he sat behind the wheel with a big smile on his face, pointing at the passenger's side. I yanked the car door open and saw a forlorn, shaggy-looking pooch with the saddest brown eyes huddled down on the seat.

"My goodness, where did you ever find him?"

"Sweets, every time I walked by Angelo's pet shop, I saw this mournful mutt sitting in a cage much too small for him. He's such a mess, it's hard to tell that he's a brown poodle. The store had a Father's Day special going on. I bought him for thirty-seven dollars."

I picked up the dirty pup, brought him into the bathroom, and plopped down on the toilet seat. Then I held and loved him until he quit shaking before I gave him a nice warm bubble bath. We named the odd looking dog Mr. Chips.

I'd never heard of a dog liking a bath, but after Mr. Chip's first bath, whenever he heard the water running, he'd scamper into the bathroom and try to leap in the tub!

I loved that Roger liked animals as much as I did. Our backyard grew into a menagerie. Quite often, Ralf and Mr. Chips would jump in the kiddies' pool and chase the ducks (left over from Easter) round and round, with the water splashing every which way. Spencer had a red longhaired guinea pig that loved the outdoors. And good old Midnight watched over and kept them all in line. No matter how much the boys would have liked it, I didn't allow snakes or lizards in our house. One big turtle was enough.

Moving to new places came with challenges, yet it created a close bond amongst Doug, Spencer, Roger and me. No matter what catastrophe we faced, I'd always say, "Honey, as long as you, me, Doug and Spencer are together, everything is OK."

Roger and I were partners when it came to caring for our family. He never liked leaving the kids with a sitter unless absolutely necessary. We worked it out so one of us would be home with the boys at all times. I was fortunate enough to land a night job at Bradford Publishing in downtown Denver, and Roger worked days.

Oh, the beauty of living at high altitude—there were no insects. Perfect weather to be outdoors, camping. On the weekends, we'd load up our tent and all our camping gear and head for the Rocky Mountains and the clear waters of the lake. Roger and the boys would go fishing while I stayed by the campgrounds with Mr. Chips and Ralf and read a good novel.

I enjoyed picking wildflowers. I'd have a pretty bouquet of Colorado's state flower, the columbine, in pastel shades of blue, violet, red, yellow and white setting on the picnic table when my family came in from fishing. Oftentimes, I'd cook a huge kettle of chili, Spencer's favorite, on the open fire. After supper, we'd sit around the campfire roasting marshmallows and telling stories with a cool, calming breeze all around us.

Roger would be the first one to crawl out of his sleeping bag in the morning, and he'd go right to work, building a fire and cooking us fresh fish for breakfast. We decided it must be the altitude that made Mr. Chips so lazy; he'd stay inside Spencer's sleeping bag and sleep until noon or later if we left him.

Nothing seemed out of the ordinary when I first woke up that Saturday morning. I showered, dressed, and made my family pancakes for breakfast, all in the usual fashion. The phone rang. I answered it—suddenly, I wasn't hungry anymore.

Jacob was on the other end. In a barely audible voice, he said, "I have da vorst news, Hannah."

It felt like there was a sledgehammer pounding in my chest. "What is it, Jacob?"

"Jour Papa died dis morning."

Papa was eighty-four years old when he succumbed to heart failure.

I felt so lonely and depressed after Papa died. To know I'd never see him again or be able to tell him stuff broke my heart.

One morning, I called my doctor and told him how melancholy I was feeling. I couldn't believe it when right off, he suggested I see a psychologist. "Really?" I responded.

That evening, when I told Roger what the doctor had said, my loving husband pulled me into his arms. "Sweets, I don't think you need a psychologist, you're sad because you're missing your Papa. I'll listen to whatever you have to say. Maybe I won't have the right answers, but for forty bucks an hour, I'll sure try." He made me laugh, and together we muddled through it.

It all happened about three years before Papa passed away. Without any warning, Lucy packed up her bags and took off with a German farmhand Papa had hired to help him with the harvest. Even though Papa spent the winters with us after Lucy left, I knew his last years were lonely.

It troubled me when Doug didn't get home from school on time, but when I saw him running up the driveway with a big smile on his face, everything was OK.

"Doogle, I was starting to worry about you. Where have you been?"

"I stopped off at the pet shop. I'm going to get my money and go back and buy the mynah bird, Mom. You saw the black mynah bird the other day, remember?"

"I sure do. He looked like a very smart bird, and he had the prettiest shiny black feathers I've ever seen."

"He'll learn to talk too, and he only costs thirty-five dollars. I have the money saved from my paper route. Mom, I've got to get going before the store closes."

It wasn't long before Doug came home carrying a big cage with the myna bird in it. Doug named the bird Sidney. In no time, Sidney surprised us all with his remarkable vocabulary.

When the phone rang, he'd screech, "Hellooooo." When he heard the doorbell, he'd holler, "Hi!"

One afternoon, as Doug rushed by me on the way to his room, Sidney shrieked, "Doug, Doug."

Irritated, Doug shouted, "Mom, I told you I was going to my room."

I busted out laughing. "Doug, it wasn't me calling your name, it was Sidney."

"Well, Mom, he sounds just like you."

One rainy afternoon, I was feeling weary—again, Doug wasn't home when he should have been. Regardless, I went to work chopping up cherries, Sidney's favorite treat. I was standing in front of Sidney's cage, not realizing I was talking out loud to myself, when out of the blue Sidney mumbled, "I wonder what happened to him."

When Roger came home after work, Sidney would giggle and screech, "Roger, Roger, Roger, Roger." He could say "Doug" real plain, but he never said "Spencer." I guess the letter S was too hard for Sidney to pronounce.

Mr. Chips became Spencer's faithful friend. He slept with him, ran behind him when he rode his bike, and when it was time for Spencer to come home after school, he would lie by the big living room picture window, patiently watching and waiting for Teber. Sometimes he'd fall asleep with his head resting on the windowsill.

"Mom, would you bring Mr. Chips to my classroom at 1:30 p.m. on Wednesday? It's my day for show-and-tell, and I want to show Mr. Chips."

"OK." I walked into Miss Berg's classroom carrying Mr. Chips. Miss Berg gestured for Spencer to take a seat on the big wooden chair in front of the class, and I plopped Mr. Chips on Spencer's lap.

Spencer proudly announced, "This is my dog, Mr. Chips."

The kids clapped.

Shaggy-brown, shy Mr. Chips sat on Spencer's lap with a curious look on his face. The kids laughed when he spun his head around and gave Spencer slobbery kisses.

Miss Berg instructed the students to use an adjective to tell something about Mr. Chips.

Christina raised her hand. "He has pretty, golden-brown eyes."

Robert said, "He has big paws."

Little Tim, who sat way over in the corner, raised his hand. "I want to be next."

Miss Berg spoke up, "OK, Tim, what do you have to tell about Mr. Chips?"

"He looks like a Colorado water buffalo."

I'd never thought Mr. Chips looked like a buffalo, but now that Tim thought so, I could definitely see a resemblance.

The following Christmas, Roger, Doug and I sat in the front row during the holiday pageant at Spencer's school and watched him play the drums. On the way home, in the car Spencer announced to all of us that he didn't want to be called "Teber" anymore. "Call me by my real name from now on."

It tickled me the day Doug called me at work to tell me, "Mom, I just got asked to the Sadie Hawkins dance. Do you know what that is?" Before I could answer, he told me, "It's when the girl asks the boy." My boys were growing up way too soon.

The following summer, I took a trip "home" to North Dakota. While I was there, a bunch of my old classmates and I sat around a campfire in Red Willow, chitchatting. Gilbert told me that Rome was very unhappy, and in the process of a bitter divorce.

"Really? I'm sorry to hear that."

Earl, Rome's older brother, spoke up, "Hannah, I think Rome has been depressed all his life because he didn't marry you."

I must tell you one more Sydney anecdote before my story ends: It happened one morning when the Dependable Gas Utility serviceman came to read the meter. He rushed past Sidney and me and ran down the basement steps. All of a sudden, Sidney let out a shrill whistle. The serviceman spun around. An expression of pure panic flew across his face.

I busted out laughing and pointed at Sidney.

He shook his head. "I didn't notice a bird sitting there when I walked by." And he bolted out the door like his life depended on it.

We were empty nesters when Roger's job sent him to Tucson, Arizona. Our stay there was less than a year when once again Roger was transferred. But this move was special. Roger was going home to California. I was anxious to move back to California as well. It'd be great to live near Aunt Maisie and Uncle Hoyt again. Thank God, our kids followed us. I couldn't imagine life without Doug and Spencer around.

By that time, I'd graduated to graphic designer status. Lucky me: right off, I landed the ideal job at Stanford University, designing ads for the *Stanford Daily* newspaper. Driving by the Stanford Barn on my commute brought back memories of Papa and me on the farm. Sometimes it was hard to believe that I was the same little country girl who rode her horse, Sally, and herded the cattle.

We seldom went out to nice restaurants during the week, but when Roger came home on a Thursday night with the good news that he'd received a promotion and a decent pay raise, we decided it was time to celebrate, and took off across town to the Fish Market in Sunnyvale. It was late by the time we got home.

"Honey, I'm going to bed."

"OK, sweets, I'll just finish watching the movie, then I'll be up."

I didn't hear Roger when he came to bed, but I woke up in the middle of the night when I felt him tossing and turning.

"Sweets, are you awake?"

"I am now."

"Do you feel OK?"

I rolled over. "Hmm, mmmm."

"I'm sorry I disturbed you, but I've got an awful gut ache. It must be something I ate."

I mumbled, "I don't think that scrumptious dinner you had at the Fish Market would make you sick," and I fell right back to sleep.

In the early morning, I heard Roger calling into work sick. That really troubled me. Roger never missed work.

"Will you be OK home by yourself?" I asked him.

"Don't go worrying about me. You go on and have a good day. It's probably some kind of flu. It'll pass."

"There's chicken noodle soup in the pantry you can heat up."

"That sounds good."

When I got home in the late afternoon, Roger was lying in bed just like when I left him.

"Did you eat some soup?" I wanted to know.

"No, sweets, I didn't feel like eating." Now, if Roger didn't eat, I knew he had to be really sick.

"Do you think you should see a doctor?"

"No, I just feel like lying here."

Around 9:00 p.m., I checked on my husband once more. That was when he told me, "The pain in my stomach is almost more than I can take." Oh, my God, his face actually had a yellowish pallor to it.

"Honey, I'm taking you to the emergency room right now."

Roger didn't argue. He struggled out of the bed, got dressed and walked very slowly to the car.

"I'm getting in the backseat and lying down. It hurts too much to sit."

I drove through San Jose as fast as I dared. By the time we got across town to the hospital, Roger was so unwell he couldn't get out of the car on his own. Medics were right there and assisted him onto a stretcher, then immediately wheeled him into a little exam room off to one side. I was told to wait.

In complete shock, I plunked down on a hard metal chair in the dreary, crowded waiting room and buried my face in my hands.

Dear God, how could this be happening? But it is, so get a grip, Hannah.

I waited and waited and waited some more. I walked outside and called my kids on my cell phone. Neither one answered. I called my friend Lexi. Thank God, she came right away.

The next thing we knew, Dr. Ebenstein, an oncologist, was standing right in front of me, saying, "We must do emergency surgery right now."

"What's wrong?" I cried.

"We've discovered that Roger's intestines have burst. The sooner we get him into the operating room, the better."

The doctor's shoes clicked on the hard tiled floor as he hurried down the corridor.

I just know as strong as Roger is, he'll come out of the surgery and be his powerful self. He has to.

After several anguished hours, a young girl in a candy-stripe uniform walked up to me with a distressed look on her face.

"Are you Mrs. Roger Victore?"

"Yes, I am."

"Dr. Ebenstein wants to see you in private. Follow me." I trailed behind the little mouse of a person through the halls and into a tiny room.

"Please have a seat. Dr. Ebenstein will be right with you." I smiled when she gave me a motherly pat on the shoulder and quickly walked away. My insides told me something was terribly wrong. I felt claustrophobic, staring at the pale yellow walls in the windowless space. I'd never liked the smell of hospitals.

After waiting for what seemed like an eternity, Dr. Ebenstein showed up. I watched him pull the green surgical mask off his face before he plunked down beside me and conveyed the god-awful news.

"Roger's large intestine was so full of cancer, we had no other choice but to insert a ostomy bag."

"Oh, my God," I wailed. "Does Roger know?"

"No, he hasn't woken up yet, but we will inform him as soon as the time is right."

"Please do."

I felt helpless.

"I'm sorry, Mrs. Victore, but there was nothing more we could do. You'll need hospice care. Please go down to the main office. They will assist you."

I caught up with Lexi in the lobby and blurted out, "The doctor said I should get hospice care. I don't really know what hospice care is, do you?"

Lexi glanced at me with a tense look on her face.

"The doctor told me to go to the main office."

"OK, let's go then."

I felt a sense of pure fear and my heart palpitated. I was having a heart attack right next to Lexi and she didn't even realize it. We turned the corner and thank God, my heart began to slow. I could breathe again. I made a swooshing sound of relief as air filled my lungs once more.

"You OK?"

"I felt really, really strange for a minute. It's gone now."

We kept on walking until we reached the administrative office.

A kindly little old woman sat behind a large desk piled high with books and papers, talking on the phone, but when she saw us walk in, she ended her call, got up from her chair and greeted us cheerfully.

I explained why we were there. She nodded and stood ringing her hands. "If they could just find a cure for cancer." Then she went on to explain what hospice was all about.

Under my breath, I mumbled, "Poor Roger."

A few days later, I took Roger home from the hospital. As I drove along, I asked him if he'd felt sick and didn't tell me. "Sweets, I felt fine, I had no symptoms whatsoever. I would have told you if I did."

My sweet Roger was more concerned about my well-being than anything else. Every morning, first thing, he'd ask me how I felt. One day, he said he wished he could hear me laugh again.

"Honey, how can I laugh when I know you're dying?"

"Sweets, I'm treating this as an adventure. I hate leaving you and the boys, but I want it to be over. I hate the son of a bitch," and he pointed to the ostomy bag.

Tears filled my eyes. "I hate the son of a bitch, too."

It hurt me terribly to see my husband in such horrendous pain. Sometimes I wondered if the morphine I administered even helped.

One day, out of the blue, Roger sat up in bed and said, "I hope you get married again."

"Why do you say that?"

"Because you're such a nice, loving person. I don't want you to live alone forever."

I couldn't imagine being married to anyone but him.

In the early morning, as I wiped Roger's sweaty forehead with a warm, damp washcloth, he murmured, "Sweets, it's getting hard to breathe."

That very night, July 29, 1995, Roger succumbed to colon cancer with Doug, Spencer, Lexi and me by his side. Roger was fifty-six years old.

After a beautiful memorial service in a San Jose chapel, Roger was buried in the San Joaquin Valley National Cemetery in Gustine, California.

During the twenty-one-gun salute, Doug nudged me and said, "Mom, us four Victores were tight. Now there's three and we're still tight."

Spencer stood on the other side of me, grief-stricken.

I couldn't imagine life without my sweet, kind husband. My soul mate, the man who made me feel entirely whole, healed and intact, like no piece was missing from the puzzle. I hurt so bad, there were times I wished I could die; yet I knew that was foolish thinking. I had my wonderful sons, good friends and so much to be thankful for—if I could just get over the awful heartbreak. Thank God for my great job at Stanford. At work, things felt normal.

To top it all off, not long after Roger passed on, our thirteen-year-old Labrador died. That was when I went out and bought the kind of dog I'd always wanted—a dachshund. I named her Gretchen. Gretchen and I went on long walks every day as soon as I got home from work. On the weekends, we drove to Half Moon Bay State Beach and strolled along the coast. Gretchen became my savior.

As time went by, I found myself doing things I'd never done before, such as purchasing a beautiful CD player; I played the kind of music I loved when I was home alone. I traded in our old Ford Tempo and bought a beautiful green VW Beetle with a turbo engine, the kind of car I'd always wanted to own.

I quit my job at the *Stanford Daily* when I was offered the perfect position at SCPD, Stanford Center for Professional Development.

The old saying "What doesn't kill you makes you stronger" proved true for me. In time, I found myself actually enjoying my independent life.

In July 2006, I traveled "home" to Munich, North Dakota, to attend the town's Centennial Celebration and all-class high school reunion. My fiftieth.

On a hot, humid summer evening, I sat beside Annabelle and Trevor on a wooden bench in the makeshift Munich Beer Gardens, sipping a cool drink when I looked up and saw a bald-headed man sitting across from me, wearing a T-shirt that said "Wallace, Idaho" across the front.

I nudged Annabelle and whispered, "Look over there at the guy wearing the Wallace, Idaho T-shirt. That has to be Rome Blom."

The next thing I knew, he was strolling through the crowd, cheerfully greeting folks and shaking hands. *Oh, my God, he's coming my way—he's right by my side.* My heart began to pound right out of my shirt.

"Do I know you?" he asked.

"Hannah Jonesen."

"Well, stand up and give me a hug."

I shifted over to make room. He spoke quietly, "Hannah, I'm sorry for the way I treated you. It wasn't right." He talked on and on about the things he regretted.

"Will you accept my apology?"

I nodded. It had been fifty-one years since I'd last seen this wonderful man. I was so choked up I couldn't talk. I just sat there, examining his face.

"Hannah, there hasn't been a day when I didn't think of you."

"Really?"

When Rome left to get more drinks, I slid down the bench next to Annabelle and took a deep, shaky breath. "Oh, my God, Annabelle, where are these feelings coming from? My heart started to pound when Rome came by me, just like it did when I was with him in high school."

Annabelle laughed, "I've heard those feelings stay with you forever."

"Well, I guess so."

I tried hard to act nonchalant, but I wasn't fooling Rome. With a big smile on his face, he handed me a drink, "You are so tickled."

I was tickled to hear his loud, familiar voice.

Rome told me he'd quit working as a miner and became a stockbroker in 1977. He still worked five days a week in his Pennaluna office in Wallace.

He grasped my hand. "Come on, Hannah, we're going dancing." Smoke from a barbecue grill hung in the air as we strolled hand in hand toward the Munich auditorium.

Once again, we danced to the tune, "In the Mood." In the wee hours of the morning, Rome gave me a ride to the lodge where I was staying with Annabelle and Trevor. I sat way over on the passenger's seat, looking out the window as we drove through the country surrounded by farmland.

Am I dreaming? It felt like it.

In the twilight, I could see silhouettes of cows grazing. But when I heard Rome say, "I would like to spend the rest of my life with you and marry you," I stopped daydreaming and gawked at him with wide-open eyes.

Is he drunk?

He made me laugh when he blurted out, "And I'm the kind of man who takes care of his woman."

Rome and I spent the rest of the Centennial Celebration together and had the time of our lives. Then we went our separate ways. But distance didn't pull us apart— Rome called me at 8:00 p.m. every night. We had lots of catching up to do. One night, we talked until 2:00 a.m. the next morning!

Back at work, my girlfriend Akiko and I were on our lunch-break walk around the Stanford campus when I confided in her that I was reluctant to give up everything in California and start a new life. I told her that Rome said, "And I'm the kind of man who takes care of his woman."

She busted out laughing, "You'll never find that in California. Why don't you just get married and quit that job?"

Yeah, why don't I?

Over Labor Day weekend, I visited Rome in Wallace, Idaho. I must say, I was quite impressed with the historic, quaint, charming city, population 993, located in the panhandle region of the state. On my very first day in Wallace, Rome and I walked to the Shoshone County Court House and bought a marriage license.

I wanted one thing in my life, and that was Rome. Could I stand leaving behind my family, good friends and the security my job gave me? But love takes chances, and I wanted to take a chance right then.

On September 23, 2006, history was made in Wallace, Idaho, when Mayor Raffaele Ormannos performed the first wedding ceremony ever on the Center of the Universe. Rome and I stood on the Center of the Universe monument, a specially cast manhole cover at the intersection of Sixth and Bank Streets, under the moon and stars and exchanged "I do's." Looking out into the crowd, I could see hundreds of smiling faces: family and friends facing us, cheering wholeheartedly.

Once more, Rome twirled me around on the slick dance floor with the lights dimmed low, but this time, I didn't care when the music stopped. I was going home with Rome forevermore.

—THE END—

Made in the USA
San Bernardino, CA
11 May 2017